A DEADLY
DISCOVERY

A DEADLY DISCOVERY

CIAR BYRNE

ACCENT

First published in Great Britain in 2024 by
HEADLINE ACCENT
An imprint of HEADLINE PUBLISHING GROUP

1

Cataloguing in Publication Data is available from the British Library

ISBN 978 1 0354 1392 8

Typeset in Baskerville by CC Book Production

Printed and bound in Great Britain by
Clays Ltd, Elcograf S.p.A.

HEADLINE PUBLISHING GROUP
An Hachette UK Company
Carmelite House
50 Victoria Embankment
London EC4Y 0DZ

www.headline.co.uk
www.hachette.co.uk

To Jon, without whom I would never have moved
to Lewes and found the perfect setting for my story

Historical Note

It goes without saying that all the events in this novel are a work of pure fiction. I have woven in historical details based on my research into the Bloomsbury set, and Lewes in the late 1920s, but I have used artistic licence liberally.

My female protagonists – Alice Dudeney, Virginia Woolf, and Vanessa Bell – are figments of my imagination. The real women of the same names kept detailed diaries that clearly show they were not where I place them on certain dates. Nelson, Mrs Dudeney's beloved Dalmatian dog, died three years before the action took place. He was replaced by Emma, but this seemed rather too human a name for my purposes. The name of Mrs Dudeney's house on Castle Banks has changed over the years, and now there is another house nearby that goes by the same.

I'm sure readers will spot other such inconsistencies and I hope you will forgive them. I have tried to stay true to the spirit of Bloomsbury, but if I have bent the facts, it is simply to attempt to write the best story I can.

1.

Alice

Lewes, East Sussex,
Sunday, 7 October 1928

The sun hadn't yet risen over Castle Banks when Mrs
Dudeney – Alice to friends – padded downstairs to the
gravy-brown drawing room and sat in her favourite mustard
velvet chair before a desk inlaid with leather the colour of
overcooked spinach. This was where she spent most of her
time, looking out of the bay window, fountain pen in hand,
imparting wit to the page. When she was not busy writing
the romantic novels that had brought her a modest degree
of fame, she was scribbling in her diary – very much not
for public consumption – or gazing out from the mullioned
panes to observe the good (and the not-so-good) people of
the country town she called home. Nothing escaped Mrs
Dudeney's peregrine eye, or her sharp quill.

But at this hour of the morning there was little to be seen
from her usual spot. It wasn't like her to wake so early; she
was normally a good sleeper. But some nocturnal intruder

had disturbed her slumber, a fox yelping, or a badger barking, perhaps. She'd tried to get back to sleep, but once the grey light started filtering through the window, she'd given up, got out of bed and pulled on her housecoat and slippers.

Nelson rose from his wicker basket, cross at being prematurely awakened, and came over to nuzzle his owner, whimpering to be let out into the garden. There was no peace to be had until she gave in, so Alice rose heavily from her chair and accompanied the Dalmatian to the kitchen door, where they both ventured out into the dawn.

The garden was just as idiosyncratic as the building to which it was attached. Built into the side of a manmade Norman motte, once home to a fortified keep, the house looked decidedly unbalanced from any angle, as if it were a series of afterthoughts. Almost entirely hidden from the street unless you stood on tippy toe and peered over the brick-and-flint wall, the garden was in shade for much of the day. But to Alice it was perfection, an oasis of trees and flowers giving way to thicket as the mound rose steeply upwards.

Lewes Castle was rare in having two mottes. From the garden, she had a good view of the second taller mound, on top of which sat the remains of the later stone castle. But she preferred Brack Mound, which she liked to think of as her own. There was a path leading from her garden to the top and the only other way up to it was a path cut through the prickly undergrowth accessed via a wooden gate from the street. This was kept locked, and only the archaeologists excavating the summit had a key.

Once they were outside, Nelson sprang to life, running

between the corners of the lower garden, relieving himself on the lawn, then, as if he had picked up an unusual scent, dashing over to the path leading up to the top of the hillock. Sighing, Alice followed.

At this early hour, she had every expectation of having the mound to herself. She took her time, listening to the rooks cawing, admiring the gleaming scarlet of the hawthorn berries against the crisp morning sky, the wispy white of the old man's beard running rampant through the undergrowth and the rust-coloured leaves that would soon fall leaving the trees winter bare.

She anticipated with pleasure the familiar view from the summit over the surrounding countryside. To the north lay the expanse of the Weald, an untamed forest quite unexpected in the south-east of England. To the east, the anatomic curves of Malling Down, or as the locals charmingly called it, the Old Lady's Bottom. To the south, the sea, changing hourly from slate grey to twinkling blue over the port of Newhaven. And to the west, more downs, rolling like ancient giants, all the way past Brighton and Worthing to Arundel, Chichester and beyond.

She thought about how beastly Mrs Woolf had been the day before. It was a word she used advisedly. Virginia thought she was the very pinnacle of culture, but there was something animal about the woman's snobbery. Like a cat looking down from a post in disdain at all who pass by. Women could be so unkind to one another. Ernest was right on that front at least. And Virginia's words of yesterday still stung. Oh, she thought her writing so modern, so superior. Yet what did that unfeminine creature know about the passions of the flesh? How different her sister

Vanessa Bell was, the heart to her head, the curves to her sharp angles.

As Alice spiralled slowly upwards, she could hear Nelson whimpering from somewhere above her. Placing her hands on her hips to support the weight of a figure that, once trim, now resembled two large apple dumplings one on top of the other, she pressed on.

What could the dratted dog be fussing about? He was a temperamental creature, it was true, but this wasn't like him at all. As she reached the top, she saw at once what it was that had upset him. One of the archaeologists was lying face down on the turf, presumably examining a find. Strange, as they didn't usually work on Sundays.

At a safe distance of a few feet, Nelson stood growling at him.

What was wrong with the fellow? Only as she drew nearer did she notice the man wasn't moving and there were flies buzzing around his downturned head.

'Hello,' she called out.

There was no response.

'Can I help you?' she added.

But even as she spoke the words, she knew he was beyond help. She bent down and put a hand on the man's shoulder. It was limp and lifeless. With all her strength, she rolled him over, then fell backwards in horror, her well-padded behind landing on the dewy grass.

Where the man's face should have been was a mangled mess of blood and bone. His features had been hacked to bits. Globules of flesh clung to his matted fringe.

Glancing around wildly, she saw the weapon that had inflicted these horrific injuries. An archaeologist's trowel lay on the ground nearby, its pointed tip black with blood. For a few moments, she sat where she'd fallen, unable to utter a word, listening to the rooks continuing to caw as if nothing terrible had just happened. Then she did the only thing she could think of. She opened her mouth as wide as she could and with all the vigour of her sixty-two-year-old lungs, she screamed.

2.

Virginia

'Get a move on,' shouted a ruddy-faced man leaning out of the window of a dust-covered coal van. He revved his engine too close behind them as Leonard struggled to make a hill start.

The roads in Lewes were awfully steep and her mild-mannered husband was still trying to get to grips with their new automobile, a second-hand Singer. They really ought to get a chauffeur, but money was tight, and they simply couldn't afford one unless the book she'd just published sold twice as many copies as the last. It was a risk, as she didn't know whether her readers would take to the whimsical tale of a cross-dressing Elizabethan aristocrat.

The essay on which she was working, about how a woman needed financial independence and a space of her own in which to write, certainly wasn't going to cover the cost of a driver. She was due to deliver it to two women's colleges at Cambridge later that month and expected to be repaid only with a homely meal of beef, greens, and potatoes. If she were lucky, it might be followed by prunes and custard washed down with water.

Leonard, bless him, remained unflustered and tried the engine once more. This time, it stuttered into life and, not wanting to lose momentum, he swung the vehicle sharply round the corner on to the High Street, sending the riders on horseback gathered outside the White Hart scattering. With a groan, she realised they'd chosen to come into town on the same day the Lewes Hunt had its monthly meet.

'Mind that dog,' she yelled as Leonard narrowly avoided running over a beagle.

He pulled the car to a halt outside the hotel. Glancing in the rear-view mirror and tucking a strand of greying hair into her tweed hat, Ginny turned the handle and climbed out, feeling the stiffness in her bones.

'Do you want me to pick you up in an hour?' Leonard called after her.

'Certainly not. I'll walk back to Rodmell. Altogether more civilised,' she said, adding, 'Enjoy your morning with the nurseryman.'

Leonard was taking the car on to a plant nursery out near Ringmer, where he was planning to buy herbaceous perennials for a new border he was digging in their garden at Monk's House.

'Ginny!'

At the sound of the name used only by family and close friends, she turned round to see her sister had just arrived.

'Good, we can go in together. I do so hate being kept waiting for breakfast. Nessa, what on earth are you wearing?'

Her sister was clad in a large flowing item of clothing. If Ginny had to give it a name, she supposed it would be called a smock. It was made of rough brown linen, covered in smears of earth and moss, and looked suspiciously as though it were held together by safety pins.

'I was up early painting the garden this morning. It's so very beautiful in the autumn light. Then I realised I didn't have time to change if I wanted to make it into Lewes for the market. They sell out of the good stuff so quickly,' said Nessa.

On her arm, Nessa carried a wicker basket laden with potatoes, a couple of rabbits and a pheasant she'd bought from the game stall. She grew most of the vegetables she needed in the kitchen garden at Charleston, the farmhouse she rented nearby with her close friend and painting partner Duncan Grant.

'Come on, then, although I shan't be surprised if they ask you to come in via the tradesman's entrance,' said Ginny.

They pushed through the double-fronted doors into the foyer of the White Hart. A smartly dressed man behind reception looked at them a little strangely.

'Breakfast for two,' said Ginny. It was a statement rather than a request.

'This way, ladies,' he said, showing them into the dining room, which was already half filled with red-coated huntsmen, farmers and their wives, sleek rosy-cheeked businessmen with hands placed over their substantial middles and silver-haired ladies dressed in their finest for Market Day.

He showed them to a table near the window looking out on to the street. Ignoring the disapproving looks inspired

8

by her outlandish appearance, Nessa tucked her basket out of the way.

'Would you like to see a menu?' asked a mousy-haired waitress, who looked as though she should still be at school.

Ginny shook her head. She knew exactly what she wanted, had been thinking about it the whole way here as the automobile bumped over the potholed roads.

'Kippers, with coffee to wash them down. No milk,' she instructed.

'And for you, madam?' the girl asked Nessa, who smiled sweetly.

'Hot buttered toast, please, with plenty of milky tea.'

The waitress grinned.

'That sounds like my kind of breakfast,' she said.

Ginny scowled, but before she could think of a retort, she was interrupted by a booming voice on a cloud of perfume and pearls.

'Mrs Woolf, what an unexpected pleasure to find you here.'

Looking up, she saw Mrs Rivers, who lived in Hollybush House, one of the grander houses in Rodmell, and was constantly thrilled to have a well-known writer for a neighbour. She rose ever so slightly from her chair, just the degree required for politeness. Daphne Rivers was powerful in the village, and it wouldn't do to get on the wrong side of her. When she and Leonard had moved to Rodmell nine years earlier, the residents had been largely farmworkers and country tradespeople – the blacksmith, the wheelwright and the like. But new money had been trickling into the village ever since, building new houses and knocking old ones together. Hollybush House was new, but made to look old, built courtesy of the fortune accrued by the late Mr Rivers as a stockbroker in the City. Having left school at fourteen, his wealth enabled him to send his only son to Eton then Oxford and Mrs Rivers never let one forget it.

'Mrs Rivers, have you met my sister, Mrs Bell?'

'Yes, we met at the village fête last summer. How do you do, Mrs Bell? An artist, aren't you?'

'That's right.' Nessa smiled. Mrs Rivers looked her up and down, then nodded as if that was all the explanation she needed for the woman's odd appearance.

'I'm here to meet my son, who's staying at the hotel,' she continued. 'You might have heard of him. Gideon Rivers? He's quite the celebrated archaeologist these days.'

'You *have* mentioned him once or twice, but we've not yet had the good fortune to meet,' said Ginny. Nine or ten times, more like it.

'Well, now's the perfect opportunity. He's leading the dig up at the castle, and he's brought his fiancée with him, a rather glamorous *Parisienne*. I'm not sure I approve, but my opinion doesn't count for much. Men don't listen to their mothers these days.'

Nessa nodded in sympathy. Her oldest son, Julian, had just gone up to Cambridge and she missed him terribly. She'd confided in Ginny that she was worried he was lonely there in the cold fens, but when she'd tried suggesting he join some university societies to meet fellow students, he'd ignored her and either stayed in his digs writing poetry or went out beagling.

'Come and join us. We're sitting just over there,' said Mrs Rivers.

Ginny was reluctant to leave their table by the window,

where they had a good view of everything that was going on in the street, for the larger table by the fireplace, where they risked being roasted alive. But Nessa had already risen from her seat, extracted her basket from under the table and was following Mrs Rivers.

'Come on, Ginny,' she whispered. 'I'm dying to meet the *Parisienne*.'

Making a face, so only her sister could see it, Ginny got to her feet, feeling the stiffness in her bones again. Perhaps the warmth of the fire might help to ease it. Mrs Rivers beamed as they joined her table.

When the young waitress returned with a tray bearing their order, she looked confused.

Ginny was about to say something sharp, but her sister got in first.

'I'm so sorry – we've moved tables,' she called out.

'Stop apologising,' hissed Ginny, but Nessa shut her up with a look. Even now that they were both well into middle age, she never stopped being the big sister. Their squabbling was interrupted by the appearance in the doorway of a glamorous young couple. The dining room fell silent as they made their way over to the table.

'Mother dearest,' called out the man. He was taller than average, slim, with broad muscular shoulders, off which his tobacco-coloured jacket hung with nonchalant ease. His golden-brown hair was flicked back from his face in a long fringe that looked as though it had been sprayed to keep it in place. He had the symmetrical features and baby-blue eyes of a Hollywood film star, with a tan to match.

Ginny had to rub her eyes to make sure she wasn't seeing things. The young man before her was the absolute spit of

11

their dear brother Thoby, whom they'd lost to typhoid at the age of twenty-six. Except he lacked Thoby's awkwardness. Her chest tightened as she remembered the pain of losing him.

The woman next to him was as petite as he was tall, with olive skin, and long-lashed eyes. Her hair was tucked beneath a fashionable midnight-blue skull cap, although a couple of glossy black strands were falling out and she had one of these caught between her slender fingers and was twisting it nervously. She smelled of, what was it? Honeysuckle, roses and something else.

'Gideon, Jasmine!' exclaimed Mrs Rivers, raising her hands in welcome.

'Yes, that's what you smell of, jasmine,' said Ginny, sniffing in satisfaction.

Mrs Rivers peered over the top of her thin-rimmed gold pince-nez.

'Her name is Jasmine,' she said, a little sternly.

'Of course,' Ginny replied, feeling her cheeks flushing.

The girl tossed her beautiful head dismissively.

'Jasmine comes from an old French Syrian family, the Zain al-Dins, perhaps you've heard of them?' said Mrs Rivers. 'She and Gideon met when he came to the Sorbonne to lecture on the dig that he was working on out in Syria with Sir Flinders Petrie at the time. It was Petrie who recommended him for the job here. Rather put old Stanley Briggs's nose out of joint, I'm afraid.'

Although she'd only met Mr Briggs on a couple of occasions, Ginny could easily imagine he wouldn't welcome the arrival of this dashing young archaeologist. He had a reputation for being slow and steady. No doubt that's why the dig's backers wanted someone with more of an energetic approach.

'What were you working on out in Syria?' she asked him.

'A dig near Antioch. Rather a sleepy place these days, but it was once one of the most important cities in Christendom, part of the Byzantine empire. Near to where we were excavating, in ancient times there was an enclosure filled with stylites, hermits who sat on top of pillars to bring them closer to God,' said Gideon.

'How unusual,' said Ginny. It sounded a strange way to connect with the divine.

'How about you, Mademoiselle Zain al-Din? Our little country town must seem very dull after Paris,' said Nessa.

'Call me Jasmine, please,' said the younger woman, her smile revealing a set of perfect white teeth. 'On the contrary, I'm enjoying the peace and quiet and the . . . Englishness of it. Wherever Gideon is, that's where I am at my happiest.'

He took her hand and they looked at one another with such intensity of feeling that Ginny felt herself blushing again.

'Mustn't let the kippers go cold,' she said, turning her attention to her plate and taking a forkful. They were just as she'd imagined, the right combination of salty and buttery. The coffee served in a silver pot was hot and strong. For a few moments, she did nothing but soak up the pleasure of good food on an empty stomach. Nessa was occupied with her buttered toast. Jasmine sipped black tea, while Gideon attacked a plate of sausages, black pudding, and bacon with fried eggs, mopped up with thick slices of buttered white bread.

Breakfast revived everyone's spirits. Once they'd eaten,

Gideon called over the waitress, who looked as though she might faint when he spoke to her, and ordered sherries all round, ignoring the protests of the women. Soon, the gathering took on a party atmosphere, which Ginny hadn't expected so early in the day.

'Gideon, you simply must take Mrs Woolf and Mrs Bell to see the dig,' said Mrs Rivers, knocking back the last few drops in her glass.

The young man opened his eyes wide as if that were the very last thing he wanted to do.

'Really, there's no need,' said Ginny, who having devoured the longed-for kippers was eager to sober up on the brisk walk back to Rodmell where she planned to spend the rest of the day reading by the fire.

'But I insist. It's not every day you get the opportunity to be shown round an excavation of international importance by the chief archaeologist. Do you know, they're uncovering treasures from the Crusades, brought back to Lewes by the third William de Warenne?' said Mrs Rivers.

'Do keep your voice down, Mother. We don't want the whole world to know about it just yet. Plus, I'm not the chief archaeologist – that's Mr Briggs. I've just been brought in to head up this dig,' said Gideon.

'Between you and I,' said Mrs Rivers at the top of her voice, 'Mr Briggs is not too happy about being supplanted by my son.'

Gideon flushed. 'You've talked me into it. Come on, ladies. I'll give you the tour,' he said, realising it was the only way to stop his mother talking. He pushed back his chair and got to his feet. Jasmine remained seated.

'I think I'll go back to my room, *mon amour*. I didn't

sleep well last night. You go ahead without me. I've seen it all before.'

Gideon planted a kiss on the top of her hair.

'I'm afraid I can't join you, either. I have some more shopping to do before I return to Rodmell,' said Mrs Rivers.

Ginny racked her brain for an excuse, but she was too late. Nessa had picked up her basket and was already following Gideon, who was striding out of the dining room in a bid to get away from his mother.

'I'd love to see the dig. I have my sketchbook with me. Perhaps I might even be able to make a quick impression,' she said.

Ginny took some notes from her purse to pay for breakfast – Nessa was always short of money – and went after them. They had to run to keep up with Gideon as he headed out of the building, cut through the hunters and crossed the High Street.

'We must stop off at the library to get the key for the gate,' said Gideon. 'They insist I put it away there every night for safekeeping. I used to have one of my own, but apparently the old dragon who lives in Castle Precincts House has complained of disturbances.'

'Mrs Dudeney?' Ginny snorted. 'You want to watch out or she might put you in one of her dreadful novels.'

3.

Vanessa

Gideon led the sisters into Barbican House, a grand, rectangular Georgian building fronting on to the High Street, behind which rose the town's Norman castle. It served both as the town museum and the home of the Sussex Archaeological Society. With her artist's eye, Nessa appreciated its classical symmetry juxtaposed against the romantic ruins that sat on a steep mound. Looking up to the castle's parapet, she thought she wouldn't like to fall from the top.

'Mr Briggs's secretary, who keeps hold of the key, is usually squirrelled away in the library on the third floor. Wait here – I won't be a tick,' said Gideon.

'We'll come up with you. I'd like to see the library,' said Ginny.

As so often, Nessa was embarrassed by her sister's forthrightness. She would have happily waited in the entrance hall, admiring the shaft of sunlight falling through the window on to the wooden floor, but Ginny was already striding up the stairs in Gideon's wake. Her basket was starting to feel heavy, so, placing it out on bottom of the stairs, she followed them.

The broad staircase led up to the first flo plaque on the door announced these were the rooms of the archaeological society. Gideon d here but led them up a second narrower flight of stps to a warren of interlinked attic rooms, with lower ceilings than the floor below. At a desk in one of these cubby holes sat a nervous looking woman wearing an unfashionable brown felt hat pulled down over her forehead. When she looked up, Nessa saw she wore thick, black-rimmed spectacles. She blinked in surprise at the arrival of the three visitors.

'Miss Bramble, this is Mrs Woolf and Mrs Bell. I'm going to take them up to the dig, but I'll need the key if that's all right?' said Gideon.

'Of course,' said Miss Bramble, whose age was difficult to guess. She could have been anything from twenty-five to forty. She appeared a little disorganised, pulling out several drawers and rummaging through them before finally extracting the key.

'Briggs keeps the main set, but he doesn't work on a Saturday. Since Mrs Dudeney complained, I must now beg dear Miss Bramble here every time I want to visit the dig out of hours,' said Gideon in an amused tone.

'And what do you do if Miss Bramble is unavailable?' asked Ginny.

'Miss Bramble is as reliable as the sun. She's here six days a week from eight o'clock in the morning until six o'clock in the evening. What she does on the Sabbath day is a mystery only she can answer.'

Gideon was waving his arms about as he spoke, but he

...ooking at Miss Bramble, or he would have seen her ...eeks flush. She cleared her throat as if she were about to tell them how she spent her Sundays, but then thought better of it.

'Do you mind if we look around?' asked Ginny.

'Not at all,' said Miss Bramble quietly.

Ginny strode from room to room, and Nessa followed behind her as she stopped to peer at the wall-to-ceiling shelves packed with leatherbound volumes, mostly covering some aspect of national or local history, archaeology, geography, or geology, although there was also a smattering of out-of-print novels.

Nessa picked up a green cloth-covered book about the smugglers of Alfriston, a large village some miles to the east of Lewes, close to her own home at Charleston farmhouse. She flicked through the pages while her sister examined the rest of the shelves. It made her think she must go there soon to paint the church, which they called the Cathedral of the Downs thank to its prominent spire.

Gideon looked on, his hands twitching in the pockets of his baggy trousers.

'I hate to hurry you, but I don't want to leave Jasmine alone for too long,' he said in a voice containing just a hint of impatience.

'Come on, Ginny. You can come back and look at the books some other time,' said Nessa.

'Can I, Miss Bramble?' asked Ginny.

'I'm sure that would be all right, although I'll have to check with Mr Briggs,' replied the secretary.

'Please do. Now I know about this treasure trove, my appetite has been whetted,' said Ginny.

She gave the bookshelves a last lingering stare and Nessa had to take her by the arm and practically pull her down the stairs after Gideon, who once again was bounding ahead.

Outside, he took a right turn on to a cobbled lane, past a narrow house clad entirely in black geometric tiles, apart from the woodwork which was shining white. Nessa had seen it before and always thought it looked like something straight out of a Charles Dickens novel. Behind this curious house rose Lewes Castle, an imposing ruin on a high grassy mound, made all the taller because the ground beneath it dipped down into a sunken garden. The cobbled lane climbed up to the east of this garden through an impressive double-arched medieval gateway.

'The first arch is thought to date from around the fourteenth century, when the castle was in its heyday,' Gideon informed them as they walked beneath stones so ancient Nessa hoped they wouldn't collapse as they passed.

'The second arch is older, built not long after the castle was first established in the aftermath of the Norman Conquest. It was home to William de Warenne, right-hand-man to William the Conqueror, and his wife, Gundrada,' Gideon added with a dazzling smile, as if he were giving a tour to a party of tourists.

He continued his lecture about the castle's founders as they walked past the aptly named Castle Gate House and Castle Lodge with the town's bowling green to their right, which he informed them was on the site of the former tilting ground, and on past a long, low malthouse belonging to one of the town's many breweries.

Brack Mound was smaller than the hill on which the castle ruins stood, covered in tufty undergrowth, with a ramshackle house set into its banks. As they walked past, they saw a woman of about sixty sitting in the window, whom Nessa recognised as Mrs Dudeney. She was waving frantically.

'Just ignore her,' hissed Ginny.

Nessa wished her sister would be friendlier to people, although she knew her literary fame often invited unwanted attention. On this occasion, it appeared such attention couldn't be avoided, as a moment later the front door of the house swung open and the woman emerged, without a hat or coat.

'Mrs Woolf, Mrs Bell, Mr Rivers,' she said, as if they might not be aware of their own names.

'Mrs Dudeney, how nice to see you,' said Nessa. 'Mr Rivers has kindly offered to show us the excavations on your mound.'

'Do call me Alice, please. You don't mind if I join you, do you? I never like to pass on an opportunity to keep up with the dig, seeing as it's on our doorstep.'

Ginny gave her sister a look as if to say she minded very much, but Nessa spoke first.

'Of course, we would be delighted. After all, it's in your back garden,' she said.

'It's been so exciting having Mr Rivers and his team here,' continued Alice. 'I like to drop by at least once a day to see how they're getting on, don't I, Mr Rivers?'

'You do indeed.' Gideon smiled unconvincingly, but the older woman didn't notice. She just carried on talking.

'It's very kind of you to take an interest, Mrs Woolf. Do you think perhaps you might find inspiration for your next book? For my part, I'm contemplating writing a novel about an archaeologist working in a country town in the south-east of England.'

'Wherever can you have got that idea from?' Ginny replied, adding, 'I imagine you and I have very different ideas about inspiration. Our writing styles are not at all similar, you must agree.'

Alice bit her lower lip and Nessa thought she could see tears welling up behind her wire-framed spectacles.

'That sounds like a jolly intriguing idea for a book. I for one would read it,' she said quickly and was rewarded with a grateful smile from the older woman, and a glare from her sister.

'That's enough literary chatter, ladies,' said Gideon, looking awkward. He went to the wooden gate leading from the street to the hill and unlocked it with the key they'd just obtained from Miss Bramble. The three of them began the climb, Gideon continued his tour.

'Might I invite you to approach the top of the mound in silence. Imagine you're stepping back in time to the eleventh century. Why have you chosen this spot for your keep? To maintain a watchful guard on the main road in case Saxon rebels approach from the north? Or to overlook the river, which in this age is navigable? Later, you realise you also need a good vantage point to the south, to monitor the ships sailing in from Normandy and further around the English coast. This first mound you have constructed, yoking local men to haul great blocks of quarried chalk and pile them up to form a gleaming white hill, doesn't offer a sufficiently expansive view in all directions. So, you build another, even taller motte. Now Lewes has not one but two viewing platforms, making it one of the best defended castles in Sussex.

This was such a crucial region for access to the continent that the Conqueror divided it into six long, thin sections known as "rapes", each with its own river inlet and castle, so no one baron could control too much of the land and threaten his own authority.'

As he spoke, Nessa found her attention drifting to the surrounding landscape, which was casting off its summer green and putting on its autumn coat of mottled hues. When she tuned back into what he was saying, they'd reached the top of the mound. A little out of breath from the climb, she stood and admired the magnificent view of the surrounding countryside. It was a warm day, but up here there was a pleasant breeze and Nessa enjoyed the sensation of the cool wind on her forehead as she stood still, a little out of breath from the climb, and took in the scenery.

Ginny had already made her way over to a deep trench dug into the ground and was lifting the corner of a tarpaulin partially covering it.

'Mrs Woolf, if you don't mind, this is a working site and it's important not to contaminate any of the artefacts,' said Gideon, rushing over to take the sheet from her.

'Allow me,' he added, tugging it back with a practised movement. Although he couldn't have been much older than his mid-twenties, there was an air of great authority about Gideon. He was clearly someone in complete mastery of his chosen subject. It helped he had the sort of looks that made both women and men stand and stare. His hair and skin were sun-kissed from working outdoors, and he had a Grecian beauty.

The removal of the covering revealed a deep, circular

hole, lined with brick. Beside this was a narrow trench, just big enough for a person to stand up in.

'It looks like a well,' said Nessa, clapping her hands together in surprise at seeing such a thing in this position.

'Indeed, it is,' said Gideon. 'This was the site of the first castle built by William de Warenne. It would have been made of wood to begin with, brought over from Normandy, ready for construction. The walls have long since rotted away, but we can find the foundations, as well as artefacts left behind. This well is evidence the keep was occupied and prepared to defend against attack. We think it may have had a double use as a repository for treasures brought back from the Holy Land. The lord and lady would have lived in grander accommodation, lower down, where there are now private houses around the bowling green.'

He was interrupted by someone clearing their throat loudly.

'Mr Rivers, I thought I'd spoken to you about opening up the dig on a Saturday.'

They all turned round to see who was speaking. A thin, balding man dressed in an old-fashioned tweed suit with a pipe hanging out of the side of his mouth appeared over the brow of the hill.

'Stanley, I thought you'd be at home mowing the lawn. I'm afraid I couldn't pass up on the opportunity to show our work to one of our leading lady novelists.'

Ginny narrowed her nostrils. She hated being referred to as a lady novelist. Alice looked close to tears again. The clear implication was her own novels were not in the first rank. Gideon didn't appear to notice either reaction as he strode over to the new arrival and clapped a hand on his back. The older man recoiled slightly as he did so.

'Mrs Woolf, Mrs Bell, meet Stanley Briggs, chief archaeologist for the Sussex Archaeological Society.'

'But somehow not in charge of this site,' Mr Briggs added, taking a puff on his pipe, then extending his arm to shake hands with the sisters, and nodding at Alice.

'No hard feelings, eh. We've both got our jobs to do,' said Gideon, grinning. But Briggs didn't look quite so sure.

'I've always wanted to see a real-life archaeologist at work,' said Nessa. 'I don't suppose either of you gentlemen would oblige?'

Briggs shook his head.

'Saturdays are outside of my contracted hours, I'm afraid, but I'm sure Mr Rivers can be convinced. His approach is rather less orthodox than mine,' he said.

'You don't get to head up a dig at the age of twenty-six without taking a few risks in life,' said Gideon with a grin. 'Come along, then. Fortunately, I have my trowel with me, and there's a section of the trench I didn't quite finish excavating yesterday.'

He crossed the grassy platform, pulled back the tarpaulin and extracted a tool with a sharp metal blade and a wooden handle from the inside pocket of his linen jacket. With all the energy of youth, he swung himself down into the pit and took up a position beside what were clearly fresh workings. Nessa was mesmerised by the way in which he moved his hands, deft and gentle, using the tip of his trowel to chisel away the earth as a piano player strokes the keys of his instrument. She took out her sketch pad and pencil and tried to capture the scene. Ginny and Alice looked on in silence.

After a couple of minutes, Gideon stopped digging.

'I think there's something here,' he said, putting down the tool and feeling the earth with his finger.

'Probably just a lump of chalk,' said Briggs, dismissively. Gideon took a small knife from the same pocket in which he'd kept the trowel and used its blade to prise the object from the ground.

He brushed away the soil from the surface with his fingertip, with surprising delicacy for someone of his size. For a moment he stood, utterly still and silent. Then he let out a long, low whistle.

'Come and look at this, Stanley,' said Gideon. The practised way in which he'd extracted the object made Nessa wonder if he hadn't planted it there in advance, in anticipation of just such an opportunity. There was undoubtedly something of the showman about Gideon Rivers.

'This is proof if ever we needed it of a link to the Holy Land,' he said, holding up the object for them all to see.

Nessa stepped closer to look and saw a tablet not much bigger than the palm of her hand. On its surface was carved a script she couldn't understand, which to her untrained eye looked like Arabic.

'May I?' she asked.

He passed the object to her, earning a scowl from Briggs.

She felt it with fingers accustomed to moulding wet clay. But something about the object made her shiver and she was glad to pass it back to Gideon.

'Can you hold it up? I would like to capture it fresh from the earth.'

He held the artefact up obligingly as she took out her sketchbook and made a rough drawing.

'It's made of clay, isn't it?' she asked, glancing up at it, then back down to her sketch.

'Yes, indeed, baked many moons ago, in the fertile basin, where civilisation began. I will need to examine it more closely, of course, but it is my guess, dear ladies, that this clay tablet was brought all the way to our cold island from sunnier desert climes. It's a link to the Crusades when the third William de Warenne went off, leaving behind his new wife and their infant daughter, Isabella. William never made it back. He perished in a skirmish in Antioch. But this find proves some of his party must have returned here to Lewes.'

'We can't draw any such conclusions for certain,' said Briggs.

'Oh, Stanley, stop being such an old stick in the mud. We all know you spend every night in your study poring over a Kufic coin with this same script on.'

The older man's cheeks coloured as all three women turned to look at him.

'Is this true, Mr Briggs? Is there a link between our old ruin and the crusading knights of yore?' asked Alice, her voice raised in excitement.

'Don't get too carried away with your romantic notions. Archaeology is a science, not one of your popular novels,' said Ginny. Nessa elbowed her sister.

Gideon came to Alice's rescue.

'You're both correct in your own way. Archaeology is a science, but it is also a creative act of imagining how the artefacts and remains of buildings we uncover might have existed in their worlds. For that, the novelist's eye is invaluable.'

26

Alice looked as though she would like to hug him.

'We have indeed found a coin, adapted to be worn as a brooch, which we believe dates to the tenth century. The inscription is in the Kufic script, a distinctive form of decorative Arabic writing. It proclaims Muhammed to be the Prophet of God,' said Briggs.

'The Crusaders wouldn't have liked that,' said Ginny.

'Antioch was on the front line of the struggle for power between Christians and Turks. Over the centuries it changed hands several times, and on the Second Crusade, most of the Crusader army was destroyed either in skirmishes with the Turks or by sickness, Earl William among them. It is thought, however, that his vital organs were borne home by his companions. In 1845, navvies constructing the Lewes to Brighton railway discovered two caskets containing the bones of his grandparents, William I and Gundreda, and nearby was a lead vessel packed with viscera believed to belong to him. Perhaps this tablet made it back at the same time,' said Briggs.

Nessa shuddered at the gruesome thought.

Briggs glanced up at the sky, where a dark raincloud was fast approaching from the east.

'It looks like rain, Mr Rivers. We should get the trench covered up again straight away. Our guests have had a taste of what we're doing here. Give me the tablet,' he added casually to Gideon. 'I'll drop it back to Miss Bramble to catalogue. This could be an important find for our dig.'

The younger man, who was already bending over to replace the tarpaulin, shook his head.

'No, it's quite all right, Stanley. I'm heading back that way.

I'll give it to her.' Without waiting for an answer, Gideon opened the leather bag he wore across his shoulder and placed the tablet inside. Briggs looked as though he would rather like to wring his neck.

4.

Virginia

As they made their way down the mound, Ginny realised she was missing something.

'My bag. I must have left it in the dining room at the White Hart. I should go back for it,' she said.

'Those clouds look ominous. I'm meeting Duncan and his friend at the castle to drive them back to Charleston. Why don't you join us when you've found your bag and I'll give you a lift home?' said Nessa.

Ginny was dressed for the weather in a houndstooth skirt suit and matching hat, with sensible brown leather brogues, but she knew Nessa worried for her health. A chill could send her into a downward spiral resulting in weeks in bed. Stubborn as ever, she shook her head.

'The walk will do me good. If I start back for Rodmell now, with any luck, I'll make it home without getting soaked. Thank you, Mr Rivers, Mr Briggs, for a most enlightening morning. Mrs Dudeney, good day,' she said.

She hoped she wasn't too late. The bag contained her latest notebook with some important jottings for the lectures she was planning, but to a waiter clearing the dining room it might look like rubbish.

Taking one last look over her shoulder at the mound, she felt a sudden premonition no good would come from the dig. But she shook the feeling off. It must be the bad weather heading this way making her gloomy.

When she reached the High Street, the hunt was still assembled in front of the White Hart. As she approached, the chief huntsman, astride an enormous chestnut field hunter, lifted a horn to his lips and blew. She watched as thirty horses made their way at a fast trot up the street, heading out of town to the west, a host of barking beagles bringing up the rear. A couple of motor cars in their path had no choice but to draw to a halt, while pedestrians leaped out of the way. Once they'd gone, the street was eerily quiet.

She went back into the hotel and made her way to the dining room, now empty, apart from one corner, where she was surprised to see Mademoiselle Zain al-Din, deep in conversation with a dishevelled-looking young man in spectacles and a suit that hung awkwardly off his thin frame. His jet-black hair shot up from the widow's peak of his brow in an almost comic fashion, and, although she couldn't hear what he was saying from where she was standing, she saw that as he spoke his prominent Adam's apple bobbed up and down. Intense brown eyes were slightly too deeply set in his face and his nose was long and knobbly, with a reddish tinge as if it had been blown one too many times, and yet there was something kindly about his countenance. If she were given the choice of spending an evening with this man or the handsome Gideon Rivers, she would choose him.

She'd always preferred intellect over appearance. Leonard was a case in point.

Jasmine and the young man didn't look up as she crossed the room and fetched her bag, which was tucked under the table by the window where she and Nessa had first sat down.

They were still whispering to one another as she left the dining room, heads bent together. As she made her way down one of the twittens, the narrow alleyways leading from the High Street to the suburb of Southover, she wondered what Mademoiselle Zain al-Din had to say with such intensity to a young man who was not her fiancé.

By the time the rain started to pelt down, she was nearly home, and had to run the last part of the way, clutching her hat to her head, her scarf flying behind her in the wind.

Back at Monk's House, the dogs barked with delight to see her. Poor old Grizzle the terrier gave a series of low woofs and nuzzled against her leg as she bent down to greet him. Pinka the spaniel jumped up in delight and licked her nose when she bent down, her affection a constant reminder of her close friend Vita Sackville-West, who'd given her to Ginny as a gift. Pinka was the daughter of Vita's own dog Pippin.

By the time Leonard returned, she was ensconced in the green sitting room, next to a roaring fire made by Nellie, their maid of many years, a cup of tea in hand, a book in her lap. As he peeled off his wet clothes – he'd been caught in the downpour while loading plants into the back of the motor – and hung them on the little wooden rack in front of the fire to dry, she told him about the morning's events and their impromptu visit to the castle.

'I should like to see this tablet,' said Leonard. 'I've read

31

about such finds out in the Near East, but it's not the sort of thing one expects to dig up on a Sussex hillside.'

'That's because you have a narrow view of the world. There have been connections between the continents since humans first walked the earth,' she said. She took a swig from her teacup then realised it was cold.

'Be a dear and put this down for me,' she said, holding it out to Leonard.

He took it from her and balanced it on top of a pile of books without watching what he was doing, so that it teetered precariously.

'They can hold great power, you know,' he said.

'What can?'

'Clay tablets of the kind you described. Ancient peoples believed magic resided in the words they wrote down, that they embodied part of the soul of the writer. There are numerous tales of bad things happening when they are unearthed. Some of the stories I've heard from the desert would make you scared to sleep at night.'

'What nonsense. You've been reading too many articles about the Curse of Tutankhamun. I didn't think you of all people would be susceptible to such superstitious humbug,' she said, placing her book down on the side table with a flourish.

'And yet you say you detected a tension between Gideon Rivers and Stanley Briggs when they spoke of it,' he replied.

'That can be put down to professional rivalry. There's no need to cast around for a supernatural explanation,' she said.

He didn't say anything else but adopted the infuriating expression he wore when he thought he was right.

That evening, they sat just the two of them opposite one another in the little dining room, on the chairs backed with an embroidery of flowerpots designed by Nessa and stitched by Leonard's mother. Nellie, who was in a mood about something or other, slammed two plates of rissoles down in front of them.

'There you are, sir, madam,' she said in an angry tone. Ginny wondered what the matter was. She'd thought Nellie would be pleased they had no company for a few days. They liked to revel in the solitude while they were in the countryside, after the busy social whirlwind of town life. That was the trouble with servants, they would insist on having feelings. One had enough trouble managing one's own emotions.

'Better tread carefully,' whispered Leonard, inclining his head in the direction of Nellie's disappearing back as she retreated huffily to the kitchen.

'I've been thinking about the tablet,' he added. 'The connection between Sussex and the Crusades would make an excellent article for the *Athenaeum*. Exactly what you were saying about trade routes and the international connections that came with them existing further back than we give them credit for. I'm thinking of a piece imagining the lifecycle of a clay tablet, inscribed a thousand years ago, before it somehow makes its way into the hands of this Warenne fellow. He means to bring it back to his cold, damp household in England and store it together with some other treasures he's collected on his travels. But, before he can do so, misfortune strikes and he dies in a foreign land, the first victim of the tablet's curse. Then, unwitting, his faithful friend and companion, Baldwin, brings it back to Sussex to give to his widow and child.'

'Baldwin?' enquired Virginia, arching her eyebrows so high that lines appeared in her usually smooth forehead.

'Humour me. It's a flight of fancy,' said Leonard, waving away her doubt with a flick of his hand.

'Baldwin arrives back with the horde, but the grieving widow can't bear to look upon her dead husband's items, and so she orders them to be buried inside the dried-up well in the oldest part of the castle, a place she rarely visits now she has a warmer, better-appointed tower on the neighbouring mound.

'Only Warenne's daughter, Isabella, who will inherit his title and lands, then pass them to her husband, the king's illegitimate half-brother, visits the well in the old keep and gazes down into its depths where she believes she can see glittering gold coins, and just make out the Arabic script on the tablet's surface.

'Little does she suspect, the tablet is imbued with an ancient curse, meaning whoever looks upon it will die without any heirs. The prophecy is realised when the Warenne family dies out, with no living descendants to pass the castle on to.'

Ginny leaned back in her chair and clapped her hands in glee.

'Leonard, you do tell a wonderful story. Although I fear you're going to turn spiritualist like Mr Conan Doyle. You've convinced me that's exactly what happened. I can't wait to hear the next instalment and find out what fresh havoc the tablet will produce now it's being stored in the attic of Barbican House.'

Leonard shook his head and took a deep breath in through his nose.

'You joke, Ginny, but no good will come of it. When

treasures are taken from the earth, she demands payment in some other form,' he said in an ominous voice. Ginny felt a prickle at the back of her neck, and, just for a moment, she believed him.

5.

Vanessa

Nessa had agreed to meet Duncan and his friend who was staying with them for a few days, in front of the castle to drive them home. Bobby Bassey was a young jazz trumpeter from New Orleans whom Duncan had invited to Charleston to nurse a broken heart. Duncan had been painting him in the private courtyard she'd dubbed Grant's Folly where he took friends when he wanted to be alone with them. Nessa pretended not to mind, but each time Duncan fell in love with a new man, she feared losing him.

They were standing in front of Barbican House when she approached with Gideon and Briggs. Bobby visibly recoiled when he saw who she was with, and she raised her eyebrows at Duncan in question. He returned a look that said he would explain later.

Gideon and Bobby gave one another a curt nod.

'What are you doing here?' asked Gideon, his usual composure clearly rumpled.

'Staying with Duncan at Charleston,' replied Bobby sullenly.

There was an awkward silence, which Duncan broke by holding out his hand. Gideon accepted and shook it vigorously.

'I know of you by reputation, Mr Grant,' he said, turning on his smile again. 'Do come and look around Barbican House. I have to take this find up to the library, then I can show you around our little museum.'

Duncan looked at Nessa, who shrugged in agreement. The party made their way back into the cool interior of the Barbican House. Miss Bramble had come down from the attic and was sitting behind a desk in the entrance hall, still wearing her brown felt hat. Did she ever take it off, the funny old thing? As they approached, she looked up and blinked several times, her eyes magnified by her glasses.

'Ah, Miss Bramble, would you be good enough to take this up to the library and put it in the safe there? Old Briggs is doing his nut in about it.'

Gideon took the tablet out of the inside pocket of his jacket and handed it to Miss Bramble, who took it but didn't move.

'Don't just stand there and stare at it, woman,' barked Briggs, who'd followed them in. 'You heard what Mr Rivers said. Take it up to the library and lock it away for safe-keeping.'

Miss Bramble flushed and hurried off up the stairs with the tablet in her hand.

'What I would give to have her predecessor back, but Miss Jenkins, as was, would have to go and get married and have a baby. Miss Bramble was all that the agency could come up with,' said Briggs once she was gone. Nessa would have liked to give him a sharp kick.

37

'Come on. There's a fascinating collection of Iron Age brooches in the shape of wild boar you simply must see,' said Gideon, changing the subject. He put his arm round Duncan's shoulder and led him off towards the exhibition rooms.

Bobby hung back.

'Are you all right?' she asked him. He nodded, but Nessa could tell he was trying to suppress some sort of strong emotion.

The museum consisted of only a couple of rooms, so the tour didn't take long. It was an odd collection of fossils, Saxon grave goods and fragments of Lewes Priory left over from the Dissolution. Aware it was nearly lunchtime, she was impatient to get back to Charleston and tried to egg the others along.

'Come on. I've left the motor just round the corner in the West Gate car park. We should be getting back. Grace is preparing lunch and she'll be furious if it's ready and we're not there.'

'What's the hurry? She's only a servant – let her wait,' said Gideon. It was all Nessa could do to stop herself from giving him an earful. Grace was so much more than a servant; she was an essential part of their household and a person for whom she and Duncan had the greatest respect.

She glanced at Duncan, hoping he would back her up, but he looked away sheepishly, unwilling to take her side against someone as handsome as Gideon. Trying to suppress her irritation, she looked around for Bobby, who was standing looking confused at the bottom of the stairs. She crossed the entrance hall, picked up the laden wicker basket from where she had left it, then linked her arm with his and tugged him towards the door.

'Goodbye, Miss Bramble,' she called out to the assistant who had reappeared from the attic, hoping Duncan would take the hint and follow.

'Goodbye, Mr Rivers,' she added. Little did she suspect that it was the last time she would see Gideon Rivers alive.

6.

Alice

The next day

No one heard her scream, and she became aware, sitting there on her mound, how very vulnerable she was. Could the killer still be at large? How long had the body been there? Indeed, who was the poor, dead soul?

Of this last, at least, she had a fair idea. She hadn't been able to look at the corpse for long, but she recognised the toned body and artfully cut casual linen suit now splattered with blood as belonging to Gideon Rivers. It was difficult to understand how someone so very alive such a short time ago could now be dead.

She couldn't bear to take another look, but what she'd already seen was seared into her memory. Now she came to think of it, the blood – so much blood everywhere – was congealed. This suggested that a few hours had passed between the murder – for that was surely what it was – and her discovery.

There was no sign of whoever was responsible for this

brutal act. They must be long gone by now. An almost uncontrollable fury began to well up from the bottom of her belly. What sort of devil did it take to cut down a beautiful young man in his prime? Her own daughter, Margery, was not much older than Rivers. The evil person who did this must be brought to justice.

The previous day, when Gideon had shown Mrs Woolf and Mrs Bell around the dig, she'd felt annoyed with him for treating Virginia as the better writer of the two of them, even though she'd sold many more books. His charming manner and handsome looks had failed to make an impression on her as they once would have.

Now, however, she regretted her annoyance. If she'd known what fate awaited him, she would have been more charitable towards the young man.

As no sign of help was forthcoming, she hauled herself to her feet, called Nelson, who was cowering nearby with the canine sense that all was not right, to her side and started making her way back down the hill, shouting for Ernest at the top of her voice. By the time she'd reached the house, her cries had roused her husband from his bedchamber, and he was not happy about it.

'What the hell is all this infernal racket about, woman?' he barked in a tone not dissimilar to Nelson when he encountered another dog he didn't like.

Usually, she would have launched into a full-blown row at this point, but it was testament to how badly shaken she was that she merely pointed up to where she'd come from and said in a weak voice, 'There's a body, on top of the mound.'

Seeing how ashen her features were, Ernest became contrite and put his arms round her.

'My poor, dear Alice, you've had a dreadful shock. Come inside and sit down,' he said.

She did as she was told. Nelson followed his mistress and curled up next to her on the old divan. Only once Ernest had poured her a large brandy, did she tell him what she'd seen.

Grim-faced, and still in his dressing gown and slippers, Ernest fetched his rifle from where it hung in the hall. Then he unlocked his desk drawer and took out the bullets that he stored there, loading them carefully into the gun cartridge. Holding his grizzled chin aloft, he made his way out of the back door to investigate his wife's claims. At that moment, Alice thought she'd never loved him more. All the ups and downs of their long marriage were temporarily forgotten.

A few minutes later, he returned, made his way back into the drawing room, where she was still nursing the brandy glass, her spirits starting to revive. She was already busy planning a letter in her head to her close confidante, Sir Philip Sassoon, telling him all about the horror of finding the body, and how no one had come to her aid, and she'd been forced to handle matters by herself so very bravely until she was able to rouse Ernest from his bed.

She felt sure Philip would be most sympathetic. He might even send flowers, and the next time they met he would hold her hand with just the right amount of delicate pressure and ask her if she could bear to tell him again about what had occurred. It was horrible to have a murder happen in one's own back garden, but she was beginning to see that the situation might also contain certain possibilities. Then she remembered the killer was still on the loose, and her fantasies of starring in her own detective novel were replaced by raw fear.

Giving a brief nod, Ernest unloaded the rifle, hung it back on the wall and poured himself an even larger glass of brandy than her own.

Only once he'd taken a swig, did he speak.

'I must go to the police station straight away and report a murder,' he said.

Lewes Police Station was only a couple of minutes' walk away in the old marketplace known locally as Commercial Square.

Alice nodded in agreement, then a thought crossed her mind.

'Do change out of your dressing gown first, dear,' she replied.

7.

Virginia

Rodmell, East Sussex

Leonard was on his hands and knees planting out the bulbs that had recently arrived in the post by mail order.

'What will they be when they come up next spring?' asked Ginny.

'The daffodils are Poet's Narcissi, so a refined yellow. But I'm afraid the tulips are a rather tarty red.'

'Oh dear, people will think us vulgar.'

'Not at all. It's very modern to have a vibrant colour scheme,' Leonard reassured her, but she wasn't convinced.

Although it was still warm for the time of year, she was dressed for cooler weather in a pale pink cotton blouse and grey cardigan with a grey flannel skirt, the hemline of which skimmed her ankles.

At the sound of the gate clinking, they both turned their heads to see who was coming round the side of the house. A man appeared with neatly parted salt-and-pepper hair and a waxed moustache, wearing a brown flannel suit. He wore a grave expression. Grizzle lived up to his name by running out of the kitchen door and growling at the new arrival. Pinka would have happily thrown herself at him with spaniel exuberance if Ginny hadn't restrained her by holding on to her collar and telling her in no uncertain terms to 'Sit'.

'Can I help you?' she called, advancing down the brick path towards the man with Pinka at her heels.

'Mrs Woolf?' he asked, in a strong Sussex accent.

She nodded. 'The same.'

'Chief Inspector Arthur Gripe of the Sussex Constabulary,' he said, climbing up the step from the back of the house to the garden and extending a hand, which she took. His handshake was brief and strong. 'I'm afraid I come bearing bad news. I've just been to see Mrs Rivers at Hollybush House to tell her that her son has been found dead.'

Virginia stopped in her tracks.

'Dead? Gideon? But I was with him just yesterday.'

'That's what Mrs Rivers told me, which is why I thought I'd drop by while I'm in the vicinity to ask if you noticed anything out of the ordinary?'

Ginny felt as if her legs might give way under her. Leonard got to his feet. The inspector, who hadn't noticed him, jumped back.

'You gave me quite a surprise there, sir.'

'My apologies. Would you like to come inside the house? I think my wife needs to sit down while she takes in this terrible news.'

Leonard stepped out of the flower bed on to the path and took Ginny's arm. At his touch, she felt instantly calmer. He led the way towards the house and through the conservatory to a long, low sitting room, the walls of which were painted a verditer green. Ginny collapsed into a saggy armchair covered in a bold patterned fabric designed by Duncan.

'Please take a seat,' said Leonard to Chief Inspector Gripe, indicating a stiffer chair with an embroidered cushion. 'Can I get you a cup of tea?'

'That would be kind, thank you.'

Once her husband had disappeared into the kitchen, Ginny felt revived enough to ask the chief inspector what had happened.

'I'm sorry to report the lady who lives on Brack Mound, Mrs Dudeney – she's a writer like you—'

'Mrs Dudeney is nothing like me,' said Ginny, batting away the suggestion with a flick of her wrist. The inspector looked puzzled by her response but continued.

'The lady in question took a walk to the top of the mound behind her house shortly after dawn and discovered a body there. Upon examination, she identified the corpse as Mr Gideon Rivers, who was leading the dig currently taking place there.'

Ginny felt as though someone had punched her in the stomach. That poor beautiful boy. Mrs Rivers had been so proud of her son. Now, instead of basking in his reflected glory, she would have to bury him. How cruel life was.

Ginny should be used to death by now. After all, she'd lost her mother and half-sister while she was still a girl, followed by her beloved brother. But one never got used to it, that was the thing.

'What happened?' she asked simply.

'That's what I'm attempting to ascertain, Mrs Woolf. Did you notice anything out of the ordinary about Mr Rivers yesterday?'

'It was the first time I met him,' she said. First and only. 'He seemed full of the vigour of youth. In love with life, with his work, with his fiancée.' She pictured the fragrant Jasmine Zain al-Din. They'd made such a beautiful couple – she'd been quite envious, but it turned out now there was nothing to envy.

'He showed you around the dig?'

'Yes, he even made quite an exciting discovery while we were with him. Some sort of Arabic tablet.'

'I see. Was it valuable?'

She considered his question.

'I'm not sure if it has monetary value, and I'm no expert, but I would have thought it's the kind of thing that's invaluable in terms of what it can teach us about the past rather than for its intrinsic worth,' she said. 'How was he murdered?' she added, curiosity getting the better of her.

'I'm afraid I'm not at liberty to divulge the details,' said Chief Inspector Gripe, puffing out his chest.

'You're quite sure it's murder? I mean, could he have fallen and broken his neck or something?'

Gripe looked her in the eye and shook his head slowly from side to side.

'There's no doubt about it whatsoever, Mrs Woolf. This was a crime of great violence. Somebody meant to do Gideon Rivers grave harm and they succeeded in their mission.'

A small amount of bile rose to the back of her throat, and she thought she might be sick. Leonard arrived bearing the tea tray just in time. Seeing her pale face, he put a reassuring hand upon the nape of her neck.

'How do you take your tea, Chief Inspector?' he asked.

'Milk and two sugars, please.'

47

Hospitality observed, Leonard poured his wife the brew she so evidently needed, a strong Darjeeling with just a splash of milk. Taking a sip, her spirits rallied.

'Do you have any idea who could have done it, Chief Inspector?' she asked.

Gripe shook his head, sending a droplet of tea that had landed on his moustache flying.

'I've spoken to Mr Briggs, the chief archaeologist at the castle, and he insists the gate to the street was locked last night. He keeps it in his study and the only spare is in the library at Barbican House. His secretary, Miss Bramble, who is also his housekeeper, was good enough to check for us this morning and the spare key was in its usual place, although it's possible someone who knew it was there came and took it and then replaced it.'

'What about the key in Mr Briggs's study?' asked Ginny. She didn't add there'd clearly been no love lost between the men. Briggs was a bit stuffy, but he surely wasn't a murderer.

'Miss Bramble is apparently a very light sleeper. Her bedroom is next to the front door, and she's quite certain that if anyone had entered the house, or left it, she would have woken and heard them,' said the inspector.

Her writer's imagination at once got to work. Mr Briggs could have drugged Miss Bramble, taken the key from his own study and returned it before she awoke. Or perhaps an intruder could have accessed the study from the window and stolen it without her noticing.

Chief Inspector Gripe struck her as a man who took people at their word and, in her experience, this was rarely advisable.

'Do you have any theories?' she asked.

The chief inspector cleared his throat and squared his broad shoulders, as if in preparation for putting forward his hypothesis.

'I suspect Mr Rivers wanted to go up to the dig site early while there was no one else around. He took the key from the library and let himself through the gate. The murderer happened to see him, thought there might be some financial gain in it and followed him through the gate. There was an altercation resulting in the death of Mr Rivers, then the murderer fled the scene,' he said.

'He or she fled the scene, but first returned the key to the library, gaining entrance to Barbican House, which would also be locked at that time of day?' asked Ginny, arching her brows.

Gripe shifted around, the hard seat not the only thing making him uncomfortable.

'There are some points to be ironed out,' he replied. 'And it must have been a "he". No woman could have used the force involved in his murder. But, there, I've said too much.'

And underestimated the female sex, thought Ginny, who knew many women capable of just as much physical strength as men.

'I'm happy to assist in whatever way I can, Inspector, but I'm afraid I can think of nothing from our encounter yesterday to aid your investigation. You could try talking to my sister, Vanessa Bell. She rents Charleston farmhouse, out near Firle, and she was with me up at Brack Mound yesterday.'

'I will indeed interview Mrs Bell, although it will be tomorrow before I get round to it. Murder requires so much paperwork these days,' said Gripe, rising to his feet. 'Thank you, Mrs Woolf, and please thank your husband for the tea. I must take my leave of you now, but if anything else occurs, however small, ask for me at the police station on Mount Pleasant.'

Ginny saw him to the door. Leonard had disappeared, no doubt back to the garden and his beloved tulip bulbs. She needed to talk to someone about what had just happened, and there was only one person in the world who shared her experience of death and grieving.

Above all right now, she wanted to be with her sister, and as Leonard was occupied in the garden and unlikely to want to drive her, she would just have to don her brogues and walk the five miles over the Downs to Charleston.

8.

Vanessa

Charleston farmhouse, Firle, East Sussex

Straw hat perched at an angle, its wide brim protecting her from the afternoon glare, Nessa was weeding in the walled garden. A shadow loomed over her, and she looked up to see her sister. Despite the autumn sunshine, Ginny was dressed in a thick walking jacket, skirt and the sensible brown leather brogues she always wore for tramping over the Downs. Beneath the heavy gear, she looked even thinner and paler than usual.

'You didn't say you were coming. We've nothing but soup to offer you,' said Nessa.

'Don't worry. I've quite lost my appetite,' said Ginny.

'Nonsense, everyone needs to eat. Just let me finish off this patch and then we can go and see what we can find in the kitchen.'

'Nessa, something terrible has happened.'

Looking at her sister's face, Nessa saw it was drawn and tense. She put down the hand fork she was using, and hauled herself stiffly to her feet, one hand on the small of her back.

'Whatever is it? You look like you've seen a ghost.'

'I had to come here to tell you at once. It's Mr Rivers.'

'Gideon Rivers? What's he done?'

'He's been murdered.'

It sounded so unlikely that Nessa peered at her sister curiously, wondering whether she was having a funny turn.

'Murdered?'

'A Chief Inspector Gripe called at Monk's House this morning. Pompous fellow. He'd just been to see Mrs Rivers to tell her that her son is dead, poor woman.'

'Wait a minute. I'm finding it difficult to take all this in. Gideon Rivers is dead? He seemed about as alive as it's possible to be yesterday. Who killed him?'

'Well, today he's dead and that's the question. Who could have wanted him dead?'

As soon as her sister spoke these words, Nessa saw the awful truth of the matter. Gideon Rivers was the sort of man around whom emotions ran high. Love, lust, envy and from there it was but a short step to hatred. Although she felt bad for even thinking it, the way in which Stanley Briggs had looked at Gideon the day before came to mind.

'Come into the kitchen and have a bowl of soup. I made it myself with some of the potatoes I bought at the market yesterday. If we're in luck, there'll be some of Grace's freshly made bread to mop it up. Don't say you've no appetite – you need feeding up, especially if you've walked all the way from Rodmell.'

Abandoning her weeding, she walked through the garden gate and past the front of the house, where the last of the roses and clematis clung on. She removed the garden soil from her shoes on the scraper just outside the kitchen door, then led her sister inside. A posy of homegrown flowers sat in a blue ceramic jug on the wooden table, illuminated by a shaft of sunlight. She made a mental note to return to capture it in oils later.

'Sit down and take your shoes off. You must be worn out,' she instructed Ginny, who for once did as she was told.

She lit the stove to heat up the soup, then checked in the stone larder. There was half a loaf left over from lunch, from which she cut three thick slices, two for Ginny, one for herself. She put them on a plate and fetched the butter dish.

'Now tell me everything,' she said once they were installed at the table, bowls of soup and hunks of buttered bread before them. Ginny repeated everything Chief Inspector Gripe had imparted.

'But it doesn't make sense. How did Gideon get up there without a key? And who can have wished him such harm. What about that lovely fiancée of his? She must be beside herself. Unless, wait, you don't think she did it, do you? *Un crime passionnel?*'

'It was probably a man, according to the inspector, or at least somebody capable of brute force. I don't think the petite Mademoiselle Zain al-Din fits that profile, do you?'

Nessa shook her head.

'And they seemed terribly in love to me,' she added.

The kitchen door opened and a slim, good-looking man with doe-like eyes and curling black hair starting to turn grey at the temples put his head round the door.

'Hello, Duncan,' said Ginny.

'Hello, Ginny,' he replied, adding, 'Have you seen Bobby?'

'Not since this morning. He said he was going for a walk,' said Nessa.

'What's up with you two? You look as though someone's died.'

'They have. Gideon, the archaeologist who showed us around the castle yesterday.'

'What's happened to him?' came a second, more urgent voice.

'Bobby, there you are. I've been looking for you everywhere.' Duncan tried to put an arm round the younger man's shoulders, but he pulled away from him.

'Is Gideon all right?' he asked again.

'He was found dead first thing this morning at the top of Brack Mound in Lewes. Did you know him?' asked Ginny.

Bobby's jaw fell open and hung there as her words sank in.

'Yes, I knew him. He used to come to hear me play at the club.'

The tone of his voice said it all. Nessa wasn't shocked. Most of the men she knew had gay love affairs.

He looked as though he might faint.

'Sit down and join us for a bowl of soup,' said Nessa, fetching two more bowls from the cupboard. She just managed to make the soup go round and cut up the rest of the loaf to go with it while Ginny filled them in on what she knew about Gideon's murder.

Bobby sat there in silence, not touching his food, and Nessa wondered just what exactly had gone on between the two men for him to be so badly affected. She resolved to get him alone later to try to coax it out of him. He wasn't much older than her eldest son, Julian, and she felt responsible for him. He was all alone in England, far away from the grandmother who'd raised him in New Orleans.

When they'd eaten, Duncan offered to drive Ginny home.

'Don't forget Chief Inspector Gripe wants to talk to you tomorrow,' Ginny called out as she climbed into the seat beside Duncan.

After they'd gone, Nessa cleared away the dishes, then picked up her trug and headed back to the garden to finish off the weeding. She loved this time of year when the sharp autumn light illuminated the garden, filled with nostalgia for the dying year. It was so peaceful here, the wind rustling through the tall beech trees that grew between the farm-house and the main road, rooks circling and cawing above.

'Nessa.'

Her reverie was interrupted by Bobby's soft Southern drawl. She sensed he'd sought her out, wanting to unburden himself of the shock of learning of Gideon's death.

'Are you all right?' she asked.

'Will you tell the police inspector I knew Gideon?' he asked with fear in his voice.

'I don't suppose I can keep it from him. He'll find out sooner or later anyway. Why don't you tell him yourself? It will look less suspicious that way. You don't have to tell him everything, of course. Leave out the fact you were lovers. You were lovers, weren't you? I can't imagine a rural police inspector being very understanding about that bit. Just tell him you were friends on the jazz scene.'

'He'll arrest me for the colour of my skin if nothing else,' said Bobby. He was right. Nessa had seen the looks he'd got when he'd come into Lewes with her and Duncan. They weren't used to seeing Black people and he'd certainly been a novelty. It was only a short step from there to the locals assuming that if a murder had taken place he was to blame.

'Do you have any idea who could have meant him harm?' she asked. If he could give the police any leads, perhaps that would serve in his defence.

Bobby shook his head, a solitary tear rolling down his cheek.

'Everyone loved Gideon. He broke my heart. When we met, he was already engaged, not to Jasmine, but to the film actress, Marguerite Muir, do you know her?'

Nessa nodded. She didn't keep up with the moving pictures, but everyone knew Marguerite Muir, the darling of the gossip press. She and Duncan had gone to see her in *The Silent Angel* at the Uckfield Picture House, in which she played a nurse who was hopelessly in love with the invalid for whom she was caring. It had been a very moving performance. When he discovered his disease was incurable, she agreed to help him end his life, even though it meant she would be left grief-stricken and alone. Now she thought of it, she vaguely remembered reading something about a broken engagement.

'That didn't stop us falling for one another. But then one day he just upped and left for Paris and the next thing I knew he'd ditched both Marguerite and me for Jasmine. I heard about it from a mutual friend – he didn't even let me know himself. I loved him, and now I'll never get the chance to tell him.'

At this, he broke into sobs and Nessa put her arm round him. Searching in her pocket, she found a handkerchief, which she offered him. It was a frilly lace affair, bought at a market in France, and he laughed through his tears, but took it anyway and blew his nose loudly. She wished she could reassure him that he wouldn't fall under suspicion, but it didn't look good that the man who'd broken his heart had been brutally murdered, and he was staying just a few miles away at the time. If Chief Inspector Gripe questioned him, he couldn't deny knowing Gideon, even if he didn't give him the full details of their love affair. It would look too suspicious if it came out later. But she had to agree with Bobby that if the inspector could pin a high-profile murder in his patch on a stranger who stuck out in this most English of country towns he probably would.

It was only a matter of time before the press got wind of Gideon's murder and descended on Lewes. If they found out about his relationship with Bobby, they would splash on it in lurid detail. She racked her brains as to how she could protect this young man who was her guest. And then it came to her. If she believed him to be innocent, and his grief was very real, then she was just going to have to solve the mystery of who killed Gideon Rivers herself. Well, not quite by herself. There was one person she could always rely on. Her sister.

57

9.

Virginia

The next morning, Ginny slept late in her little bedroom in the eaves of Monk's House, drunk with dreams of dead bodies and deep trenches.

When she eventually awoke, to the sound of the church clock on the far side of the garden chiming nine, she was relieved to see sunshine filtering through the lace curtains. Seized by a sudden urge to put pen to paper, she swung out of bed, took her dressing gown from the chair next to it and flung it on loosely. She ran down the stairs and out of the back door on to the narrow brick path between the cottage and the lawn. Tying the belt of her dressing gown tighter around her, she padded across the lawn, glancing over to the curving heights of Mount Caburn in the distance. But before she could reach her writing hut her path was impeded by the solid figure of their gardener, Fred Hobbes. A man of few words and long pauses, today he was visibly agitated, and it seemed he'd been waiting for her to emerge.

'Mrs Woolf, may I have a moment of your time?'

Her brain was still clouded by the fog of sleep, but she attempted to shake it off.

'Of course, Fred. What is it?'

She had a soft spot for these old-fashioned country types, who seemed to her almost to blend with the landscape.

'It's my Betsy. Well, it's her husband. They were only married this summer. He's a good lad is Danny. He would never have done such a thing.'

'Never have done what thing?' asked Ginny, trying to understand what Fred was saying.

'He's been arrested for the murder of that young Rivers fellow. *He* had it coming to him, but Danny would never have taken it into his own hands. Not when he's got Betsy and the baby to think about.'

'Slow down. You're telling me your daughter's husband has been arrested for the murder of Gideon Rivers? What on earth would his motive be?'

She couldn't imagine how the gilded Mr Rivers could exist in the same universe as Fred Hobbes's son-in-law.

The gardener looked at her. He was silent, but his eyes were filled with meaning.

'Betsy is beside herself,' he said at last, speaking more slowly this time. 'She walked all the way from Kingston to Rodmell first thing this morning to tell me and the wife what's happened. She's at home with us now, and the little one. It's lovely to see them, but not in these circumstances. I thought perhaps you could go and speak with Inspector Gripe, tell him Danny Lamb has nothing to do with it.'

'I'm not sure how much my word counts for with the inspector,' said Ginny, wondering what she should do. Normally, she would have consulted Leonard, but he'd taken the early train up to London for a meeting about their printing press.

'Give me five minutes to change into some proper clothes and I'll come with you to talk to Betsy,' she said.

Fred nodded in agreement. She returned to her bedroom, splashed herself with some cold water from the bowl on the dresser, towelled herself dry and dressed. As promised, five minutes later she emerged wearing a brown flannel skirt and cream blouse with a sage-green woollen cardigan.

The gardener led the way out of the gate and down the lane to a cluster of smaller cottages, one of which was his own. As they entered, Ginny heard a baby crying with a piercing yell.

A plump but shapely young woman with flaxen hair, who couldn't have been much older than twenty, sat on a wooden stool with tears streaming down her pretty cheeks, while an older, stouter woman jiggled a red-faced infant up and down on the kitchen table.

'Dry your eyes, Betsy. Mrs Woolf has come to ask you about Danny,' said Fred.

The young woman mopped away her tears with her white apron and looked Ginny up and down.

'Tell her what happened, Betsy,' said the older woman, prodding her with her finger. The girl seemed uncertain, but started speaking.

'They came for him last night, after dark it was, the inspector and two police officers. Told him anything he said might be used in evidence against him, so he was too scared to speak, wasn't he? They clapped a pair of handcuffs on him and dragged him out into the night. I heard the police van driving away and that was the last I saw of him.

Didn't sleep a wink, and at the crack of dawn I fed Baby and made my way here on foot. Forty minutes it took me. I had to walk on the road, what with the perambulator. You can't push that across fields. I don't know what Baby and I will do without Danny.'

At this, Betsy started crying again in great uncontrollable sobs. Ginny tried not to show her revulsion.

'Is there any reason they suspect Danny of the crime?' she asked.

She was met by more silence. Heavens, they were a surly lot, these Sussex types. Husband and wife and daughter looked at her, but didn't say a word.

'Did Danny know Mr Rivers?' she pressed.

Betsy shook her head.

'He never met him.'

'There must be something. The police don't just arrest someone for no reason.'

There was an awkward silence. Then Fred cleared his throat and spoke.

'Betsy knew him. She was in service with Mrs Rivers at Hollybush House until this summer,' he said.

'What happened in the summer?' asked Ginny, then as her brain caught up with her mouth, she realised the implication. 'Oh, I see,' she said. But just to be sure she added. 'How old is your baby, Betsy?'

'He's coming up to four months.'

'And when were you and Danny married?'

The girl flushed a deep shade of pink.

'In April.'

It didn't take Ginny long to do the sums in her head. It was as she thought.

61

'So, the police suspect jealousy as a motive?'

Betsy shook her head vigorously, her mouth forming a circle of outrage.

'Danny isn't the jealous type. We've known one another all our lives. He's always been sweet on me, and he knew what he was letting himself in for. We've been happy as anything the three of us since Baby came along. He makes a wonderful father.'

'Yes, but that's not how the mind of the law thinks. How did they find out about this? Did someone tell them?' asked Ginny.

Betsy nodded woefully.

'I bet it was Mrs Rivers. There was a dreadful scene when she found out what happened. She blamed me, used some terrible language for such a refined lady, she did. Called me a slattern.'

Ginny cleared her throat.

'Yes, well, that's not very kind. One would have thought she might hold her son to account rather than a simple village girl.'

Betsy frowned.

'Forgive me. I was thinking out loud. I meant simple in the sense of honest – I don't doubt your intelligence, my dear. Nevertheless, you must see that Danny did have a motive for wanting harm to come to Mr Rivers.'

'He didn't care. He got used to the idea long ago,' the girl said in a petulant voice.

Ginny ignored her.

'Where was Danny in the early hours of Sunday morning?' she asked.

'He was with me. Until he got up as usual to go and milk

the cows at Howe Farm where he works as a labourer. Cattle don't respect the Sabbath, you know.'

'I see. What time does he usually leave for milking?'

'Sometime between four and five. I'm not sure exactly. I woke up for a few moments, but it was pitch black and, as Baby was quiet, I went back to sleep. Got to get my kip where I can these days.'

She chucked the infant under the chin, and he gurgled with pleasure.

'And what time did he return?'

'I wasn't paying much attention, but it was light, I know that much. That's when I got up. He had a wash like he normally does, because I can't stand the smell of the cows on him.'

Ginny wondered if Danny would have had time after milking the cows, or possibly before, to run from Kingston to Lewes, murder Gideon Rivers, then run back again. The fact that he'd washed could be suspicious. It would have removed any traces of blood. But then again, Betsy said it was his habit always to wash after milking the cows, so perhaps she shouldn't read anything into it. There was also the matter of how he would have convinced Gideon to meet him by Brack Mound at such an early hour on a Sunday. She supposed he could have sent him a letter asking to meet, but then there would be evidence, and wouldn't Gideon have been suspicious? Her curiosity was well and truly piqued. There was nothing for it – she was going to have to pay Chief Inspector Gripe a visit and get more information out of him about the circumstances of Danny's arrest.

'Leave it with me. Do I have your permission to say I'm

representing your family?' she asked Fred, who nodded vigorously.

'Yes, of course, thank you ever so much, Mrs Woolf. I said to Mary here that you would be the person to consult, and she wasn't sure, but I was right, see.'

He looked at his wife, who said nothing, but nodded curtly, still dangling the baby from her arms with his chubby little feet just touching the table.

Ginny went home and breakfasted on tea and eggs on toast. She was just digging her teaspoon into an egg, which Nellie had boiled to perfection for once, when the doorbell rang. It was the postman with a letter from Nessa.

Dearest Ginny,

I've arranged to meet Chief Inspector Gripe at the castle at midday. He sent a messenger boy to say he was going to come out to Charleston, but I told him I was coming into town today anyway. Why don't we meet beforehand, and you can come with me? I've got some news of my own.

Meet me at the White Hart at eleven, Nessa.

'What's your news then?' Ginny asked her sister over a strong pot of coffee at the hotel, which they both decided they needed ahead of their interview with the chief inspector.

Nessa took a deep breath.

'It turns out Duncan's jazz musician Bobby Bassey, who you met at Charleston the other day . . .'

Ginny nodded and hurried her along with a wave of her hand.

'Well, he and Gideon Rivers were lovers. He says Gideon broke his heart, and he's terrified he's going to be framed

64

for his murder. But now you say this Danny Lamb has been arrested – that changes things.'

Ginny poured out two cups of black coffee. Nessa added milk to hers and offered the jug to her sister, but Ginny, who preferred it black, waved it away and took a sip of the scalding liquid. Its bitterness made her scowl, but she relished the kick of caffeine.

'Betsy and her parents want me to protest Danny's innocence, but it's in the interest of your house guest that he stays in custody. Where does that leave us?'

'Perhaps we should try to extract as much information as possible about why Danny has been arrested,' said Nessa.

Ginny considered this, nursing her coffee cup in both hands.

'I think you're right,' she said at length. 'But if we want information from Chief Inspector Gripe we must give him something in return. Is there anything you can think of?'

At that moment, the door of the hotel lobby opened, and a slim figure entered, dressed entirely in black, with a netting veil attached to a pillbox hat covering her face, and a black silk rose pinned to her breast. Even though they couldn't see her face, the sisters recognised Jasmine Zain al-Din at once. Nessa got to her feet and hurried over to the young woman.

'Mademoiselle Zain al-Din, what a terrible shock you've had. You must be completely beside yourself. Come and sit with us. What can we get you? Coffee? Brandy?'

The black-clad figure shook her elegant head.

'Just *une tisane*.'

Ginny clicked her fingers. 'Waiter, mint tea, if you please.'

'We've only got English Breakfast,' said the man.

'That'll have to do,' said Ginny.

The sisters ushered Jasmine into a seat at their table. Her features were stricken with grief.

'*Ma pauvre chère*, this must be too awful for you. Do you have anyone you can confide in?' asked Nessa.

Jasmine shook her head, her eyes downcast.

'I'm completely alone here, apart from Mrs Rivers, but I don't want to intrude on her grief.' Her English was heavily accented, but otherwise flawless.

'It's decided, then. You can't remain here wallowing by yourself. You must come and stay at Charleston. We have a spare bedroom where you'll be quite comfortable and at least you'll have people around you. It doesn't do to be on your own at a time like this.'

The young woman looked at Nessa uncertainly, but her mouth broke into the faintest hint of a smile.

'Yes, perhaps that would be good, but not until after the funeral,' she said, her voice barely louder than a whisper.

'Is there anything you can tell us about the morning of the murder?' asked Ginny. Her sister glared at her, but Jasmine didn't seem to mind the question.

'He must have left early because I didn't notice him go. We were sharing a room, you know. Are you shocked?'

Ginny let out a brief laugh, before remembering there was nothing funny about the situation and stopping herself.

'Very little shocks us, my dear,' she said.

'The next thing I knew is Inspector Grape came knocking on the door. I wasn't even dressed. I had to receive him in my dressing gown. When he said Gideon was dead, I thought it must be a practical joke. Even now I can't believe it.'

'It's Chief Inspector Gripe,' Ginny corrected her, amused.

66

Nessa took Jasmine's hand and patted it.

'It must be very terrible for you. Tell me, Jasmine, how did you and Gideon meet?'

'He came to the Sorbonne, where I was studying archaeology, to give a lecture on the dig he was working on out in Syria in the ancient city of Antioch. It's a unique site with finds dating back all the way from the time of the Crusades to pre-Christian antiquity. I've never experienced anything like the lecture he gave that day. He conveyed such passion for his work. I just knew I had to be a part of it, and I persuaded my parents to let me stay with my uncle in Syria, so that I could join him on the dig. That's when we fell in love.'

She paused and her eyes were shining with the memory.

'That's why he was recruited to work on the dig at Brack Mound,' she continued. 'After they discovered a Kufic coin, which must have been brought back from the Crusades, the Sussex Archaeological Society felt they needed an expert in the field. Stanley Briggs knows a lot about British prehistory, but he lacks international experience. He wasn't happy about Gideon leading the excavation at all.' At this she shook her head.

'Do you think he might have had anything to do with the murder?' asked Ginny.

Jasmine shrugged.

'I am told he has . . . How do you say it in English? An iron alibi.'

'Cast-iron alibi,' came a new voice.

The sisters had been so intent on listening to what Jasmine had to say that they hadn't noticed the arrival of a tall, thin man, with jet black hair, wearing a crumpled suit. Ginny nudged Nessa and made an expression to let her know this was the man she'd told her about, who she'd seen with Jasmine on the day before Gideon's murder.

'Harry,' exclaimed Jasmine, looking a little less distraught than she had done a moment before. Perhaps she was not quite so alone as she made out.

'These ladies are friends of Gideon's mother. I'm so sorry – I've forgotten your names, with all that's happened.' She turned to the sisters apologetically.

'I'm Virginia Woolf and this is my sister Vanessa Bell. I'm a neighbour of Mrs Rivers.'

Harry raised his eyebrows, indicating he had heard of them. He extended his hand.

'Pleased to meet you, Mrs Woolf and Mrs Bell, even if it is under such tragic circumstances. I'm Gideon's oldest friend, Harry Dryden. I came a few days ago to help on the dig. Never in the world expected anything so terrible to happen. I'm staying with Mrs Rivers in Rodmell, but she's absolutely beside herself as you can imagine, so I thought I would get out of her way and come and see how Jasmine is faring. I still can't believe it. I mean, who could wish Gideon any harm? Everyone loved him, me included.'

'Love and hate are often not so far apart as we think,' said Ginny.

'I suppose that might be true,' said Harry.

'And what about you? Do you have a cast-iron alibi?' Ginny asked.

Harry turned to look at her, clearly surprised at her abruptness, then he nodded grimly.

'It's only natural everyone who knew him should fall under suspicion, but I can assure you, Mrs Woolf, that Gideon and I were like brothers. I've been staying out at

Rodmell the whole time. Mrs Rivers can vouch for me, and I'm sure you'll agree she's unlikely to cover up for her son's murderer.'

Nessa gave her sister a stern look. 'Ginny, we need to leave now if we're to make our appointment with the inspector. It was a pleasure to meet you, Mr Dryden, despite the sad circumstances. Jasmine, don't forget my offer. You're welcome to come and stay at Charleston whenever you like.'

'Thank you. I'll stay here at the hotel until the funeral, but after that it might be a relief to have other people around me,' said Jasmine.

The sisters wished the young people good day and made their way out of the dining room. Once the door had swung shut behind them, Nessa leaned towards her sister and whispered, 'Jasmine and this Harry Dryden fellow seem very close, don't you think?'

'Oh no.' Ginny shook her head firmly. 'Jasmine was devoted to Gideon – anyone could see that – and he was infinitely more handsome than Mr Dryden.'

But even as she said it she thought of how Jasmine and Harry had turned to one another as they'd left the room, and doubt crept into her mind.

10.

Vanessa

Chief Inspector Gripe was late. As they crossed the street, she felt the first flecks of rain, and suggested they take shelter inside Barbican House. Miss Bramble had emerged from her eyrie in the attic and was sitting behind the desk in the entrance hall, which now had a sign on it announcing visitors could pay tuppence to look around.

'Would you like to buy a ticket, ladies?' she asked, before they turned to face her, and when she recognised them she said, 'My apologies, Mrs Woolf, Mrs Bell. I thought perhaps you were day-trippers, here to see the castle ruins.'

They explained they were waiting for the chief inspector, and Miss Bramble nodded and went back to looking at a ledger on the desk, in which she appeared to be doing some sort of cataloguing.

A few minutes later, Gripe arrived.

'Mrs Bell, you've brought your sister with you. Very good. As I have both of you here, perhaps we could walk back up to the scene of the crime if it won't distress you too much, to see if it stirs your memory.'

They nodded in agreement. He turned to go, then remembered something. Taking a key from his pocket, he laid it on the desk in front of Miss Bramble.

'Thank you for the loan of the key. My men have taken a copy of it, which I assure you will be for police use only,' he said. Miss Bramble nodded, but didn't say anything. She just scooped the key up and tucked it away in her skirt pocket.

'Funny old bird that one,' said the inspector as they walked out of the building and turned into the cobbled street leading under the Norman archways to Brack Mound. 'Very protective of that key, although I suppose I shouldn't blame her, given what happened. She was beside herself at the thought that someone might have come in and taken it while she was asleep.'

'I hear you've made an arrest,' said Ginny, changing the subject.

The chief inspector swung round sharply.

'Who did you hear that from?' he asked.

'My gardener, Fred Hobbes, who also happens to be Daniel Lamb's father-in-law. Lewes is a small place, Chief Inspector. Everyone knows everyone else. You should know that better than most.'

The chief inspector took his clay pipe from his pocket, a pouch of tobacco from the other pocket and sprinkled a little into the bowl, then lit it with a match. It took a couple of puffs before it was properly alight.

'As you already seem to be aware, Mrs Woolf, we are holding the suspect Daniel Lamb in custody. I suppose, given your knowledge of the family, I don't need to explain his motive to you.'

'Quite,' said Ginny, holding up her hand as if to push the

71

unpleasant thought away. 'But what evidence do you have against him? His poor young wife is beside herself and she insists he isn't the jealous type. Do you have any proof he was in Lewes at the time and not out at Kingston milking the cows as he claims?'

Chief Inspector Gripe took in a lungful of smoke, puckered his mouth and blew out a perfect ring.

'I'm afraid I'm not at liberty to divulge details, but if you're in touch with the family you might let them know there was a sighting of Mr Lamb walking into Lewes from the Kingston direction around five o'clock on Sunday morning,' he said.

Ginny flared her nostrils as she always did when she was put out. Nessa reached out and gave her hand a squeeze as they walked along. They'd reached the gate up to Brack Mound. Fortunately, Mrs Dudeney was nowhere to be seen. Nessa didn't think she could cope with any spikiness between the lady novelist and Ginny today.

'Have you spoken to Harry Dryden?' she asked the chief inspector.

'Harry who?'

'He's a friend of Gideon's who's staying with Mrs Rivers. We saw him just now in the White Hart with Mademoiselle . . . Miss Zain al-Din.'

'I see,' said Chief Inspector Gripe, taking a small black leatherbound notebook from his seemingly bottomless pockets and turning to find a blank page, on which he started to write with a stubby pencil. 'What was the name again? Barry Dryden?'

'Harry,' Nessa corrected him. She hated to snitch, but she needed to keep his attention away from Bobby, whom she was certain was innocent, and help Ginny in her bid to prove Daniel Lamb's innocence too.

'Can you walk me through what happened when you came up here with Mr Rivers the day before his death?' he asked.

Nessa breathed in, catching a whiff of late honeysuckle rambling over the undergrowth at the bottom of the slope. It was only a couple of days ago, but so much had happened in between that the details were already hazy.

'We met Mrs Dudeney who lives in Castle Precincts House and were all talking as we walked up this path. Just before we got to the top, Gideon – Mr Rivers – told us to close our eyes and imagine we'd stepped back in time to when the castle was first built. He related a little of the history of William de Warenne, the first baron, and his wife Gundrada. When I opened my eyes again, I thought the view was marvellous, but I must say I was disappointed with the mound itself. I mean it's just a lump of earth, isn't it, with a hole dug into the top.'

'Typical painter,' said Ginny. 'You see the wider land-scape, but the whispers of the past are lost on you.'

Nessa tried to stifle her rising sense of irritation with her sister.

Chief Inspector Gripe took another puff on his pipe.

'As I see it, the work of an archaeologist is not dissimilar to that of a detective. You must dig down beneath the layers to get to the kernel of truth.'

He was looking up into the air as he said this, giving Ginny the opportunity to widen her eyes at her sister as if to say 'what a pompous fool'. Nessa knew what the man was getting at, but had to agree he was giving himself airs.

Ginny interrupted his reverie. 'Then Mr Briggs turned up. And I think it's safe to say there was some tension between him and Mr Rivers. Something to do with who oversaw the dig. While we were watching, Mr Rivers found the clay tablet with Kufic script on it that I told you about. I must take the credit for that because it was I who asked Gideon to give us a demonstration of his work. That's when he found it, tucked inside the trench over there.'

She gestured in the direction of the tarpaulin, which was once again stretched over the gaping hole in the ground.

Gripe walked across the grass and lifted the corner of the sheet. He looked distinctly unimpressed with what he saw.

'Beats me how these fellows manage to find out so much about the past from a muddy ditch. What was this Kufu tablet you mentioned?'

'I believe the term is "Kufic", Chief Inspector. It refers to an early form of Arabic script, such as that used in writing the Quran, although in this instance the script is to be found on coins and a clay tablet. One can't imagine how the clay survived all these centuries. It must have to do with the unique drying qualities of chalk,' said Ginny. It always amazed Nessa how authoritative her sister could sound on a wide range of subjects about which she knew next to nothing.

'It's all over my head, I'm afraid. Do you think this ... professional rivalry between Mr Briggs and Mr Rivers could have led to anything more sinister? To violence, perhaps?' asked Gripe.

'That would seem rather extreme over an archaeological artefact, however old and rare they are, but who can know for sure the mind of an expert in their field?'

Nessa saw what her sister was trying to do. Not to point the finger of blame at Stanley Briggs exactly, but to obfuscate to such an extent that the pedantic chief inspector might doubt the wisdom of keeping Daniel Lamb in custody for much longer unless further evidence came to light.

But, before she could say anything, they were interrupted by a cross, whining voice.

'I thought I told you not to come up here without consulting me first. This is an important archaeological site. You could cause irreparable damage by poking around without knowing what you're doing.'

Over the brow of the hill appeared Briggs, a slight sheen of sweat on his forehead from the climb as he was overdressed for the day in a thick cream cotton shirt, a grey woollen V-neck sleeveless pullover and a thick tweed jacket the colour of a house sparrow.

'Don't you worry yourself, sir, I was just doing a spot of imaginative re-enactment with the ladies here in case there's anything that might spark their memories about their meeting with Mr Rivers shortly before his death, to shine a light upon the case. No stone unturned – that's my motto.'

'Yes, well, my motto is to be jolly careful about which stones you turn over and make sure you leave them where you find them,' said Mr Briggs.

Chief Inspector Gripe narrowed his eyes as though he were seeing the archaeologist in a new light.

'While you're here, Mr Briggs, would you mind going over your alibi for late Saturday night and the early hours of Sunday morning?'

'In front of the ladies?'

'We can go down to the station and make a written statement there, if you prefer, sir, or I could take it down in my notebook now and save you the bother. It's up to you.'

'Very well, then. Let's get it over with.'

'Where were you on Saturday night?'

'Where I am every night, tucked up in bed with the Victoria History of Sussex and a cup of cocoa made for me just how I like it by Miss Bramble, who can account for my whereabouts as she is a very light sleeper. There I stayed until the church bells chimed at nine o'clock on Sunday morning. I'm not a churchgoing man, Chief Inspector Gripe, but I do like to mark the hours by the clock at Saint Anne's.'

'I'm a Chapel man myself,' said the chief inspector, puffing his chest out and chewing on his pipe. 'Well, your secretary has already confirmed your whereabouts on the night of the murder, so you're in the clear.'

'If that's all, may I suggest we all make our way back down to the castle and lock the gate behind us? The last thing we need is curious members of the public making their way up on to the mound out of ghoulish fascination with the murder once word gets around,' said Briggs. Did Nessa detect a sense of relief in his voice that the inspector had accepted his story so readily?

'One last thing before we leave, sir. The ladies here mentioned a tablet with some sort of Arabic writing on it that was found up here. It seems there was a disagreement about who discovered it.'

There was no mistaking it: Stanley Briggs's eyes flashed with sudden anger. But when he spoke his voice was calm and reasonable, perhaps a little too much so, as if he were exercising monumental restraint.

'There was no argument. Mr Rivers found the tablet, but we were engaged in a friendly debate as to whether it should stay in Lewes or be sent to the British Museum.'

He clenched his jaw as he said this, and Nessa doubted there was anything friendly about the debate at all. As usual, though, it was Ginny who got to the crux of the matter with her penetrating logic.

'Now that Mr Rivers is out of the picture, I suppose the debate is at an end?' she said, as though it didn't really matter.

'Yes, it will be up to me now as chief archaeologist to decide on the best course of action,' agreed Briggs, not realising he'd walked straight into the trap of providing himself with a motive for removing Gideon from the scene. After all, secretaries can lie, or a sleeping draught could be slipped into their night-time cocoa to ensure they don't hear a thing.

Chief Inspector Gripe put a hand up to his forehead and pushed back a strand of greying hair that was falling into his eyes. Nessa understood his frustration. He'd begun the morning with a suspect in custody who had a strong motive for the murder. Now he'd been presented with at least two other possibilities. Either Harry Dryden had something to do with the murder of his best friend, or Stanley Briggs had evaded his secretary and done his young rival in out of professional jealousy.

11.

Virginia

Although she wouldn't have dreamed of calling on Mrs Rivers in her period of fresh mourning, it was quite a different matter when she saw her standing over her late husband's grave in the churchyard that lay nestled on the other side of the flint wall from the garden of Monk's House.

Even then, if Mrs Rivers hadn't looked up and seen her advancing up the path, Ginny would have continued to her writing hut and left the grieving mother in peace. But, as their eyes met, Mrs Rivers lifted a hand in greeting, so Ginny had no choice but to lean over the churchyard wall, balanced on a tall tussock of grass, and talk to her.

'I'm so very sorry . . .' she began. But Mrs Rivers held up a black-gloved hand and gave the slightest shake of her head.

'I've been discussing the matter with Cyril,' she said, nodding in the direction of the gravestone upon which her late husband's name was carved.

'Cyril says Gideon is to be buried alongside him. They were very close in life, you know.'

Ginny nodded in a manner that she hoped conveyed both

sympathy and understanding. She barely remembered Cyril Rivers, who, despite having moved to the countryside, had spent most of his time in the City working to fund his wife's ambitions for genteel country living. Following his retirement, he'd only managed to enjoy the fruits of his labour for a couple of years before his heart gave out. Whether it was his job or his wife that had taken its toll on the organ was the subject of much discussion behind closed doors in the village, with many suspecting the latter.

'He insists we catch the evil soul who took our son's life. Mrs Woolf, you are one of the cleverest people I know. Perhaps the most intelligent. And you met Gideon shortly before his cruel murder. If anyone can get to the bottom of this matter, I feel you can.'

Ginny wasn't sure how to respond. It was a heavy responsibility, and yet hadn't she already set about that very task?

'I'm happy to assist in any way I can,' she said, without committing to specifics. 'I believe they've already arrested a man,' she added.

'Yes, the foolish husband of my former housemaid, the little hussy. I don't believe he did it. He took Betsy as a wife in full knowledge of her condition and as far as I know they've lived quite happily together until now. You don't need to look at me like that, Mrs Woolf. I'm not completely heartless. I've kept a close eye on Betsy and her baby and send her money regularly to help with the expense of feeding and clothing an infant. The child is my grandson, after all, even if he is illegitimate, and I don't want it known more widely. Danny Lamb married her knowing they would receive this extra income, so you see it wouldn't be in his interest to take revenge on Gideon.'

'Perhaps he couldn't bear the idea of another man having touched his wife.'

Mrs Rivers shook her head. 'These country types are more pragmatic than you give them credit for, Mrs Woolf. They are surrounded by nature in all its glorious fecundity, after all. No, I feel sure Chief Inspector Gripe has arrested the wrong man. I know it isn't your area of expertise, and you're very busy with your writing and everything that goes with the literary life, but it would mean a great deal to me if you could turn your extraordinary powers of perception to my son's death. Anything at all you can find out that might lead us to the murderer.'

'I'll do what I can, Mrs Rivers. As it happens, Fred Hobbes, our gardener and Betsy's father, has also enlisted my help in proving Daniel Lamb's innocence.'

At Fred's name, Mrs Rivers narrowed her nostrils and drew in a sharp, angry breath.

'Mr Hobbes and I do not see eye to eye on many things. He's a man with a vicious temper.'

As she said this, a thought clearly occurred to her, and she reached out and touched Ginny's hand.

'You don't think it could have been Fred, do you? He was so angry when he found out about Gideon and Betsy. He said he wanted to kill him and I believe he meant it. He came to the house and hammered on the door so loudly I had to get Watkins to send him away in no uncertain terms. Perhaps now he's finally carried out his threat.'

Mrs Rivers clasped her hands to her chest in horror. Ginny thought of how mild-mannered Fred was in the presence of her and Leonard. A quiet man, usually to be found in the middle of a border, turning the earth with his fork, halfway up a ladder pruning branches, or wheeling a barrow down the brick paths of their garden. She found it difficult to imagine him being angry. But she supposed it was only natural for a father to react that way when his daughter had been taken advantage of by someone who should have behaved better.

'Let's not jump to any conclusions, Mrs Rivers. I'm not sure how much use I can be to you. My talents lie in words and imagination, and I don't know if that prepares me for the stark facts of a murder case. But I do have a knack for noticing things, and for persuading people to tell me about matters they wouldn't usually divulge. I promise that, insofar as I'm able, I'll use these quirks of mine to find out any information I can that might lead to the discovery of your son's murderer. It's such a terrible crime, and I'm so very sorry for your loss. Aside from your feelings about Fred Hobbes, is there anyone else who would have a reason to wish Gideon ill? How about his friend Harry Dryden?'

'Harry? He's like a second son to me. He and Gideon have been friends since they were young boys at boarding school. Harry's mother died when he was a baby, and his father is a rather distant professor type. He used to spend all the school holidays with us. He and Gideon were like brothers.'

And yet brothers had been known to hate one another, even to kill one another, thought Ginny, although she didn't say so out loud. Besides, she had taken a shine to Harry.

'Why is he here now?'

'Gideon invited him to come and help with the dig. They've both been fascinated by archaeology since they were boys, but only Gideon got the chance to pursue his passion. Straight after he left university, Harry's father insisted he took a job as a clerk in an insurance company. Said he wanted to make sure he was set up in a steady job for life in case anything happened to him. It's such a shame. Harry is a romantic at heart and sitting behind a desk all day is killing him. When Gideon invited him here, he jumped at the chance and took a week's leave from work to help him on the dig. He was the first one there in the morning and the last to leave at night. Until now, that is. Work has been suspended until after the funeral. He's been a great support to me, though – won't let me do a thing. He's organised everything and he's almost as cut up about it as I am. It's just a shame about Jasmine.'

'What about Jasmine?'

'Harry can't stand her. He tried to be civil for Gideon's sake, but we all knew he didn't think she was good enough for his friend. If she comes into a room, he leaves and barely acknowledges her. Gideon told me I was imagining it when I mentioned it to him, but I have a woman's instinct for such things.'

'I see,' said Ginny. But she didn't see. Not at all. Because the look on the face of the young man she'd observed talking to Jasmine Zain al-Din in the dining room of the White Hart Hotel was not one of dislike. Quite the opposite, she would have said.

She didn't have time to mull this over, though, as at that very moment the shaggy-haired subject of their conversation appeared round the grey flint corner of the country church.

'There you are, Mrs R. The funeral director has arrived to discuss arrangements, and everyone is looking for you. I thought I might find you here.'

Mrs Rivers put out a hand and touched the young man's arm.

'That's because you know me so well, Harry dear. I don't know what I'd do without you.'

While they'd been talking, the older woman had been calm and dignified, but now her lip trembled, and Ginny saw what a tremendous effort she was making to control her grief. She too had been touched by grief more often than most and she sympathised acutely with Mrs Rivers's pain.

Harry nodded in her direction. 'Mrs Woolf.'

'Mrs Rivers has just been explaining to me that you also have a passion for archaeology,' said Ginny.

A red flush spread up Harry's neck. 'I dabble,' he said. Before she could ask him any further questions, he placed his hand gently on Mrs Rivers's forearm.

'Better not keep the funeral director waiting,' he said.

She watched as the pair left the churchyard, Mrs Rivers stooping a little more than she had done a few days ago, supported by Harry.

Once they were gone, she turned back to the garden where the last of the dahlias were still putting on a show. Leonard liked to plant those of unusual colours, some were nearly black, others hot pink and peach. Behind an old flint wall, which had once been part of an outbuilding, but was now used for growing climbers, she found Fred Hobbes, weeding in between the perennials. Had he overheard her conversation with Mrs Rivers? She thought not, as from this position he wasn't within earshot of the churchyard. But, then again, he could have moved away when he heard her coming.

'Fred. How are Betsy and the baby? I've spoken to Chief

Inspector Gripe. He's not prepared to release Danny from custody just yet, but I have a feeling they don't have much to go on and it won't be long.'

'Thank you, ma'am,' said Fred with a brief nod. 'Betsy has calmed down a little and the wife is delighted that our grandson has come to stay, although of course we would prefer it wasn't under such circumstances. Did the inspector say any more about why Danny was arrested in the first place?'

'There was a sighting of him walking into Lewes in the early hours of Sunday morning, but it sounds rather flimsy to me. It could easily have been someone else who looked like him. For what it's worth, Mrs Rivers doesn't think Danny is the murderer either. The bad news is I'm afraid she's got her sights set on you.'

Having casually lobbed this into the conversation, Ginny observed Fred's reaction carefully. He didn't say anything for a moment or two, just moved his mouth around as if he were chewing on something.

'Interfering old biddy,' he said finally. 'I would use stronger language if I weren't in the presence of a lady,' he added.

'I shouldn't worry about it, so long as you have an alibi for the early hours of Sunday morning.'

Fred's eyes darted from side to side.

'I would just have been doing the usual. I wake up early, before the missus, and go for a walk down the lane to stretch my legs. Then I come back and make a pot of tea and take her a cup in bed. That's what I do every day and Sundays are no different. Never been one for a lie-in.'

'Did you see anyone who could vouch for you?'

'Not many people up at that time. I sometimes bump into one of the other folks from the village, but I can't remember seeing anyone on Sunday. The days all start to blur into one another when you get to my age.'

'Oh well, hopefully it won't come to that. Did you know about the money Mrs Rivers was giving to Betsy, by the way?'

'Money? What money?'

'For her and the baby. Mrs Rivers is no fool. She knew Gideon bore a responsibility towards them even if she insists on blaming your daughter for the affair. Apparently, she sends Betsy a regular allowance. Didn't you know?'

A strange look crept over Fred Hobbes's face. Surprise, mixed with something else. If Ginny didn't know her gardener to be a solid, earthy type, she would have said it was horror. Once again, he nodded, more slowly this time.

'P'raps she's not so bad, after all,' he said in a strangled whisper.

There was another element to the gardener's expression and, as he spoke, it occurred to Ginny exactly what it was. Guilt.

12.

Vanessa

Soho, London

Divided only by the cheerful emporiums of Oxford Street, Bloomsbury and Soho are as different as any two places can be. One is the staid preserve of mansion blocks, university halls, hospital wards and museums. The other is a warren that never sleeps of shops, restaurants, bars and nightclubs and other less salubrious establishments.

It was to Soho that Nessa now made her way from her house in Gordon Square. Her destination was the Sylvan Rooms, a small, but infamous jazz club just off Wardour Street, run by the infamous Diana Underhill and frequented by the demimonde. Bobby had told her this was the place he'd first met Gideon.

At this early hour, she was confronted not by strains of music wafting on the autumn breeze, but by a locked door and a miserable pile of cigarette butts. A bored-looking lady of the night leaned out of a window opposite, a fag dangling from her lips, her deep cleavage spilling out of a faded silk dressing gown.

'You looking for Diana?' she called.

Nessa glanced up and nodded. 'Is she around, do you know?'

'No one's been in or out all morning, so either she's fast asleep on the sofa in her office, or she's not there. This is my quiet time, see, nothing to do but have a smoke out the window and keep an eye on things.'

'I see,' said Nessa. 'I'm a friend of Bobby Bassey. Do you know him?'

If the woman spent half her life looking out at the club from the window of her backstreet boudoir, she might have some useful information.

'Lovely boy. Such a talented musician. I come and listen to him sometimes on my nights off, not that I have many of those. Shame he got his heart broken.'

'That's why I'm here. About the man who broke his heart. I'm afraid he's been murdered.'

The woman in the window gasped.

'Never,' she exclaimed. 'Old Goldenballs got himself done in.' She took a deep drag on her cigarette. 'Mind you, he had it coming. Breaking hearts left, right and centre, men and women – he wasn't fussy. Just wanted everyone to adore him, and they did, with looks like those. I'd have done him for free, but he never asked. I'm Lily, by the way.'

'Nice to meet you, Lily.'

At that moment, the door of the Sylvan Rooms swung open and a tall woman with ivory skin thick with powder and a red bob in a shade never seen in nature stood in the doorway.

'What's all this racket about?' she demanded in a husky voice.

'Morning, Diana, nice to see you too. Gideon Rivers only went and got himself murdered. This lady's come to talk to you about it,' said Lily.

Just a fraction too late, Diana's jaw dropped open. Taking in Nessa's middle-aged respectability, her tone changed.

'My goodness, what terrible news. I'm Diana Underhill, a pleasure to meet you. Do come in,' she said, holding out her hand to shake Nessa's then standing back and ushering her through the door, which she closed firmly behind them.

'Never mind Lily. She's a dreadful gossip. My office is just down the corridor. I'll make us a pot of tea.'

Nessa wasn't sure she wanted to allow anything in the place past her lips, but out of politeness she followed Diana Underhill along an artificially lit tunnel into a windowless room, furnished with a saggy red velvet sofa and a large wooden desk and chair. Diana indicated Nessa should sit on the sofa. Doing her best to avoid the suspicious-looking stains she lowered herself on to it. The club owner busied herself at a little stove in the corner, boiling water for the teapot, which she carried over to the desk with two chipped china cups on a tray. Pouring out a cup for them both and apologising for the lack of milk, she took a seat behind the desk and leaned forward, pressing her palms together and resting her chin on her fingertips.

'Now tell me how I can be of assistance,' she said.

'There's not much to tell. Gideon's dead body was found at the archaeological dig he was working on in the country town of Lewes on Sunday. My sister and I both have houses nearby and my sister – Virginia Woolf, you may know her – is acquainted with Gideon's mother, Mrs Daphne Rivers.'

Here she paused and Diana Underhill looked suitably impressed.

'Everyone's heard of Virginia Woolf. In that case, you must be Duncan's friend Vanessa?'

Of course the woman knew Duncan and what he was, but Nessa didn't let it bother her. She'd long ago learned that if she wanted him in her life she would just have to put up with his indiscretions.

'I don't think Mrs Rivers knows Gideon frequented Soho nightclubs,' she added.

'The mothers never do. They like to imagine their darling boys are innocent,' said Diana. Nessa thought of Julian, her own firstborn. She wasn't under any illusions about his innocence, but, then again, she probably didn't know the full extent of his love life, nor did she want to. One's offspring must have their own secret lives. She cut straight to the reason she'd made the journey from her sedate apartments to this seedier side of town.

'The thing is, we have a young man staying with us, a friend of Duncan's with whom I believe you are acquainted, Bobby Bassey.'

Did she imagine it, or was there a flicker of warning in Diana Underhill's heavily mascaraed eyes?

'You want to know whether Bobby did it? Whether he killed his former lover because he couldn't bear to see him marrying a Parisian heiress? You needn't look so surprised, Mrs Bell – we all knew about it. Gideon liked boys and girls and he was ambitious, knew he needed a marriage with the right connections. Not that he would ever have admitted it,

89

but did you know his father was a grocer's son before he made his fortune in the City? Plus his fiancée is beautiful enough. But Bobby took it hard. It stopped him playing music. When Duncan suggested he go and stay at your house in the country, I encouraged him. Told him there would always be a place for him here in the band when he was back to his old self. If anyone can make him forget his heartache, it's Duncan.'

Nessa thought about the sounds she'd heard from the private courtyard, where Duncan liked to entertain his guests, and couldn't help but agree.

'To answer your question: no, I don't think Bobby could have killed Gideon. He had the physical strength, for sure, but he's the gentlest man I've ever met. I can't imagine him carrying out such a violent crime.'

How did she know Gideon's death was violent? Nessa had told her his dead body had been discovered, but she hadn't gone into any more detail than that. As for Bobby, sometimes it was the most gentle, quiet types who were capable of the greatest violence.

'Do you have any idea who else might have done it?'

Diana placed a black cheroot in the end of a gold cigarette holder and lit it with a silver lighter. She leaned back in the mahogany chair and propped a pair of slim ankles in emerald slippers with a feather trim up on the desk in front of her. She inhaled deeply and blew the smoke out through her thin nostrils.

'Plenty of people had it in for Gideon Rivers. He left a trail of broken hearts and jilted lovers wherever he went. Members of the aristocracy, film stars, you name it. He was even engaged to Marguerite Muir before he met Jasmine,' she said in a confidential tone.

'So I've heard. She was splendid in *The Silent Angel*, but I haven't seen her in any films since,' said Nessa.

'She hasn't made any recently. The rumour is it's because she was too distraught to act after Gideon ditched her,' said Diana.

'Thank you, Mrs Underhill, for setting my mind at rest about Bobby, although I don't think we're any closer to identifying the murderer,' said Nessa, rising to her feet to leave, the tea untouched.

'Surely that's a job for the police. And it's Miss Underhill, I've never married,' said Diana.

'I'm not sure how much confidence I have in our local constabulary solving the murder. They're rather . . . blinkered, to put it kindly. That's why my sister and I have taken it upon ourselves to find out what we can on behalf of his poor mother. If you think of anything at all, don't hesitate to call me. I'll leave the telephone number of my Bloomsbury house.'

She took a card out of her purse and handed it to Diana, who examined it briefly, then tossed it on to the desk in front of her.

'If I hear anything of interest, I'll be sure to let you know.'

Lily had disappeared from the window when Nessa stepped back out into the daylight, which made her blink even though she was in a shaded alleyway. She was about to turn back into Wardour Street when she felt a tap on her shoulder.

'Carry on walking. I don't want Diana to see us talking.'

It was Lily. She slipped her arm into Nessa's, and they

picked up pace as they walked along the busier street. She was so close Nessa nearly choked on her cheap perfume.

'Did she tell you about Gideon's fiancée, that French bird?'

'Jasmine Zain al-Din. What about her?'

'She was here, a few days ago, at the club. On her own, not with Gideon. She and Diana were deep in conversation, and they went into the office together for half an hour.'

'You saw all this from the window?' asked Nessa sceptically.

'No, I was in the club. Diana lets me come in to scout for punters if it's quiet. In return, I run a few errands for her, passing on messages, that sort of thing. I noticed it because Jasmine seemed agitated, and Diana had to calm her down.'

Nessa thought of the coolly self-confident young woman she'd met and wondered what could have happened to make her so flustered.

'Do you have any idea why?' she asked Lily.

Her companion shook her head.

'I didn't get close enough to hear what they were saying. I was too busy drinking champagne with a gentleman who paid for my company for the rest of the night, but I do remember thinking it was strange. When I'd seen her before, she was inseparable from Gideon. Wouldn't let him out of her sights in case some former lover of his came up and tried to steal him away from her.'

'Thanks, Lily. Can I give you something in return for the information?'

Lily broke away from her and stood back, opening her mouth in horror.

'What do you take me for? I was passing on the information

from the goodness of my heart. I wouldn't take a penny for it.'

'I'm so sorry. I didn't mean to insult you.'

Lily's face broke into a broad smile and she started laughing.

'Don't worry, I'm only having you on. Price of a packet of fags would be lovely.'

Nessa reached into her purse and took out a crown, which she pressed into the woman's palm.

'Thanks, dearie,' said Lily, leaning in to kiss Nessa on the cheek before she could back away, then skipping back off down the street in the direction of her flat.

Nessa stood still for a moment, amid the bustle of Soho, trying to take in what Lily had just told her. Was there more to Jasmine than just a glamorous fiancée? Was she somehow involved in Gideon's murder? They'd seemed far too much in love for that, and with her petite frame, she was hardly a violent killer. And yet there must be something behind Lily's story. Jasmine had promised to take up her invitation to stay at Charleston, which would be the perfect opportunity to find out more about her solo trip to the Sylvan Rooms. The only problem was how to find a way to probe her about it without putting her on her guard.

13.

Alice

Rodmell, East Sussex

It was several years since Alice had ventured out to Rodmell. On that occasion she'd taken Nelson on a particularly long walk across the Downs, dropping down from Kingston Ridge into the Ouse Valley.

That was shortly after Mrs Woolf and her husband had moved into the village, a few miles south of Lewes. Out of curiosity, she'd walked past Monk's House, the white weather-boarded cottage they'd bought at auction, and found Leonard out the front, pruning the roses. When she introduced herself and asked after his wife, he disappeared inside the house to find her, but soon reappeared to say she was indisposed. Even though everyone knew Mrs Woolf suffered from periods of depression when she was unable to rise from her bed, Alice had taken the hump and it had set the tone of their relationship in the years to come.

As she'd written in her latest missive to Philip, she'd rather not have attended the funeral, especially as she was of the

Roman Catholic faith and the service was to take place in an Anglican church. But, as the person who'd found the body, it was expected of her. Ernest had a bad head cold and had made his excuses, so she had no choice but to come alone.

Now she was here, though, she relished the opportunity to observe those present. The pews were full, and it seemed the whole of the village of Rodmell had turned out to bid farewell to their young man, together with half of Lewes. Mrs Rivers was not popular exactly, but influential. Her son, on the other hand, had clearly been loved.

It was the first time she'd seen his fiancée. Jasmine Zain al-Din was just as lovely as her reputation suggested. Today, she was wearing a plain black silk dress and a black lace veil, which accentuated her large sad eyes. Although they were filled with tears, Alice couldn't help noticing they were a rather revolutionary shade of green. She was holding the arm of Mrs Rivers and it was not clear who was supporting whom. Both looked as though their legs might give way at any moment. As a mother herself, her own daughter and grandsons far away on the other side of the Atlantic, Alice's heart went out to the two women.

Mrs Woolf and her husband were already seated towards the front of the church. They didn't have far to come as their garden backed on to the churchyard. Rather than acknowledge Virginia and risk not being greeted in return, Alice chose a seat in a pew several rows behind them.

Having secured her place halfway down the nave, she turned her head to watch who was coming through the church door just in time to see the party from Charleston farmhouse arrive. Mrs Bell had made an effort for once, putting on a black dress and coat that made her look

95

almost respectable. Alice had little time for the loose apparel favoured by these bohemian types. What was wrong with a well-tailored jacket and fitted skirt? Beside her was Mr Grant, raffishly dishevelled, and wearing brown rather than black. Behind them, oh how delicious, was a young man she recognised. It was not often one saw a Black man in their sleepy country town, but it took her a few moments to remember where she'd seen him. That's right, it was from her bay window a few days earlier, when she'd spied him deep in conversation with Gideon Rivers. The two men had stood out a mile in Lewes, one dark, the other fair, both in fancy suits with slicked-back hair.

Could there be a link between that meeting and Gideon's murder? She would mention it to Chief Inspector Gripe if he ever got round to speaking to her. A junior policeman had taken a statement from her immediately after she'd found the body, but she was surprised that since then no one had been in touch from the station. She would have thought she would be the main witness, but it seemed they had other lines of inquiry to pursue. If they wanted to find out what she knew, they would just have to come to her. She had no intention of being one of those attention-seeking hangers-on to police cases one heard about. Perhaps she would mention it in her next letter to Philip and see what he thought about the matter.

After the Charleston lot, who sat down beside Mr and Mrs Woolf, came Mr Briggs and Miss Bramble. The chief archaeologist removed his hat as he entered the church and stared at his feet, looking thoroughly miserable. The hypocrite. He'd detested Gideon Rivers while he'd been alive. More than once she'd heard him shouting at the top of Brack Mound from her garden down below. Odious man. Whenever she'd been up to check on progress at the dig he'd treated her presence as an inconvenience to be got rid of as soon as possible. He'd failed to understand that as the nearest neighbour she had a special interest in the excavations.

Now Briggs nudged his secretary sharply and gestured that she should remove her hat. There he went again, throwing his weight about the place. Trembling and looking as though she might burst into tears at any moment, Miss Bramble obliged, revealing mousy hair cut in a most unflattering style. As the pair took a seat in the pew behind Mrs Bell and her party, she took out a large handkerchief from her sleeve and blew into it noisily.

The vicar emerged from the chantry and the congregation fell silent. At the back of the church, the parish clerk closed the heavy wooden door. The service was about to begin, and the vicar climbed up the few steps to the raised pulpit and laid down his notes before him. But before he could start speaking there came a loud banging. Everyone turned round and craned their necks to see who it was. The parish clerk reopened the door and in staggered a young man with tousled black hair and an open shirt, who was clearly inebriated. How disrespectful, on this of all days. Mrs Dudeney would have sent him packing. However, Mrs Rivers got to her feet and opened her arms.

'Harry,' she said, and the young man stumbled down the aisle towards her.

Jasmine rose to her feet and went to his aid, taking his arm and guiding him towards the front pew, where he took a seat between her and Mrs Rivers. That must be the best friend, but how disgraceful to get drunk before the funeral. Afterwards might be understandable, but beforehand showed a lack of self-control. Then again, grief did strange things to men.

Once the disruption was smoothed over, the vicar began the service. His words were heartfelt, painting a picture of a young man who had been a favourite of almost everyone he met. No mention of his ill manners towards those he considered his social inferiors, which Alice had heard all about from the coal merchant whose sister lived in Rodmell. Nor of the child born out of wedlock to a serving girl, which was common knowledge in the village.

As the packed congregation rose to their feet to sing the first hymn, 'The Lord is My Shepherd', she looked over to where Mrs Bell and Mr Grant were sitting and couldn't help noticing the young man with them, the one she'd seen with Gideon. He was looking up at the ceiling, so she could just glimpse his face. His back was convulsing with sobs, and there were tears streaming down his cheeks.

14.

Virginia

Nature was calling her outside. The October sunshine pierced through the clouds scuttling across a fresh blue sky. Ginny had a mind in need of clearing. Tying on her stoutest brogues with grey worsted tights and the old tweed skirt she wore for hill walking, she made her way up the lane to where Rodmell met the outcrop of the South Downs known as Kingston Ridge.

As she approached Hollybush House, she saw someone coming out of the gate. It took a moment or two for her to recognise Harry Dryden. She was still far enough away that he hadn't seen her, and his mind appeared to be somewhere else. At the funeral the day before, he'd been visibly drunk, but now he looked like a man on a mission and his gaze was fixed on the hills ahead. It seemed he was set upon the same route as her.

She considered catching up with him, but she was in a mood for solitude, and it was likely he was too. Instead, she decided to hang back, allowing a decent time for him to stride ahead. He was at least two decades younger than her and a good foot taller, so his youth and longer legs would soon carry him out of sight.

Having paused to examine a neighbour's display of autumn-flowering nerines – it was rather fine; she must mention it to Leonard – she continued along her way. As she'd predicted, Harry had surged far ahead of her and was a distant figure slipping in and out of view. Now she could relax into being alone in the countryside on a fine autumnal morning. She hadn't realised how much the events of the last few days had oppressed her. Familiarity with death didn't make it any easier. Being faced with the brutal murder of a young man who had died too soon at the same age as her brother had opened old wounds.

Once she'd passed the last houses of the village, she met an old hollow way leading up to the bald tops of the Downs. The path was enclosed by a hawthorn hedge covered in crimson haws and ivy flowers still brimming with bees despite the lateness of the season. As she trudged along, she could smell the peculiar meaty scent of the hedge. Soon the track emerged into open countryside, where the Downs undulated like the waves of the sea. From time to time, she spotted Harry ahead in the distance, marching uphill with a determined stride. He was too far ahead to notice her following.

She soon met a slope so steep it was only good for grazing cows, a couple of which had strayed on to the path, so she had to scout around them nervously. When she reached the highest point, she was rewarded with a magnificent view of green fields pouring down towards the English Channel. For a moment or two, she stood and admired the panorama, but, keen to remove herself from the cattle advancing slowly towards her, she picked up her pace and walked along the ridge, until she reached the point where it dipped back down to Kingston, a large village lying just off the road between Rodmell and Lewes.

She was about to start the descent when she heard voices floating up from the steep chalk track below. It sounded as though she'd caught up with Harry, but she didn't fancy coming upon him and whoever he was talking to, so she sat down on the turf, now she was at a safe distance from the cows, hidden from view by a clump of stunted hawthorns growing at an angle in the salt winds.

'Did you bring it with you?' said a voice that sounded like Harry's.

'No, it would be missed. I don't think it's safe to move it while the police investigation is on. It's been mentioned as an important find from the dig and it's possible they might ask to see it. What would I tell them if it was gone?'

Ginny thought she recognised the clipped tones as belonging to Stanley Briggs, but she didn't dare stand up and get closer to find out. That would reveal she'd been listening, and it sounded as though what they were discussing was confidential.

'What do you propose we do, then?' asked the younger man impatiently.

'We'll just have to wait it out until all this hoo-ha over the murder dies down. It's unfortunate timing, to say the least. That chief inspector has picked up there was some argument over it, but he presumed I was the one who wanted to keep it in Lewes and Gideon was keen for wider publicity. I have no intention of alerting him to the fact it was the other way round.'

The coldness of his words made Ginny shiver. To describe the brutal killing of a young man as 'unfortunate timing' revealed a callousness she hadn't suspected of Briggs. What could they be talking about? It didn't sound like a conversation they would want anyone to overhear. She retreated further into the hawthorn thicket. The branches were scratchy, but she pushed in, her heart thumping loudly. From this uncomfortable position, she could still hear the men's voices as an indistinct hum, but she couldn't make out individual words.

She didn't dare move until the voices had disappeared and even then she waited a good ten minutes to make sure the men had left. Emerging from the bushes, she felt her cheek and realised she had the indentation of a twig there. Rather than descending the steep chalk path to Kingston as she'd planned, she returned the same way she'd come, suddenly longing to be back in the safety of her writing hut in the garden of Monk's House. Although she'd wondered if there was something between Jasmine and Harry Dryden, she hadn't imagined for a minute there was a link between him and the sour-faced Briggs. The only thing she knew that the two men had in common was Gideon Rivers, and he was dead.

Thankfully she didn't meet a soul on her descent, and once she was back in the village she scurried along, head down. The villagers were used to her being aloof, so if anyone had seen her, they would have thought her behaviour unremarkable.

'Why do you think they met in such a remote spot, and what do you think they were discussing?' she asked Leonard later over tea and toast with a thin scraping of Bovril.

'It's not that remote,' he pointed out.

'But they clearly didn't want to be overheard.'

'Didn't reckon on you lurking in the bushes, then,' teased Leonard, who was highly amused by his wife's account of pressing herself into the thicket so as not to be seen.

'Briggs said it was an important find from the dig. Could he have been talking about the tablet Gideon found while we were with him?'

'It sounds distinctly possible. I warned you that clay tablet would be trouble. Perhaps they're trying to sell it on the black market.'

'Leonard, you're a genius. That sounds like exactly the sort of underhand enterprise two men would want to be alone in open countryside to discuss. You don't think, do you, it could have been a motive for murder? Briggs said Gideon was the one who wanted it to stay put. Perhaps the darned thing *is* cursed, after all.'

Her husband's bushy eyebrows knitted a little closer together as he considered this proposition. Then he shrugged.

'All seems a bit far-fetched for quiet old Lewes, doesn't it? The whole thing is like one of those detective novels you despise so much.'

Ginny narrowed her nostrils.

'I don't despise them all. Only the inferior ones. Yet here I am, behaving like one of the interfering old women in those stories. I'm probably going to end up as the next victim.'

Her husband leaned forward and placed his hands on top of hers.

'Now that's something I very much don't want to happen.

Be careful, Ginny. You don't know what you've got yourself into here. I have no idea who killed Gideon Rivers, but I'm quite certain I don't want you to get on the wrong side of them.'

15.

Vanessa

Charleston farmhouse, Firle, East Sussex

'This is your room. It's quite the nicest bedroom. You have a marvellous view of the walled garden from the window,' said Nessa.

Jasmine glanced around the long, rectangular room with its north-facing window looking out over the garden. Nessa had painted the walls a soft primrose, with custard-coloured beams, after reading that yellow invoked a cheerful humour. The bed was a grey French affair, which she hoped would make Jasmine feel at home. She'd decorated a high corner cupboard with abstract paintings of flowers, vases and waving lines in black, mustard and slate blue. Crossing to a smaller, east-facing window, she added, 'And from out here you can see the pond.'

'*J'adore les jardins*,' said Jasmine, giving Nessa a grateful smile. All the radiance seemed to have gone out of her. The poor girl. How could Nessa have thought she might have something to do with her fiancé's murder? The best she could do for her was to offer her a place to rest for a few days and try to tempt her with some nourishing food. She would ask Grace to make beef broth with the last of the greens from the kitchen garden and serve it with some of her homemade bread and creamy butter from the farm up the lane. That would soon put roses back in the girl's cheeks.

'I'll leave you to rest for a while, then you can come down and meet the others before dinner. There's Duncan and Bobby Bassey, whom I think you've met before, as well as our good friends John Maynard Keynes and his wife Lydia.'

A momentary look of horror crossed Jasmine's face at the mention of Bobby's name, but she quickly rearranged her features. Nessa remembered what Diana had told her at the Sylvan Rooms about Bobby taking the engagement badly. She still needed to get to the bottom of Lily's information about Jasmine visiting Diana alone, but now wasn't the time.

She kicked herself for not realising sooner that it might be awkward bringing Jasmine here to Charleston, where she and Bobby would be forced together. Well, she would just have to do her best to smooth it over. She couldn't uninvite the poor girl now.

Heading back down the wooden staircase, leaving Jasmine to unpack her things, she spied Duncan sitting painting at his easel halfway down one of the paths that criss-crossed the walled garden. She would go and ask his advice; he was always so good at negotiating tricky social situations. His own complicated love life often demanded it.

But as she stepped out of the French windows and down the couple of steps to the gravel, Angelica appeared from round the side of the house and flung her arms round her. Her daughter was dripping wet and covered in mud.

106

'Mummeee! Come and see what I've been doing. Quentin has been showing me how to dam the stream and we're stopping the water coming into the pond.'

Her nine-year-old daughter took her by the hand and led her through the grey garden gate to the large fishpond in front of the house where her big brother was hard at work. He was up to his knees in pond water, constructing a barrier made of fallen branches. He gave his mother a cheerful wave.

'Don't blame me for the mess, Ma – it was all Angelica's idea,' he said with a grin.

'Quentin!' The little girl ran over to her brother and punched him. 'That's a total lie! You said you were going to show me what you and Julian used to like doing when you were younger.'

'*Still* like doing, by the looks of it,' laughed Nessa, going over to inspect the results of her offsprings' labour.

She sat down on the grassy bank by the edge of the pond, stretching her legs out in front of her, then leaned back on both hands, closing her eyes and lifting her face to feel the sun's rays. It was amazing how the sounds of the countryside came alive when you shut off your sight. The leaves rustled in the breeze as they clung on to the trees for as long as they could. In the distance, she could hear the cowman making the same herding cry to the cattle his father and grandfather had made before him. Only now that she was allowing herself to relax did she realise how tense this whole business was making her. She let the tension seep out through her fingertips into the chalky earth, enriched by alluvial deposits from the ridge of Firle Beacon, the hill to the south of the old farmhouse.

'Have you seen Bobby?'

Her reverie was broken by Duncan, calling out to her as he emerged through the gate of the walled garden. She sprang to her feet and went to meet him. At forty-three he was six years her junior and still possessed of the sort of looks men – and women – went wild for. He was wearing a blue flannel shirt, opened a couple of buttons too many to reveal an almost hairless chest without an ounce of extra fat on it. But it was his face that drew people in, with large soulful eyes, a little like Nessa's own but dark and impenetrable where hers were watery blue. His black hair was artistically long and, without thinking, he pushed it back from his face with slender fingers speckled with oil paint.

'I was going to ask you the same. Listen, you know the Parisian girl I was telling you about, Jasmine Zain al-Din? Well, I've invited her to stay.'

Duncan's jaw dropped.

'Nessa, she can't stay here. She was the cause of all Bobby's misery, the reason I invited him here in the first place to forget about Gideon.'

'Keep your voice down. I'm afraid it's too late. She's already here, resting in Clive's bedroom, and I don't want her to hear you being so unfriendly. It's not her fault Gideon dumped Bobby. Not that it's done her much good. At least they've got something in common now they're both grieving for him.'

Duncan raised his eyebrows. He didn't look convinced. 'Bobby's terrified he's going to have the murder pinned on him just because of the colour of his skin. Once the police realise he's staying here, they're bound to jump to conclusions. Now you've invited that girl, no doubt she'll go and blab to the police.'

'I don't think that's the sort of thing Jasmine would do. Wait until you've met her. At first, I thought she was full of herself, but now this terrible thing has happened I just want to look after her.'

Duncan leaned forward and planted a kiss on Nessa's forehead.

'That's just like you, Nessa, a mother hen, always looking after other people. When are you going to learn not everyone in the world is your responsibility?'

He would have said more, but a small muddy girl, eager to show off her creation to as many adults as possible, slipped her hand into his.

'Come and look at our dam, Duncan,' she pleaded.

As someone still possessed of many childlike qualities himself, Duncan couldn't resist such an offer, and dutifully trotted off hand in hand with Angelica, although he drew the line at getting his white linen trousers wet.

Nessa left them to it and made her way to the kitchen to let Grace know they had an extra mouth for dinner and ask her about the broth.

That done, she found Maynard and Lydia in the garden sitting room, listening to music on the gramophone.

'Too early for a drink, Nessa?' asked Maynard.

She shook her head.

'Never too early for a sherry,' she replied, feeling she needed one more than ever this evening. He poured her a glass and she sat back in an armchair and listened to the music. It was a jazz record Bobby had brought with him, Louis Armstrong's 'West End Blues'. The notes wafted on the air out to the garden, bringing Duncan back in to join them. But there was still no sign of Bobby.

Jasmine must have heard the music from her bedroom because she soon came down, a little flushed in the face, as if she'd just woken from a nap.

'Sounds like quite the party,' she said, and Nessa was glad to see she was smiling.

'Come in and join us. Jasmine, this is Duncan, John – but we all call him Maynard – and his wife, Lydia. Everyone, this is Jasmine Zain al-Din.'

'*Enchantée*,' said Jasmine, reaching out an elegant hand for the men to kiss, and curtsying to Lydia. She was delighted when the Russian ballerina replied to her in perfect French and soon the pair of them were chattering away.

Only Duncan didn't seem as relaxed as the rest of them, constantly glancing over to the door. Realising he was watching out for Bobby, Nessa went over to him and laid her hand upon his arm.

'He probably wants to be by himself, with everything that's happened,' she said.

'Do you think he's found out Jasmine is here and is making himself scarce?'

'If he is, what can we do about it? We'll just have to wait for him to come round to the idea. Come and have a sherry and try not to worry.'

Duncan let her pour him a glass and did his best to join in the conversation, although there were still anxious lines around his eyes. After a couple of glasses, Jasmine came out of herself. She'd stopped speaking to Lydia in French, and switched back to English, which she spoke nearly fluently, regaling Maynard with tales of life at the

Sorbonne and the ridiculous pretensions of some of her fellow students there.

'That's why I was so attracted to Gideon. He was so English, so practical, so real,' she said.

At the memory, the smile fell from her lips. Nessa quickly racked her brains for a way to cheer the girl up before she sank back into her grief.

'We haven't shown you around yet, have we? There's still half an hour until it gets dark, and dinner isn't ready yet. Come on. I'll give you a tour of the garden.'

Jasmine looked as though she might protest, but then thought better of it. Rising to her feet, she accepted the forearm Nessa held out to her, linking her own arm round it, and the two women set off through the French windows into the garden.

Nessa showed her the wallflowers she'd planted underneath the apple trees, in the hope their flowers would emerge next spring at the same time as the blossom. The borders were starting to look a little windswept, but there was still much to appreciate: purple asters, red bistort and orange marigolds tumbling out of the flower beds on to the gravel paths. As they walked out of the walled garden and past the pond, the fish flocked to the edge, opening their mouths in expectation of food.

'I'll come back and feed you later,' Nessa promised them, as if they could understand her. She turned to Jasmine.

'I didn't want to mention it in front of the others, but I dropped by the Sylvan Rooms the other day and spoke to Diana Underhill.' She paused here to observe the young woman's reaction, but her expression remained perfectly calm and still.

111

'Gideon used to love that place,' was all she said in reply.

'How about you?' asked Nessa, as casually as she could.

'Oh, I've been there once or twice,' said Jasmine lightly. 'What's round here?' she added, making her way to the side of the farmhouse.

In the twilight, the barn and outbuildings looked dark and threatening. Nessa hurried past them, through to the pottery garden, where Duncan kept his kiln. Usually, she didn't disturb him here, but knowing he was safely indoors with the others she led Jasmine through a passageway between outhouses into the courtyard.

'We have a little plunge pool here, perfect for cooling down in summer. Duncan is particularly fond of naked bathing,' she confided with a knowing look.

Jasmine took a couple of steps closer to get a better look at the pool and let out an ear-piercing scream. Surely the thought of Duncan without any clothes on wasn't that disturbing. Then Nessa saw what it was that had frightened her. Floating in the pool, fully clothed, but clearly lifeless, was a man's body. There was no mistaking his identity, even in death. It was Bobby.

16.

Virginia

'What's the matter with Mummy and Duncan, Aunt Ginny?' asked Angelica, who'd had the bonus of extra breakfasts untouched by the grown-ups to eat, although she'd had to fight Quentin for her half.

'They've had a terrible shock, dear. Duncan's friend is dead,' said Ginny, who didn't believe in protecting children from the truth.

'I know that. I'm not stupid,' replied Angelica. 'What about the pretty French lady?'

'That's the question we're all asking,' said Ginny, patting her niece on her soft brown hair. 'You didn't see anything, did you?'

The girl shook her head.

Ginny had done her best to console her sister, but Nessa was a wreck. After they'd found Bobby's body, it was she who had to go and tell the others. Duncan took it as badly as might be expected. If it hadn't been for Maynard, Nessa had told her sister, she wouldn't have been able to get through it. But he'd had the presence of mind to go to the farmhouse up the road and telephone Chief Inspector Gripe, who'd come out at once, bringing a couple of duty police officers with him. They'd cordoned off the scene, not that there were many passers-by at Charleston, and then questioned each member of the household one by one about their movements that night. By the time they got to bed, it was long past midnight. Nessa had to administer a sleeping draught to Duncan, but hadn't taken one herself and had lain awake all night trying to understand how such a dreadful crime could have been committed here in their rural idyll.

The following morning, the household awoke to another shock. Jasmine had disappeared without leaving a note. No one knew how she'd left, whether by foot, or by some other mode of transport. Was she alone, or did she walk to the motor road where someone picked her up? It was all too much for Nessa, who found herself unable to eat or drink. When Ginny arrived in answer to a phone call from Lydia, she found her sister sitting staring into space, and swiftly put her back to bed.

At the same time Ginny and her niece both heard the purring of an engine and ran to the window of the study. A smart black automobile swung into the yard next to the house and drew to a sharp halt. Chief Inspector Gripe climbed out, wearing a brown tweed suit and trilby hat, accompanied by a uniformed officer.

Ginny went to the door and opened it before they had time to knock, much to the surprise of the policemen on the other side.

'Ah, Mrs Woolf, we're here to give your sister an update,' boomed Gripe.

'I've just put Nessa to bed with something to make her

sleep. Come in and tell me what you have to say, and I'll pass it on when she wakes up. She and Duncan – Mr Grant – need to rest after what happened last night.'

'We could all do with a good night's sleep,' said the chief inspector pointedly, but he followed her into the study and motioned to his sidekick to do the same. Angelica trailed along behind them like a curious kitten.

'Please take a seat. Would you care for a cup of tea, gentlemen?' asked Ginny, ignoring his sarcastic tone.

They accepted and she rang for Grace to bring three cups of tea, then gestured to the policemen to take a seat in the pair of antique armchairs flanking the fireplace. Gripe looked at it curiously as he sat down. She had to admit the hearth was rather unusual, built by Roger Fry, and decorated by Nessa in circles of grey and ochre, with putty-coloured criss-cross lines descending in Doric columns on either side of the grate. When Quentin and Julian were young, they used to bake objects modelled from a vein of clay they found in the pond here. Blue toy soldiers and cannons that exploded into pink.

'Run along and find your brother,' she said, gently pushing Angelica out of the door in the direction of the garden. 'Now, what is it you wanted to tell my sister?' she turned to ask the policemen once the child was gone.

'We've alerted the ports to stop Miss Zain al-Din from boarding any ships,' said the inspector.

Ginny waved his words away with a languid flick of her hand.

'I don't see what the use of that is. She'll have taken the early morning sailing from Newhaven. No doubt she's in Dieppe by now.'

'Do you mind if I smoke?' asked the inspector.

'Not if you offer me one,' Ginny replied.

'I'm afraid I'm a pipe smoker,' said the chief inspector, taking the instrument from his jacket pocket along with a box of matches. It took him a couple of minutes to light it. Ginny wrinkled her nose as he blew out a cloud of wood-scented smoke.

'Do you think she did it?' asked Ginny.

'My job is to examine the evidence. It's highly suspicious that she disappeared directly after the murder. But it's possible she didn't want to get any further mixed up in the matter, especially after what happened to her fiancé, and went back to her family in Paris while she still could.'

'How did Bobby die?' Ginny asked.

'I'm afraid I'm not at liberty to divulge such matters, but I don't think it's any great secret that he drowned,' said Gripe.

'Would someone as petite as Jasmine have had the strength to keep him under the water for all that time? Surely, he would have fought back, and won.'

'That's why the pathologist is examining the body as we speak. There are suspicions the young man might have been drugged before he entered the water, although there are some signs of a scuffle in the gravel around the plunge pool.'

'Could it have been a vagrant trying his luck? I know my sister has complained about one or two such fellows sleeping over in the barn.'

'I assure you we will explore every avenue to get to the bottom of this. What I want to ask your sister is whether there was a connection between this young man and Gideon Rivers.'

Ginny drew in a deep breath and let the air out slowly through her long nostrils as she thought about how best to answer the inspector's question without bringing shame upon Mrs Rivers.

'I believe the young men were acquainted. When she was up in London earlier this week, my sister visited a jazz club in Soho they both used to frequent.'

At the word 'Soho', Chief Inspector Gripe raised his eyebrows. Even a rural Sussex policeman knew the reputation of that part of London. His brow creased.

'Have you ladies been conducting investigations of your own? Because, if so, I would remind you that this is strictly a police matter.'

'We wouldn't dream of doing such a thing, Chief Inspector. My sister and I were merely making discreet enquiries on behalf of a friend and neighbour in her time of need.'

'I see. And did these discreet enquiries throw up anything else of interest?'

Ginny considered telling him what Nessa had found out about Bobby being jealous of Jasmine. But it was mere hearsay, and she didn't want to get the girl into any more trouble than she was already. There was no proof she was involved in either murder. Perhaps she had just been in the wrong place at the wrong time, although she had to admit it didn't look good for her.

Grace appeared with the tea tray and Ginny took the opportunity of pouring to gather her thoughts. If suspicion didn't fall on Jasmine, the police might start probing Bobby's relationship with Duncan. While she had little doubt that Jasmine was safely in Paris, under the protection of her rich and powerful family, Duncan was an old friend who had just lost his lover. She didn't want him coming under any more scrutiny than was necessary.

'I wasn't here last night, but I gather you've taken statements from all those who were and, except for Miss Zain al-Din, they were all gathered in the garden room for drinks at the time of the murder. Far be it from me to tell you how to do your job, but I do think you should investigate whether there have been any rough types hanging around lately.'

Gripe took another puff on his pipe.

'Would you mind if we took another look at the spot where Mr Bassey's body was found?' he asked.

'I'm sure my sister would permit it. I can show you round there now if you like.'

The uniformed policeman quickly drained his teacup, clearly fearing it might be his only chance. His superior glared at him.

'Lead the way, Mrs Woolf,' he said.

Ginny got to her feet and walked with purpose out of the front door and through the gate on to the quiet track that ran past the side of the farmhouse. To the rear of the house, a separate entrance led into the pottery yard. Despite being a regular visitor to Charleston for more than a decade, it was not a part of the property she'd visited often.

The yard was not large, paved with brick, with blue periwinkles growing with abandon in narrow flower beds hugging the walls. Fragments of discarded pots lay on the ground. In the centre of the space was what amounted to little more than a large rectangular hole filled with water. This was the plunge pool where Duncan and his friends would cool off on hot days. It was usually out of bounds to

118

the rest of the household. To think the body of that talented and kind young man had been found here made her ache with sadness.

She stopped and looked around her. Chief Inspector Gripe was right, there were signs of a struggle. Bare earth streaked the gravel where it had been dragged by some heavy object. The body perhaps? Several twigs had been ripped off a nearby bush, leaving bare wounds. By the looks of it, Bobby hadn't given in to his attacker that easily, after all.

17.

Vanessa

'I can't stop thinking about those two poor boys with so much life ahead of them,' said Nessa, leaning back on the wooden recliner in the spring sunshine later that day. She had slept until early afternoon. The sisters were sitting in the 'piazza', a sunny corner of the walled garden at Charleston that she and Duncan had created to remind them of La Bergère, their house in the south of France. What she would give to be there now.

'Are you going to let Bobby's relatives in America know he is dead?' asked her sister.

Nessa nodded.

'I'm planning to write to his grandmother who raised him, but it's hard to find the words.'

She closed her eyes, and felt the warm sunshine on her lids, reminding her life continued. Then a shadow passed over, and she opened her eyes again to see a young man standing before them. She nearly cried out, thinking she had summoned one of the poor dead boys to life, then realised it was Harry Dryden, looking as dishevelled and unkempt as usual. He cleared his throat, sending his Adam's apple popping out.

'I'm so sorry to disturb you. I'm looking for Jasmine. I heard she was staying here,' he said.

Nessa and her sister exchanged a look. Then Ginny got up from where she was sitting and gestured to Harry that he should take her place.

'I think you need to sit down to hear this.'

He hesitated, but when she gestured a second time he did as she said.

'I'm afraid to inform you there's been another murder,' said Nessa.

Harry's mouth dropped open.

'Not Jasmine, my God . . .'

Nessa held up her hand.

'No, not Jasmine. The young man who was staying with us here, Bobby Bassey, but it seems Jasmine may have had something to do with his murder. Particularly as she's disappeared.'

'God, that's awful. I knew Bobby, he and Gid were . . .' Harry's voice petered out.

'Yes, we know,' said Nessa.

He shook his head, struggling to take on board what he'd just heard.

'What do you mean, Jasmine has disappeared?' he asked. 'Has she been abducted?'

'We don't think so. She took all her belongings with her and there was no sign of a struggle. The likelihood is she's returned to Paris. She's from a rich and powerful family and if she's managed to make her way back to them, she'll be virtually untouchable,' said Ginny.

Harry leaped to his feet.

'Don't you see, that's just what a kidnapper would want you to think. Jasmine isn't capable of murder! She's the sweetest, gentlest . . .'

He stopped as he felt the gaze of both sisters upon him.

'Mr Dryden, I must ask you, were you and Miss Zain al-Din close? Gideon's mother seems to think you detest her, but from what you say that doesn't sound like an accurate reflection of your feelings at all,' said Nessa.

Harry sat back down on the whitewashed garden chair and put his head in his hands. When he looked up again, his eyes were red, and tears ran down his cheeks.

'I adored her from the minute I set eyes on her out on the dig in Antioch. I'd never believed in love at first sight until then. Only trouble was she was engaged to be married to my best friend, which of course meant she was completely out of bounds.'

'And were your feelings reciprocated?' Nessa asked.

'Neither of us would ever have done anything to hurt Gideon. You met him, didn't you? He was like a beautiful child. All I've ever wanted since we were boys was to please him, and I think Jasmine felt that too. But he had the temper of a child. If he'd suspected there was anything between us, who knows what he would have done. He sometimes had violent impulses he couldn't control.'

'But his death removed that obstacle. How convenient for you. The perfect opportunity to step in and console his grieving fiancée,' said Nessa.

Ginny nudged her. Nessa suspected her sister had a sweet spot for the young man.

'I swear I had nothing to do with Gideon's death. I

loved him like a brother. I would never have hurt him,' said Harry with passion. 'But I would be lying if I said the thought hadn't crossed my mind that Jasmine and I could be together now.'

'And what does she think about that?' asked Nessa.

'Jasmine said her head was all over the place and insisted it was too soon to think about anything except Gideon. That's why she accepted your invitation to come here, to give her space to grieve. I was meant to leave her alone, but I couldn't bear it. I just had to see her.'

'What do you mean by "the minute you set eyes on her in Antioch"? I thought only Gideon was out in Syria on the dig,' said Ginny.

'He invited me to come and join him and I took a couple of months' sabbatical from my job at the insurance brokers, much to Father's displeasure. Neither of us knew then that Jasmine was going to arrive and take his world by storm. In fact, he was already engaged at the time, to an American film actress, Marguerite Muir.'

'So we've heard,' said Nessa.

'She was considered quite the catch, but then Jasmine turned up, fresh from the Sorbonne, where she'd heard Gideon lecture on the dig. She had Syrian family connections and was determined to come out and join him. If you ask me, it wasn't just the archaeology she was interested in. She'd set her sights on Gideon. I can still remember the day she arrived. We'd both been up since before dawn. You must start work early out there before the day gets too hot, even in spring. By ten o'clock, there was sweat dripping down our foreheads, we'd rolled up our sleeves and probably stank to high heaven. We stopped work to smoke a pipe and were sitting on one of the low walls we'd uncovered, part of the old Roman city. A silver motor car drew up and out of it stepped Jasmine, dressed in a white trouser suit and a broad-brimmed white sun hat. She lowered her sunglasses and I thought I'd never seen anything as beautiful as her eyes. The purest emeralds don't compare. Neither of us said anything, we just stopped and stared. Then Gideon remembered his manners.

'"Miss Zain al-Din, isn't it? You came to see my lecture at the Sorbonne."

'She nodded in agreement.

'"I hope you don't mind me turning up like this, but I was visiting my uncle in Aleppo, and it seemed too good an opportunity to miss to come here. I found your lecture so intriguing."

'Turning to Gideon, she fluttered those long black eyelashes. I remember he blushed, which is most unlike him, and cleared his throat, momentarily lost for words. Finding his voice at last he spoke.

'"You're very welcome here, Miss Zain al-Din."

'"Call me Jasmine, please," she said.

'He said, "In that case, Jasmine, may I show you around the site?"

'In answer, she held out her arm to him. Without asking if I wanted to join them, he took it and started leading her around the dig, pointing out the different sections and bringing them to life with his descriptions, something he was expert at.'

Harry closed his eyes as he recalled the scene and took a deep breath before continuing.

'I wasn't going to be cast off quite so easily, though. To

my mind, Gideon was already attached, and Jasmine was fair game. I don't get to meet many women through my work, certainly not any quite like her. I followed them around the site and made a few comments of my own whenever I could get a word in edgeways. Gideon glared at me every time I did so, making it perfectly clear he wanted me to make myself scarce. Usually, I would have taken the hint, but the casual way in which he was so ready to forget about both me and Marguerite riled me, so I persisted. It was only later that evening, back at camp, that we squared things. He asked me if I would back off and said he was planning to break things off with Marguerite. It turned out Jasmine had invited him to Aleppo, to her uncle's house. I saw I didn't stand a chance, and so I did the only thing I could and stood aside. That was the thing about Gid – he was very good at getting his own way. He acted as if he was the only one that mattered. It could be quite stifling at times, I tell you. I realise that doesn't paint me in a very good light, but I assure you that I soon came round to the idea of Gid marrying Jasmine. I had nothing to do with his murder, I swear.'

Nessa exchanged a glance with Ginny, who was looking at Harry with shining eyes. She clearly believed everything he said, but Nessa wasn't so sure.

'What's your relationship with Jasmine now?' she asked.

'We're friends, that's all. But I must admit that one day I hope we can be something more.'

'Then it is with a heavy heart I must tell you it's suspected she might have something to do with Bobby's murder.'

Harry shook his head with vehemence. 'Not Jasmine, no. She wouldn't be capable of such a thing,' he said.

'And yet she's left without a word to anyone. By now she's

probably back with her family in Paris, where I believe she has diplomatic immunity.'

Harry jumped to his feet. 'I'm sorry. I've already taken up too much of your time. If Jasmine has gone, there's nothing for me here. I'm heading back to London. I don't mind if I never set eyes on Lewes again.'

Ginny reached out and put a hand on the young man's arm. 'Be kind to yourself. You've lost your best friend in horrific circumstances. A woman you admire has gone missing. You're bound to be confused.'

Nessa was not going to let him off so easily.

'Do you have any idea who might have wished Gideon so much ill they would kill him in this way? And how that might be linked to Bobby's death?' she asked.

Harry shook his head vehemently. Then, looking deflated, he sank to the seat again and put his head in his hands. When he looked up through his fingers, there were tears running down his cheeks.

'Gideon was just one of those people. Everyone loved him. Men and women. Me included. Not in that way – my love for him was purely platonic. But he enjoyed making people fall in love with him. Jasmine was the first time he'd met his match, and I think the first time he really fell in love himself. But being able to inspire love like that, it has a dark side. Bobby felt it, and I'm sure you're right, his death has something to do with Gideon. If he were still alive, I would have said it was him who stoved Gid's face in like that – he certainly was passionate enough to do it. God, Bobby was heartbroken when Gideon ended their affair. The way he did it was cruel, leaving him to find out the truth from someone else. Bobby was furious and he let half of Soho know about it. I didn't often go to nightclubs with Gid, it's not really my scene, but he asked me to go with him after Bobby found out about Jasmine. Said he couldn't trust him not to do something stupid. There were other men too whom he dallied with, some of them quite rough types. I think that's where the police need to be looking.'

Nessa felt a sudden lurch of fear in her stomach. If the police went down the line of inquiry of asking about men on the nightclub scene, Duncan was sure to be caught up in it.

18.

Alice

Alice was woken by a crashing sound. Lying in bed, beneath pressed cotton sheets and an embroidered quilt, she listened to the night, alert for any other noises that might suggest an intruder. But none came. All she could hear was the solitary hooting of an owl and her own heartbeat pounding in her ears. From down the corridor came the strangled cry of a wild boar. That was just Ernest snoring. The crash had been of quite a different order.

Unable to get back to sleep, she prised herself from under the covers and padded over the wooden floorboards to the window. As she approached, she could feel a draught coming through the cracks in the frame. With her index finger, she pulled back the curtain ever so slightly, carefully enough that anyone standing in the street below wouldn't notice it move. Then she pressed one eye to the gap to see what was out there.

All she could see were the familiar dark shapes of the lane that ran between her home and the long, low flint-walled brewery building opposite. Perhaps the wind had blown a barrel over in the yard. There was sure to be a simple explanation.

Now she was out of bed, she realised she needed to use the water closet that opened off her bedroom. Such were the discomforts of growing older. She heaved her girth on to the wooden seat and, as she was relieving herself, was once again startled by a sound. This time it was a banging, followed by the familiar clink of the latch on the gate from the street leading up on to Brack Mound. She hadn't imagined it. There must be someone out there. She watched for a few moments, and then she saw it. A dark figure disappearing into the night, although it was impossible to tell from this distance whether they were male or female.

She considered waking Ernest and asking him to go outside and look, but reminded herself that his days of battling burglars were well behind him. Plus, he was so bad tempered if woken. She could have taken a poker from the fireplace, put on her slippers and dressing gown and gone out there herself, but she knew she wasn't brave enough.

Instead, she washed her hands at the little basin, dried them on the starched hand towel hanging from the mahogany stand and climbed back into bed, pulling the quilt up to her chin, and closed her eyes. For a while, she feared she would never get back to sleep. She lay there, alert to all the creaks and groans of an old house. But at some point she drifted into unconsciousness. When she awoke again, the sun was pouring through the gap in the curtains, and she wondered whether the whole episode had been a dream.

Emboldened by daylight, she rose, quickly washed and dressed, then let herself out of the kitchen door, and headed straight for the path leading from her garden to the gate.

When she reached it, she tried rattling it with her hand, but it was locked from the outside and barely shifted. Whoever opened it must have had a key.

She went back the way she'd come, examining the ground for any trace of footsteps. The grass underfoot was a little flattened, but it hadn't rained for a few days and the chalk mound was completely dry. It was impossible to tell whether anyone had walked here in the night. The path had been well-trodden by policemen and the remaining archaeologists who had temporarily packed up and put the dig on hold. Still puzzled, she continued back to the scene of the crime, now wiped clean of all traces of the bloody deed. It was the first time Alice had been up to the top of the mound since discovering Gideon's body. She'd avoided coming here until now, fearful it would provoke violent emotions, but instead all she felt was a curious flatness. There was no point in lingering. She would just take a quick look around to see if there was any sign of disturbance. But she could see nothing. The trench was covered in the same tarpaulin, weighed down with heavy stones round its edges. Apart from that, there was nothing to see except grass, sky and the surrounding landscape. Beautiful as it was, today her spirits were not in a mood to be lifted. Strangely disappointed, she turned round to go back home when she saw something flashing in the turf. With a groan, she bent over and squinted her eyes. What was it? A foil wrapper tossed carelessly aside, perhaps? Although she wouldn't admit it, she couldn't see so well without her reading glasses these days.

She put her hand to the ground and felt around until her fingers ran over a tiny, slender metal object. Picking it up between thumb and fingernail, she lifted it up to her face to take a closer look. It was a sharp silver needle. It must have been one of her embroidery needles, but how it had come to be up here she couldn't imagine.

How silly – she must have dropped it from her skirt on one of her visits up here before the terrible thing happened. Funny the police hadn't come across it in their search of the area. They'd spent long enough up here looking for clues. But then she supposed it was the proverbial needle in a haystack, easily overlooked had the sun not happened to hit it from a particular angle just then. Plus, policemen these days were not as assiduous as the officers of her youth. Yet another sign of the fraying fabric of society.

Taking a deep breath, she let out a loud sigh to relieve the tension that had been building since she'd woken and thought about what had happened in the middle of the night. Now, in the bright morning sunshine, she felt sure it was nothing, after all, and that her imagination had just got carried away with her. It was probably just a cat crash-landing on a dustbin lid, then striking the latch as it made its return journey. She must have dreamed the dark figure. Still, something about the noise had frightened her half to death, and one couldn't ignore that completely.

19.

Virginia

'Why is there no way to drive into this town without going up a hill?' asked Ginny with a groan, as Leonard struggled once again to start the motor.

They were approaching Lewes from the west, where the road from Rodmell joined the old Juggs Road up which milkmaids used to carry their wares to Brighton. They passed a jolly old inn called the Swan and made it smoothly up the hill past the cemetery. It was only at the crossroads at the top that Leonard had to stop to check for traffic and the engine stalled.

Thankfully, he managed to get it started again without too much difficulty and the approach into town from the west was all downhill. Leonard parked in the little Westgate car park underneath the high town wall beside the castle. Glancing up, Ginny spotted the octagonal Round House, the former windmill which had once nearly become their home. She'd bought it on a whim, but they'd never lived there because a few days later they saw an auctioneer's lot for Monk's House and Leonard had pointed out how much better it would suit them. He was right, of course. How claustrophobic they would have been in the heart of the town. Out at their cottage in Rodmell with its generous garden they had room to breathe. Now they'd bought a field adjacent to their garden, she felt they belonged in the landscape more than ever.

'Are you sure you don't want me to come with you?' he asked, peering at her with the concern usually reserved for a sick child.

'No, you go and buy your brass treatment, or whatever it is you're planning to spray on your roses,' she said.

'Copper fungicide,' he replied, shaking his head. 'Very well, but I insist on waiting for you afterwards. I'll be here when you've finished.'

''Scuse me, sir. Thruppence to look after your automobile?'

They both looked down to see a small boy smelling strongly of carbolic soap as if he had been recently scrubbed. He'd already managed to spoil the effect by wiping the back of his hand, covered in oil, presumably from another vehicle in his care, across his pink cheek, leaving a large black smear.

'Very well, then,' said Leonard. 'But it's tuppence and make sure there are no scratches on it when I get back.'

'Right you are, sir,' said the small boy, standing to attention and saluting them. Ginny had to suppress a laugh.

'Do your job well and I'll make it thruppence,' she whispered in his ear as she passed.

They walked along the High Street together then parted at the Barbican House, Leonard continuing to the hardware store. Ginny had telephoned ahead to let Miss Bramble know she was coming, but when she rang the bell, there

133

was no reply. She tried the door, and it was open, so she let herself in. Seeing there was no one behind the desk in the entrance hall, she decided to try the library. Perhaps Miss Bramble hadn't heard the doorbell from three floors up.

But when she reached the third floor there wasn't a soul to be seen in the warren of little attic rooms either. She was sure she'd said eleven o'clock to Miss Bramble on the telephone. Never mind, it was hardly the worst fate in the world to be left alone in a library. She was about to start scouring the shelves when something on the assistant's desk caught her eye. It looked like a brass rubbing on tracing paper. Picking it up, she brought it closer to her eyes. She really should have brought her reading glasses with her. The markings were made in charcoal, revealing what looked like Arabic letters. What a pity that language was indecipherable to her.

'Please don't touch that,' said a high voice. Looking up, she saw Miss Bramble, flushed in the face with a couple of strands of mousy brown hair hanging loose beneath the felt hat she always wore, having clearly just run up the stairs. Ginny placed the sheet of paper back on the desk.

'I thought we had an appointment at eleven. I was just looking around while I waited. I didn't mean to pry,' she said.

'I'm so sorry,' replied Miss Bramble in a more conciliatory tone. 'It's just that paper belongs to Mr Briggs and he's very protective about his work.'

'Did you ask him whether I can use the library?'

Miss Bramble nodded.

'He's quite happy for you to come in and consult the books here, so long as you make an appointment in advance.'

'Can I ask what it is?' Ginny nodded at the tracing paper.

Miss Bramble took a deep breath and looked from side to side.

'I don't suppose there can be any harm in telling you. It's a rubbing of the tablet they found up on Brack Mound.'

'What does it mean, do you know?'

Miss Bramble blinked behind her little round glasses.

'I'm not sure, I'm afraid. I'm just the general dogsbody. But I do know there's been a lot of argument about it.'

'Argument?'

Miss Bramble sat down at the desk and put her head in her hands. 'Oh dear, Mr Briggs told me not to say anything about the dig and here I am spouting off about it to a stranger.'

'I'm hardly a stranger, dear. I'm an interested party. And if this argument might shed light on the case, you'd be better off mentioning it. Why don't you tell me about it, and we can decide together whether it's something Chief Inspector Gripe needs to know about?'

The poor woman looked as though she were about to burst into tears, but she nodded. 'You're right. I've been worrying about whether I should say anything. It will be a relief to tell someone about it.'

Ginny put a hand on her arm and realised the secretary was trembling. 'Take your time,' she said.

'It began when Mr Rivers found the tablet up at the dig. I think he would have liked to keep it to himself, but once Stanley – Mr Briggs – realised its importance, he said it was essential to his research and should be handed over to him.'

As she spoke, Miss Bramble fingered the sheet of tracing paper on the desk, as if awestruck even now by the beauty of the script.

'That's why there was such a fuss over who found it, you see. Mr Rivers was the one who uncovered it, but Mr Briggs is the foremost expert on the Warenne family – they were the Norman barons of Lewes. He has a particular interest in the third William de Warenne who fought in the Crusades and died at Antioch, and he immediately realised the tablet must have something to do with him. Gideon has worked out in Syria on a dig, so he claimed the superiority of being on the ground out there. They nearly came to blows over it in this very office. There was a great shouting match. I honestly think if I hadn't been here as a restraining presence, they might have started punching one another.'

'Have you told this to Chief Inspector Gripe?' asked Ginny.

Miss Bramble shook her head, sending another strand of mousy hair flying, which she hastily tucked behind one ear.

'I don't want to get Stanley into trouble. He's been so good to me and I'm quite sure it has nothing whatsoever to do with Gideon's death. Working here, I've seen how passionate men become about archaeology. It might seem like dusty old bones to some, but to them it's the very stuff of life. It's the story of how we've come to be who we are today, what's brought us here. It's not like history, filtered by someone else's point of view. There's something pure about it.'

'Yes, I see that, and how the inspector could easily misinterpret such a disagreement. He's not the most imaginative of men,' said Ginny.

Miss Bramble gave her an appreciative smile. 'I knew you'd understand,' she said.

Having been granted permission to use the library, Ginny

stayed on for another half an hour, until it was time to go back to the car park to meet Leonard. She used the time to read up about the connections between Lewes Castle and the Crusades, recorded in the journal of the Sussex Archaeological Society. It included an article on the Kufic coin Briggs had mentioned, which had somehow made itself to the south coast of England all the way from the Near East. There was a drawing of the coin, a beautiful and intriguing object, and a translation of the inscription, which declared Muhammed to be the prophet of God. The writing was the same as that on the rubbing of the clay tablet. How had these two items, bearing the script of a distant land, come to be here on a Sussex hillside?

When she'd wished Miss Bramble farewell and returned to the car, the boy with the black smudge was sitting on the footboard of their motor car, chin in his hands, whistling to himself. As soon as he saw her approach, he jumped to his feet and saluted again.

'Good job,' said Ginny. There was something about the child's nonchalant air that appealed to her. She reached into her purse for the promised extra penny and slipped it to him, just in time as Leonard rounded the corner. She put a finger to her lips and winked to show the third penny was a secret between them.

'You owe this young fellow tuppence for looking after our motor,' she said loudly to Leonard, who felt around in his pocket and obliged.

20.

Vanessa

Firle, East Sussex

While the entire village had turned out to say goodbye to Gideon, Bobby's funeral promised to be a much more modest affair. With what little family he had thousands of miles across the Atlantic in New Orleans, Nessa felt she had to do the best for him she could.

The night before the ceremony, she sat down in the study at Charleston, looking out over the pond. A solitary moorhen was swimming across the opaque surface of the water. The light in the room was fading and she lit the oil lamp and threw an old but much-loved shawl that had belonged to her own mother over her shoulders. Once white, over many years of being worn and only occasionally washed, it had faded to a soft beige. It was more than three decades since her mother, Julia Stephens, whose ethereal beauty some said she'd inherited, had passed away. Nessa was only a girl at the time, left to deal not only with her own emotions, but also those of her younger sister, Ginny. To the outside world, she was the intimidating Virginia Woolf, a woman who knew her own mind and wasn't afraid to speak it. But to Nessa she was still that thirteen-year-old girl, left bewildered and devastated by the death of the woman who'd cared for her most in the world. Ever since, she'd felt the pressure to take their mother's place and look after Ginny. Even though she could be infuriating at times, she would, if necessary, defend her sister with her life.

These were the thoughts running through her mind as she dipped her old fountain pen in the pot of black ink on the desk before her, and took out a sheet of thick, creamy writing paper from the drawer.

She thought of Bobby's grandmother, who'd brought him up in New Orleans, receiving the news of his death. He'd described his childhood home to her, a small house in a working-class neighbourhood, with an old wooden deck out front where his Gramma would sit in her rocking chair, watching the world and calling out to friends and acquaintances who passed by. That was the house where he'd learned to play the trumpet, bringing it home from school when he was just ten years old, and practising as if his life depended on it. Which it did in a way, as it was his passage out of the poverty of his youth. She hoped the old woman would be sitting in that rocking chair when she read the letter. Otherwise, she would stumble, her world diminished forever. She would carry on rocking for a while, keeping the news to herself, aware that speaking it aloud would make it real.

In her closing words, she promised they would give Bobby the best funeral they could. She'd wanted to take his body to London at least, so that his friends on the jazz scene could give him a good send-off. But Chief Inspector Gripe had refused to sign the release for the body to travel, insisting it could adversely affect the investigation into his murder, although she couldn't see how. The pathologist had concluded his report for the inquest and Bobby's body was ready to be collected from the morgue by the undertakers.

Instead, after some discussion, she and Duncan agreed Bobby's funeral would take place in the little church at Firle, a quiet village under the Downs that couldn't be further away from the busy streets of New Orleans.

'Remember that day we walked there together, not long after he arrived at Charleston? He said it was the most peaceful place he'd ever visited, and he could stay there forever,' said Duncan. Little did he think when he spoke those words how soon his wish would be granted.

The next morning, Nessa drove a party over from Charleston, including Duncan, Julian and Quentin. She considered Angelica too young to attend such a sad event, so she was to stay home with Grace.

As they pulled up outside the church, they saw Maynard and Lydia, who had walked over the fields from their cottage. The undertakers were already parked, ready to unload the coffin. Ginny and Leonard were waiting for them inside. There were barely enough of them to fill the front two pews.

The grey-haired vicar emerged from the vestry and came over to talk to Nessa and Duncan about how they wanted the ceremony to proceed. Together they'd chosen the readings, a poem about a trumpeter in Harlem, where Bobby himself had often played, and Isaiah 40, one of his grandmother's favourite chapters from the Bible.

'We would have liked to have music,' said Nessa.

'Yes, I'm so sorry there was no one available to play the organ,' said the vicar.

'Perhaps I can help?'

Nessa turned around to see a woman walking through the church door, dressed in a dark green suit, with a leopard-print scarf wrapped artfully round her neck. She wore black stilettoes and silk stockings, and on her head was a jaunty little black hat with a small netting veil, worn at an angle on her Titian red hair. She was smoking a cigarette in a long black holder.

'Diana Underhill,' said Nessa and Duncan at the same time.

The woman looked over her shoulder.

'Come on in. Seems like we're just in time,' she said.

Those few already gathered in the pews watched in amazement as a dozen men and women, of varying ages and races, all dressed in dark clothing and carrying a variety of instruments in cases ranging from tiny to enormous, followed her into the church.

'Welcome to those mourners who have just arrived,' said the vicar, beaming.

'My sincere apologies. The bus I hired to bring us from London was late. These are Bobby's friends and colleagues, and they wouldn't have missed the chance to say goodbye to him for the world,' said Diana in a theatrical whisper. 'Do go ahead, Vicar,' she added, with a flourish of her hand.

Nessa felt a warm rush of emotion. This was more like it. Ginny delivered the jazz poem, in her steady, confident voice, then Duncan read the chapter from Isaiah, ending with the verse: 'Those who hope in the Lord will renew

141

their strength/They will soar on wings like eagles; they will run and not grow weary, they will walk and not be faint.'

Nessa had a vision of Bobby's soul rising from the coffin before them and soaring over the Downs, flying back to his Gramma in New Orleans. Then his musician friends came up to the front of the church. Some of them had brought instruments with them, a clarinet, a trumpet. Someone else played the organ like a jazz piano and they sang songs by Duke Ellington and Louis Armstrong, so the country church rang out with joyous jazz music so loudly that she imagined the dead jiving in their graves.

After the ceremony, the body was taken to the new crematorium at Woodingdean and they all piled into automobiles and the bus to follow. There was another short ceremony, in which the coffin was cremated, and they were told to return a few days later to collect Bobby's ashes.

Nessa and Duncan had decided that rather than have Bobby buried in a foreign land, they would scatter his ashes out at sea. At least that way Bobby had an outside chance of making it back home to New Orleans. After the crematorium, they invited everyone back to Charleston.

When the crowd arrived at the door, Grace gave them one look and disappeared into the kitchen. As it was a sunny afternoon, Nessa took everyone out to the lawn, where she put down blankets for them to sit on and instructed Duncan and Leonard to ensure everyone had a drink. Then she followed Grace into the kitchen, fearing she would find her in a fury. But she was pleasantly surprised to find her raiding the larder for every item of food she could find. There were rolls of cheese, sides of ham, a large green salad, and loaves of bread, which she arranged on plates and trays. Grace had grown fond of Bobby during his short stay with them and nothing was too much for his friends.

'Always had time to chat to me,' she recalled, her eyes misting over.

Nessa helped her carry the spread out into the garden where they all tucked into an impromptu picnic, washed down with wine and whisky.

Later, the jazz band struck up again, and played tunes through the afternoon and into the dusk. Nessa sat next to Ginny on a tartan woollen picnic rug listening to the music and, as the day turned into night and the air temperature dropped, she was glad of the heat from her sister's body.

Diana, who had been singing with the band, came over.

'Do you mind if I come and sit with you?' she asked. She was holding a glass of whisky and slurring her words slightly.

'Not at all,' said Nessa, patting the rug beside her.

Diana sat down beside them, tucking her elegant legs, still in the high heels, beneath her slender frame.

'Thank you for this,' she said, gesturing at the now-empty plates.

'It's you we should be thanking for bringing his friends down to say goodbye to Bobby. Now I can write to his grandmother and tell her what a splendid affair his funeral was. I hope that gives the poor woman some comfort,' said Nessa.

Diana took a cigarette case from the top pocket of her jacket, took one out and placed it in the holder. She lit it with a match, took a long drag, then exhaled, a cloud of sweet tobacco encircling her heavily made-up face.

'I hope they catch whoever did it. Bobby was like a son to me. Such a dear, sweet soul. I'll murder them with my bare hands if I find out who it was,' she said. 'If the law doesn't get to them first.'

Nessa shivered. Despite Diana's slim stature, she felt suddenly certain she would easily be capable of such an act if she chose.

21.

Virginia

Rodmell, East Sussex

'Where would Sherlock Holmes begin? Or Philip Trent?' asked Ginny. *Trent's Last Case* had been published fifteen years earlier and was to a large extent a send-up of the genre, but it remained to her mind the finest piece of detective fiction ever written.

'If you're Sherlock Holmes, what does that make me? Dr Watson?' said Nessa, frowning.

'It was simply a figure of speech. What I mean is we ought to have some system, go through each of our suspects one by one. Who had the opportunity to kill both Gideon and Bobby, and, more importantly, who had the motive? Isn't that how one goes about it?'

'I'm not sure there's a blueprint for amateur sleuths, although I'm certain the police have their own set of procedures,' said Nessa.

'One which ties their hands with red tape,' said Ginny with a dismissive toss of her head.

'Let's start with motive,' said Nessa. 'How about Briggs? Could he have been overwrought with professional jealousy? Desperate that a younger man shouldn't claim the credit for an exciting discovery on his patch?'

The sisters sat side by side in dark green canvas deck chairs balanced on the small brick terrace beside Ginny's writing hut.

Ginny lifted a languid arm, draped in a lace shawl, and put her cigarette to her mouth, taking a drag and exhaling sharply.

'It's too obvious. If he was going to do it, wouldn't he have chosen a more subtle method than bashing him to death with his own trowel on the dig where they both worked?'

'Perhaps he wanted to claim all the credit for discovering the clay tablet,' said Nessa, wrinkling her nose at the smell of the tobacco smoke.

'Then who killed Bobby? You're not saying Briggs somehow made it out to Charleston, drowned him in the plunge pool, then hotfooted it back to Lewes without anyone noticing?'

'Stranger things have happened. Whose word do we have for it that he was at home at the time of both murders? That of his secretary, whose livelihood depends on her loyalty to her employer? Bobby could have seen some confrontation between Gideon and Briggs that proved he was guilty of murder, and so he had to remove him from the picture,' Ginny continued.

Nessa shook her head.

'I spoke to Bobby shortly before his death and I'm quite sure if he knew anything then he would have said. He was terrified the blame was going to be pinned on him.'

146

They both let out a deep sigh, then laughed at their synchronicity.

'What about Harry Dryden?' said Nessa. 'Always living in the shadow of his richer, more successful friend. Gideon got to pursue a glamorous career as an archaeologist out in the field, while Harry was stuck behind his desk at the bank. Then Gideon gets the beautiful girl whom Harry is secretly in love with and suddenly it becomes too much to bear.'

'Sounds like a marvellous plot for a detective novel, but I'm not convinced,' said Ginny, although they still hadn't got to the bottom of what he was doing meeting Briggs up on Kingston Ridge.

'I swear you've got a soft spot for that young man,' said Nessa. 'Well, if you're adamant it couldn't have been Harry, then that brings us back to Danny. You can't deny jealousy is a motive for him?'

But Ginny shook her head.

'He knew Betsy's condition when he married her, plus they were receiving money for the child. I think he's just a convenient suspect for the police to pin their case on, because he's poor and doesn't have the resources to defend himself. I feel sure there's more to this murder than Chief Inspector Gripe's limited imagination can allow for.'

'Where does that leave us, then, Ginny? We're no closer to unravelling this mystery.'

'Come for a stroll around the garden. Walking helps me to think things through,' said Ginny. She jumped to her feet, dropping the end of her cigarette and stubbing it out with the toe of her tan leather shoe. Nessa hauled herself out of the deck chair less gracefully, letting out a groan and rubbing her back. Ginny looked at her sister with concern. She'd always thought of her as so strong and capable, but she was approaching fifty. Was she starting to feel her age? She couldn't bear to think of Nessa getting old.

Linking arms with her sister, she pulled her along the path cut through the long grass of the orchard, where a trio of beehives stood. From there they joined the brick path leading past flower borders, which they'd put in where once there were old outbuildings. It was higgledy-piggledy, but it suited them just fine and was on a scale that was manageable for the two of them, with Leonard as chief gardener and she as his assistant. They continued round the side of the house until they reached the cool shade of a strip of lawn by the side of the house. Here Ginny lit another cigarette as they both turned back to admire the borders.

'The garden really is looking splendid. Old Fred Hobbes is doing a grand job. Will you thank him for the hollyhocks he brought over the other afternoon? I've planted them around the piazza. They should come up beautifully next year.'

'What afternoon? When?' asked Ginny. Fred hadn't mentioned any visit to Charleston to her recently. She would have remembered if he had.

'Now I come to think of it, it was the day Bobby died,' said Nessa. 'I completely forgot about the plants he'd brought for a day or two afterwards and I've only just managed to get them in the ground.'

Ginny took a drag on her cigarette as she absorbed this new information.

'Fred didn't tell me he was paying you a visit. He usually lets me know in case I want a lift with him, or if there's anything else I want to send you.'

148

'He did mention it was a last-minute visit. He was coming to see his cousin on the farm near to us who isn't well. Perhaps it slipped his mind, or he didn't have time to tell you.'

Ginny narrowed her nostrils as she always did when she was suspicious.

'You see what it means, don't you?' she asked.

Nessa shook her head. 'I'm afraid I don't. Enlighten me.'

'It means Fred had an opportunity to kill Bobby, as well as a motive to murder Gideon.'

Nessa clapped a hand to her mouth. 'You're right, Ginny. I hadn't thought of that. Oh dear, you're rather fond of old Fred, aren't you? You don't really think he's the murderer?'

'I don't know what to think. Would he have come to me asking for my help to prove his son-in-law innocent if he'd done it all along?'

'He might have been trying to cover his tracks,' said Nessa, but she didn't look convinced.

'What about Jasmine?' said Ginny. 'We haven't included her in our list of suspects, but I suppose we should. I can't see what her reasons would have been, but she doesn't have an alibi for the murder of either Gideon or Bobby. Why did she flee to Paris so suddenly if she wasn't guilty?'

It was a question that had been niggling at Ginny for some time now. They'd walked past the back of the house, around the stepover apple trees and out through the gate by the old tool shed to the croquet lawn, where a more expansive view over meadows and the newly acquired field, down to the river Ouse, suddenly opened before them.

'I can't believe someone so lovely could be capable of such a brutal act,' said Nessa.

149

'Just because someone is beautiful doesn't mean they can't also be bad,' said Ginny.

'There's only one way to find out,' said Nessa. 'I've made up my mind. I'm going to Paris.'

Ginny was so surprised she dropped her cigarette. It landed on the bare earth and she stubbed it out with the toe of her shoe.

22.

Alice

Mayfair, London

London was overcast with a bite in the air and hard spits of rain that hit her at a horizontal angle. She hailed a cab to take her to 25 Park Lane and, when they got there, hurried as fast as she could from the vehicle to the door of Philip's townhouse.

What a relief it was to be inside the voluminous entrance hall, filled with large gilt mirrors and huge blown-glass vases of scented arum lilies. The butler, who knew her well, showed her into the drawing room, where a fire crackled in the hearth. She took a seat and was offered coffee or champagne, to which she answered, 'Both, please.' Coming to Sir Philip Sassoon's was always a treat and he liked her to indulge herself.

Theirs was a curious relationship. He'd written to her twelve years ago, at the height of the war, to tell her how much he admired her work, and invited her to tea in this very house. They'd hit it off at once and been inseparable ever since, spending numerous weekends together at one or other of his country houses. She was ten years his senior, and there was nothing romantic in their bond. Philip was not that way inclined. But they were devoted to one another.

When she was a younger woman, Alice had a passionate love affair with a man who wasn't her husband. His wife said the pair of them would have trampled over her dead body to be together. She'd left Ernest, taking their daughter with her, and caused immeasurable pain all round. If it hadn't been for the income from her books, she doubted she would ever have had the courage to follow her heart.

But it turned out that leaving the husband of her youth wasn't as easy as she'd imagined, and her lover's wife wasn't ready to let go of him either. They'd parted, and she'd moved to Lewes, and invited Ernest to join her there. It was a tribute to him that he'd put aside his pride and done so. Or perhaps it was just that he didn't know what else to do with himself. Either way, they muddled along these days, even though he was even more cantankerous than ever. At least he was tolerant of her friendship with Philip, who always cheered her up.

'There you are, dearest one! I've missed you so,' he cried upon entering the room and seeing her. He came over and sat down beside her, taking her hands in his own and kissing her on both cheeks. 'Tell me all about this horrid murder you mentioned in your letters. How are you bearing up?' he asked.

'There have been two murders now. That's why I came here today. I want to ask your advice,' she replied.

She told him all about the recent events in Lewes, the gruesome discovery of a body on top of her mound, the subsequent death at Charleston and her uneasy dealings with Mrs Woolf, who appeared to have taken it upon herself to investigate the crimes together with her sister.

'I'm not sure why she believes herself qualified to play detective. As if she weren't already inflicting enough damage on the world with her difficult fiction,' said Alice.

'Miaow,' said Philip, turning his hand into a scraping claw. 'My poor darling. It's all too ghastly. Of course I knew Gideon,' he added. 'Everyone knew Gideon.'

'What was he like?' she asked.

Philip drew a deep breath sucking in his nostrils and leaned back on the sofa with his eyes closed. After a long pause, he fluttered them open again.

'Gideon was the sort of man you either loved or hated. He provoked strong reactions in men and women. His looks were to die for –' At this he stopped and opened his mouth in horror. 'Forgive me – I didn't mean it like that.'

She waved away his concerns. 'Carry on.'

'What I meant to say is for everyone who fell in love with him, there was someone else who detested him. He could be very cutting if he didn't get his own way. I was once at a nightclub when he asked the pianist to play his favourite tune. The man refused and later the same night he was accused by the manager of stealing tips from the tables and sacked on the spot. Gideon was long gone by then, but I've always wondered whether he set the manager on the poor man.'

A footman arrived with a tray bearing coffee, cream, a

bowl of sugar lumps and a plate piled high with pastel-coloured macaroons, followed by another carrying a silver ice bucket containing a bottle of champagne and two crystal flutes. This feast was arranged on the smoked-glass table in front of them. Alice poured the coffee, adding the cream and three sugars she knew Philip liked, while he nodded at one of the footmen to pop the champagne cork and pour them both a glass.

Alice took a ladylike sip of coffee.

'Did you know Bobby Bassey' she enquired.

'Heard of him. Jazz musician, wasn't he? Now you come to mention it, I did hear he and Gideon were . . . close friends for a while.'

Philip winked, in the way he was accustomed to when discussing the affairs of others, although he was notoriously discreet about his own.

'I wish they would hurry up and find out who the killer is, so I can rest easy in my bed. My cottage just doesn't feel as homely as it did before this all happened. I've a good mind to get it exorcised again,' she said. When she'd first moved into Castle Precincts House, having finally managed to eject the tenant who plagued the early years of her ownership, she'd had a priest in to rid it of evil spirits.

'I don't think it's the supernatural you have to worry about, unless poor old Gideon comes back to haunt you. It's the living you need to watch out for. Take care of yourself, dear heart, for I simply couldn't bear to think of anything bad happening to you. Until the police have solved the case, make sure you lock your doors and windows at night.'

She snorted.

154

'I don't have much faith in Chief Inspector Gripe,' she said, draining the champagne flute. 'But I've got a strange feeling that, much as I dislike her, Virginia Woolf and her sister are the ones who are going to get to the bottom of this.'

23.

Vanessa

Paris

It was strange being in Paris on her own without Duncan or Angelica. The children sailing their toy boats on the circular pond in the Jardins de Luxembourg made her think of her daughter with a pang. She usually brought her with her when travelling to France, but, given the sensitive nature of this trip, she'd left her behind at Charleston with Grace, on the promise they would return together soon to their house at Cassis.

It was one of those autumn days when the air is still as warm as summer. She'd removed her gaberdine coat and folded it over one arm. Her outfit of a brown linen shift and faded red espadrilles was attracting a few disdainful looks from the women of Paris, but it didn't bother her too much. At least she was comfortable and at her age that's what mattered most.

The sky was as blue as the butterflies on the South Downs, with chalky clouds reflected in the water of the pond, together with the white sails of the toy yachts, which the children manoeuvred with a system of wooden poles and brass hooks.

She made her way to the café in the park where she'd arranged to meet an old friend and gallery owner, Marcel, at eleven. While she waited, the waiter brought her a glass of crème de cassis and sparkling white wine. It made her think with a pang about La Bergère, the little farmhouse on the Côte d'Azur, which had been turned into a holiday home for her and Duncan.

'Vanessa, *belle comme toujours*.'

She turned round to see a small stocky man with a shock of black hair and a large expressive mouth. Rising to her feet, she accepted his embrace and returned his kisses.

He sat down and waved at the waiter who brought over a second Kir pétillant.

'What can be so urgent that you wanted to meet with me *immediatement*?' he asked after they had toasted one another and sat back in their chairs, drinks in hand.

'Marcel, do you know the Zain al-Din family?' she asked.

He inclined his head. '*Mais bien sûr*. They are one of the most notable families in Paris *en ce moment*.'

'I need to speak with their daughter, Jasmine. Between you and me, there's been a murder back in England, near to where I live in Sussex. The dead man was her fiancé. Then another man was killed, and she was on the scene. Naturally, she feared she would become a suspect and fled back to France. I'm convinced she's innocent, but I need to talk to her, to find out if she can shed any light on the killings.'

'The British police are employing artists to help with their investigations now?' asked Marcel, lighting a cigarette.

She patted his arm. 'You're teasing me. I'm most certainly not working for the police. But my sister and I are making some discreet enquiries. The mother of the first young man who died is an acquaintance of hers.'

'Ah, the famous Virginia Woolf, novelist and now it seems detective too. It is like a *roman policier*. Come to Le Boeuf sur le Toit tonight and I'll see what I can do,' he said, referring to the famous nightclub favoured by artists and writers where she and Duncan usually hung out when they were in Paris. 'Now tell me, how is Duncan? Why didn't you bring him with you? We miss him,' he added.

'This trip is strictly business and not pleasure. He'll be here soon enough on his way down to Cassis,' she replied.

As they said goodbye, she noticed Marcel's hand shaking slightly and wondered if it was the result of too many Pernods, or something more serious. None of them was getting any younger. As she turned and walked away, she was about to mention it to Duncan before remembering he wasn't there.

Leaving the park, she made her way to the Rue de l' Odeon to Sylvia's bookshop, Shakespeare & Co, intending to see if they had a copy of *To The Lighthouse* with her design on the cover. When she got there, she paused by the door and strained her eyes to see who might be inside. A strong desire to be by herself washed over her and she quickly turned round before anyone recognised her. The constant glances at her unconventional footwear were finally getting to her, so she went into a shoe shop and bought herself a pair of black leather shoes with buttons on the straps.

She returned to the Hôtel de Londres on the Rue Bonaparte where she always stayed when she visited the city. Asking the young man behind the counter for the key to her room, she hurried upstairs before anyone of her acquaintance spotted her.

In the safety of her hotel bedroom, she slept for most of the afternoon, exhausted by all that had happened and finding she was relieved to be away from Duncan's nervous energy.

She dreamed she was back at Charleston, trying to rescue Bobby from the tiny plunge pool, which turned into a vast ocean with waves that threatened to engulf them both. When she awoke with a start, dusk was falling. She hadn't closed the curtains and for a while she lay on her bed, watching the silhouette of the rooftops against the yellow glow of the city sky.

Then she remembered she'd arranged to meet an art dealer she knew for dinner at seven and forced herself to get up from the double bed, a luxury after the narrow beds at Charleston, to wash and dress. She strapped on the leather shoes and, unused to the height, she was a little unsteady on her feet, although there was no denying they made her look and feel more elegant.

On the short walk to the Rue de Tournon where the restaurant was situated, she passed a poster for an exhibition at the Louvre which caught her eye. The words '*Trésors des Croisades*' were emblazoned in gold against a black background. There were fragments of pottery on the sign, inscribed with Arabic writing that jogged something in her memory.

Only as she stepped into the cavernous restaurant, alive with the hum of voices and cutlery, did she realise what it reminded her of. The tablet Gideon Rivers had found at the top of Brack Mound. But how could that possibly have anything to do with an exhibition at the biggest museum in Paris?

The art dealer, Jean-Claude, flirted outrageously with her throughout the meal, and she wasn't sure whether to be flattered or embarrassed. After coffee, he escorted her to Le Boeuf sur le Toit. From the street it didn't look like much, but as soon as you entered you were in another world. Gypsy jazz rang out from a piano in the corner. Groups of women in flimsy silk and men in dinner jackets and bow ties crowded together conspiratorially in plush red velvet banquettes. Silver helium balloons floated up towards the ceiling. Surveying it all was Francis Picabia's *L'Oeil Cacodylate*, a painting that always made her laugh, depicting a large brown eye surrounded by the signatures of all the friends who'd come to visit the artist while he was sick in bed with an eye infection.

Couples were already dancing, and the small round tables covered in starched white linen cloths were all occupied. Shaking off her escort, Nessa looked around for Marcel. He was nowhere to be seen, but her eye was immediately drawn to a beautiful young man sitting by himself at a table next to the piano. He had slicked-back hair, an aquiline nose and eyes of tourmaline green. In his hand dangled a cigarette holder, from which he occasionally took a drag. There was something very familiar about him. She must have been looking for too long, because he glanced over in her direction and raised one eyebrow.

At the same time, she felt a tap on her shoulder and turned round to find Marcel behind her.

'There you are, *chérie*. I was wondering when we might expect you.'

'It was hard to escape from my dinner date. He's still here somewhere,' she replied, hoping the art dealer had found someone else on whom to lavish his attention. 'Is Jasmine here yet?' she continued.

Marcel held his sides and let out a long, deep laugh.

'But, *chérie*, you are looking right at her,' he said.

Glancing back over to the young man, Nessa realised why he looked so familiar and at once felt like a dreadful idiot. It was Jasmine, her black bob greased back, wearing a sharply cut pin-striped suit with a mustard-coloured silk cravat. Marcel led the way over to her table, and Nessa followed. As they approached, Jasmine got to her feet and Nessa threw her arms round her and hugged her. Then she stepped back and held her at arm's length.

'My dear, I didn't recognise you. You look simply marvellous. How are you? Why did you leave without telling anyone where you were going? We've all been so worried.'

Jasmine didn't answer immediately. She looked away as if trying to decide what to say in answer to Nessa's flurry of questions. Finally, she spoke.

'I had to get away before the police came to investigate Bobby's murder. Don't you see how it would look for me? The lover of a murdered man ends up in the same place as his former lover, then he too is killed. It is too much of a coincidence.'

'You knew about Gideon and Bobby, and you didn't mind?'

'Of course I knew that Gideon had male lovers. So what? You too are in a similar boat, I think. You love Duncan and

161

he loves men, lots of them. In such situations, you can't escape jealousy, and Bobby was broken-hearted when Gideon told him he was marrying me, and it was over between them. What else could he say? Our love was *un coup de foudre*, it eclipsed everything that had come before for both of us.'

'Did he continue to take lovers after you were engaged?'

A shadow passed over Jasmine's lovely features. 'I suppose he did. That was Gideon's way. Even though he'd pledged himself to me, he didn't want to deny himself to others. It was different for me, of course. He was terribly jealous and wanted to make sure I had no other lovers. Now he's gone, I can do as I like.' She threw back her head in a gesture of defiance.

Nessa nodded. Now Jasmine explained, it all made sense, but there was something else she wanted to ask her about.

'What's your connection to Diana Underhill at the Sylvan Rooms?'

Jasmine narrowed her eyes. 'We're old acquaintances. A friend took me to the Sylvan Rooms when I was first in London and we've kept in touch ever since. There's really nothing more to it than that.'

She'd paused a moment too long before speaking and Nessa saw her eyes dart up to the left, a sure sign she was withholding the truth.

The conversation was clearly at an end. Jasmine looked over at a pretty girl dancing to the music. Their eyes locked and she gave her a meaningful look then patted her knee. The girl came straight over as if pulled by an invisible string and perched on Jasmine's slender thigh. She leaned back and their mouths met. Nessa looked away. Pulling back from the embrace, Jasmine rose to her feet.

162

'I think you know all about jealousy,' she said.

Nessa said nothing, but it was true. Even now, she was wondering what Duncan was doing in her absence. When she'd left for Paris, he'd travelled up to London from Charleston on the same day.

'I'm going to paint. It's the only thing that gets rid of the pain,' he'd said before she left. But was he still painting in his studio flat off Fitzroy Square, or had he downed his brushes and headed off into Soho, to a place where she couldn't follow him? With each new love affair, she feared she was going to lose him, and yet it went against everything she believed in to pin him down and so she just had to live with the uncertainty.

Jasmine joined her girlfriend on the dance floor, moving with a physical confidence Nessa envied. There was a time when she too had been such a sensual creature, living purely in her body, but these days she was never able to shake off entirely the intrusion of her thoughts.

It had been foolish to come to Paris in pursuit of a young woman who clearly knew her own mind. Feeling suddenly very old and tired, her feet aching in the new shoes, she decided she would find Marcel, say her goodbyes and go back to the hotel and from there to Charleston. There was nothing more for her to find out here.

24.

Virginia

Rodmell, East Sussex

Sunlight sliced through the windowpane of her writing hut, falling on to the desk, and illuminating the little jam jar containing a late rose, cut from the garden that morning. Unlike summer roses, its colour was dappled pink and white, as if someone had bled on to it. She lowered her face to smell it, remembering that the scent of roses had been Thoby's favourite.

Closing her eyes, she inhaled its myrrh-like perfume, then opened them again quickly when she heard a sharp rapping on the door. Sighing, she rose to her feet and answered it to find Leonard standing there. He wasn't holding the customary cup of tea, so there must be some other, more urgent reason for his intrusion.

He put an apologetic hand on her arm. 'I wouldn't have interrupted you for the world, Ginny, only I've got Betsy at the front door and she's half hysterical, poor girl. I can't make out what she's trying to say, so I said I'd fetch you.'

There was a sinking feeling in her belly. If Betsy was in such a state, it couldn't be good news. Had they found evidence against her husband? Abandoning her notebook open on the desk, she pulled on her mohair cardigan and accompanied Leonard back down the brick path and through the house to the front door. Outside, Betsy was pacing up and down the small front garden.

'Do come in, won't you?' she said, not wanting the neighbours to overhear any more than was necessary. When Betsy looked uncertain, Ginny reached out and practically pulled her inside. Once the girl was over the threshold, she remembered her manners and accompanied her hostess into the green sitting room. Ginny indicated a seat and Betsy obediently sat down.

'What's happened to upset you so?' asked Ginny, sitting in the armchair opposite and leaning forward, her forearms on her knees, palms pointing upwards to support her chin.

'It's Dad,' Betsy said in a strangled voice.

'Calm down and speak clearly. What's happened to your father?'

'They've released Danny and arrested Dad in his place. Why have they got it in for us? I was the one who was badly done by and now we're getting all the blame. Neither of them is guilty, I promise you, Mrs Woolf. They wouldn't hurt a living soul, not Danny or Dad. It's that so-called friend of Gideon's they want to keep an eye on. Pretended to be like a brother, he did, but secretly he was mad with jealousy. I keep in touch with one of the girls who works there, and she told me there was something between Harry and Gideon's fancy French fiancée. That's who they want to be looking at, but it's always us poor folk who get the blame.'

165

With this outpouring of words, Betsy burst into tears, snot dripping from her reddened nose. Ginny felt inside her sleeve for the handkerchief she always kept folded there, discreetly checked that it was clean, then shook it out and handed it to the girl. Accepting it, Betsy blew her nose loudly.

Ginny thought of how she'd followed Harry Dryden over the Downs and spied on his rendezvous with Stanley Briggs. It did seem strange given what had happened and she wasn't a woman to believe in coincidence. But Nessa was right – she'd warmed to the young man from the first time she'd met him. There was an earnestness about him that reminded her of the men in her friendship group when they were young and meeting in rooms in Bloomsbury to discuss ideas and art. Living with her siblings, at last liberated from paternal restrictions, it had been a time of freedom of intellect and spirit. Was this affectionate association clouding her judgement when it came to Harry?

Having thoroughly vacated her nasal passages, Betsy recovered some of her composure.

'I didn't know who else to turn to. Dad has always spoken well of you, and I know he's done you good service over the years. Oh, please can you have a word with the inspector on our behalf? He won't listen to me, but he'll respect what you have to say if you tell him Dad couldn't possibly have done it.'

Ginny found the girl's faith in her father touching, but wondered if she knew just what human beings were capable of – how much fury might lurk in his soul at the thought of Gideon Rivers making free with his daughter and leaving her quite literally holding the baby? Still, she was right:

they owed it to Fred, who had always been loyal and hard-working, to intervene on his behalf.

'Leonard, can we drive into Lewes this afternoon? I think we need to pay Chief Inspector Gripe a visit. He'll pay more attention if I have a man with me.'

She knew full well she could argue Fred's case by herself, and she was without a doubt the more forceful of the two of them. But one had to give the appearance, at least, of conforming to social norms if one wanted to get things done.

'Thank you, ma'am. I knew you would help,' said Betsy, jumping to her feet and looking as though she would like to throw her arms around Ginny, who took a step backwards.

'I can't make any promises. The police must have had their reasons to arrest your father, some piece of evidence against him, even if it's only circumstantial. But I'll get to the bottom of it and report back to you. For what it's worth, my husband and I can both vouch for his character. Now you'd better get back to that baby of yours.'

She ushered Betsy out of the front door. The young woman tried to hand back the handkerchief, but Ginny held her palms up.

'Keep it. I have plenty more.'

As she watched Betsy close the garden gate behind her and trot back down the road to her parents' cottage, she was sure she saw a curtain twitch in one of the nearby houses. Rodmell might seem a sleepy, peaceful place, but its residents were always on alert for scandal, particularly when it was linked to a woman who until the untimely death of her son had considered herself the queen bee of the village. Now it looked as though Daphne Rivers's star was falling.

* * *

That afternoon, they drove into Lewes, parking near to the police station on Mount Pleasant, where the duty officer told them it was the chief inspector's afternoon off.

'Surely he can't have time to take an afternoon off in the middle of a murder investigation?' asked Ginny.

'He's most particular about it, madam. Spends every Wednesday afternoon up on his allotment. Very proud of his potatoes, he is. I believe he's planning to pull up the last of them today.'

Upon further questioning, the duty sergeant revealed the chief inspector's allotment was not too far from the police station on the other side of the railway track near a crescent of large Victorian houses. Although they could have walked it, Ginny insisted on getting back into the car and driving the short distance.

'This is the place,' she called out.

Leonard rapidly pulled the vehicle to a halt at the top of a dirt track leading down over fields into the river valley. They got out and set off on foot to find Gripe. In the first plot they came to, an elderly gentleman in a knitted V-neck vest over a starched white shirt with the sleeves rolled back to his elbows leaned on his long-handled fork, and watched them go by. When he saw Leonard and Ginny, he started chuckling to himself. Despite being keen gardeners themselves, they had dressed in their town clothes in anticipation of speaking to the chief inspector and looked decidedly out of place between the rows of cabbages.

'Those dahlia tubers will need to come up soon,' said Leonard, pointing to a patch of colourful blooms beside the old man. The expression on his face changed and he nodded with a newfound respect.

'You know your flowers, then, sir,' he said.

'Indeed, I have a large garden of my own at Rodmell. I'd value your advice on growing dahlias; you look to have some very fine specimens there.'

'My secret is I shake off all the soil from the tubers, cut the stems right back and store them in boxes of sawdust in the dry woodshed over winter,' said the old fellow, putting his thumbs in his pockets and puffing out his chest.

'I see. That's a good system you have there. By the way, you wouldn't happen to know which plot belongs to Chief Inspector Gripe?' asked Leonard.

'Third one down on the right,' said the old man. They looked to where he was pointing and saw Arthur Gripe using a large fork to dig up potatoes.

'Thank you for the advice,' said Leonard, and they continued down the path between the allotments. As they approached, Gripe looked up. When he saw them, he let out a deep sigh.

'Mr and Mrs Woolf, I'm afraid you've caught me on my afternoon off. Mrs Gripe is very partial to her potatoes,' he said, sticking his fork into the ground and leaning on it. His brow was sweaty and his cheeks ruddy.

'Never mind potatoes. Here you are digging the soil when an innocent man is behind bars, terrified he will never see his grandchild again. Arresting Fred Hobbes was a mistake. My husband and I can vouch for his honesty,' said Ginny without pausing to take a breath in between her words.

'He may be an honest worker, but he was seen walking towards the castle in the early hours of the morning before Gideon Rivers was found there brutally murdered. What's more, he had a strong motive to want to see the young man dead,' said the chief inspector.

'That's where you're completely wrong. We both know Gideon fathered Betsy Lamb's baby, but Mrs Rivers pays the family a handsome sum of money every month towards the child's upkeep. The last thing her father would want is to cut off the source of that income,' replied Ginny.

Gripe stood up stiffly, putting a hand on his lower back. He looked Ginny straight in the eye.

'Is this true?' he asked.

She nodded. 'I have it from Mrs Rivers herself.' She didn't add that Fred Hobbes hadn't known about the money either until she'd told him about it, and that had been after the murder.

The chief inspector shook his head and swept a soiled hand across his brow, leaving a dirty brown smudge on his forehead.'

'That may put a different light on things, but we still have to explain what Fred was doing in Lewes in the early hours of Sunday morning.'

'Have you asked him?'

'That's the thing. He doesn't have a decent explanation. At first, he denied it, and when he was told there was a witness he said he'd just gone for a walk to clear his head and couldn't remember exactly where he'd ended up.'

Ginny paused. That didn't sound like the practical Fred Hobbes she knew.

'The thing is, Chief Inspector, you seem to think this murder has to do with an affair of the heart between a serving girl and the young man of the house. But what if the real cause is something much more exotic? Gideon Rivers was working in a new field. One where exciting discoveries are being made all the time, and professional jealousy is rife. Have you considered the work he was doing at the dig on Brack Mound and whether the motive might lie there?' she asked.

The policeman snorted at the indignity of being spoken to in such a way by a woman. Ginny imagined Mrs Gripe would never dream of talking in that manner to a professional man, and, if she did, he would have something to say about it.

She ignored him. As a woman who frequently spoke her own mind, she was used to such a reaction from men. Her only interest was in finding out the truth.

'Have you interviewed Mr Briggs yet?'

The inspector looked at her sharply. 'We have taken a statement from the chief archaeologist, but he is a well-respected professional man,' he answered.

'And well-respected professional men have never been known to commit crimes?' asked Ginny, raising one eyebrow.

Gripe filled his cheeks with air, then puffed out a breath.

'Mr Briggs is an Oxford man, Mrs Woolf, and his secretary can vouch for his whereabouts on the nights of both murders,' he said.

'So you prefer to pin it on an honest working man who happened to be in the wrong place at the wrong time,' said Ginny. Her long, thin nostrils flared, and she and the chief inspector looked at one another for a long moment, holding one another's gaze, each daring the other to look away. Gripe blinked first.

'At present we're merely keeping Mr Hobbes in for

questioning. If it turns out he can come up with a good reason for being near Lewes Castle at the time of the murder, we'll release him on bail. And I can assure you we'll continue to pursue every other angle.'

'How much?' asked Leonard.

'How much for what?' said the chief inspector, looking a little confused.

'For bail? Fred Hobbes has a wife and daughter who need him. He's not going to do a disappearing act and my wife and I will act as surety for him if you release him now.'

The chief inspector pushed the prongs of his fork deep into the earth and drew a loud breath as he contemplated this suggestion. Then he nodded to himself as if he'd reached a conclusion.

'Come back tomorrow at noon with fifty pounds. We'll have finished our questioning by that time and if you can stand bail for him, Fred can go home with you then.'

Leonard nodded and turned to Ginny.

'Looks like we'd better pay a visit to the bank on our way home.'

Ginny opened her eyes wide as she took in this arrangement. Trust men to reduce everything to the base matter of payment. And yet it offered a practical solution when she could see no other. Throwing her hands up in the air, she nodded her head.

'I suppose we have no other choice. To the bank it is,' she said.

25.

Vanessa

Paris

When she woke, her mood had changed. A day to herself in Paris. What luxury. Eager as she was to get back to Charleston and her children, her train was not due to leave until the evening and she might as well make the most of it.

Rising from her hotel bed, Nessa crossed to the window and opened the shutters. The sun was rising, pink and silver, over the city, washing away the dark glamour of the night before when she'd seen a different side to Jasmine, a more complicated woman than the beautiful heiress she and Ginny first encountered in the White Hart.

She washed and dressed in a tailored blue frock, her concession to Paris fashion, although as her new shoes were rubbing her badly, she packed them away and slipped back into her comfortable red espadrilles.

At breakfast, missing her daughter, she dunked a slice of baguette laden with *confiture des fraises* into a bowl of milky coffee, thinking of how Angelica loved to do the same with her *chocolat chaud*.

Then having left her baggage at the hotel's reception she ventured out. What to do? She would have dearly loved to go shopping, but money, as always, was tight. The poster of the forthcoming exhibition at the Louvre pasted to the wall across the street from the hotel caught her eye. It was not until later that year, but it was a long time since she'd visited the museum. To the Louvre it was, but first she'd promised Marcel to drop by at his gallery to discuss a forthcoming show of her pictures.

The streets of the Latin Quarter were slowly coming to life. She nearly tripped over the leg of a prostitute leaning against the wall, smoking a cigarette, and noted her stocking seam was painted on with kohl.

As she passed *Les Deux Magots* she heard someone calling out her name. Turning round, she saw Roland Penrose, the young surrealist artist she'd met last time she was in Paris with Duncan. A tall, thin man of aristocratic gait, he was sitting with a young woman with a shining face, her brown hair tied neatly back with a black ribbon.

'Mrs Bell, I didn't know you were in Paris. Do come and join us for a coffee,' said Roland, his upper-class English vowels oddly jarring just as she'd acclimatised herself to French. But she liked the look of his companion, so she crossed to the table, and took the seat he offered.

'Call me Nessa, please,' she said as she held out a hand to the woman, who took it in her own soft palm and looked her directly in the eye. There was a passion in the young woman's gaze that reminded her what it was to be young in the heart of a busy metropolis. These days she spent far too much time hiding in her garden; it was good for her to be out in the world like this.

'Meet my wife, Valentine. She is a poet, the intellect in our marriage, the wordsmith to my simple daubs.'

Nessa laughed. 'You sound like my sister and me. She's the brains and I'm the poor painting peasant, holed up in the Sussex countryside. You must come and visit us at Charleston.'

'Nessa's sister is the writer Virginia Woolf,' Roland explained to Valentine. The young woman's eyes lit up and she placed a hand on Nessa's arm.

'I cannot believe it. Your sister is such an inspiration to me, to women writers everywhere,' she said.

Roland coughed, in the fashion of an Englishman who doesn't like to make a fuss.

'We would love to come and visit. I've heard great things about Sussex.'

Nessa smiled and nodded, then, remembering the scene she'd left behind, her face fell. Roland and Valentine were so young, so earnest, and yet she felt compelled to speak, to tell them about all the emotions swirling around in her stomach like paints on a palette.

'To be honest, we've been having a difficult time of things lately. I don't know if you've heard, but there have been two murders in the town close to where we live. The first was that of a rising star in archaeology, Gideon Rivers.'

Valentine made a sharp intake of breath and pressed her hand to her chest.

'*Mon Dieu*, but we knew Gideon. How could someone so alive be dead?'

Worry lines appeared in Roland's brow. 'That's jolly bad news. What happened?'

She told them the facts of the case as she knew them, leaving out the worst of the gory detail.

'The police have arrested a young local man, but my sister and I think they have the wrong person. That's why I'm in Paris, not for pleasure, but because I wanted to speak to Gideon's fiancée.'

At this, a look of recognition crossed Roland's face. 'Ah, yes. The enchanting Jasmine Zain al-Din. So beautiful she lured him away from Marguerite Muir. It's quite something to break the heart of a Hollywood star. There was a great scandal when it happened here in Paris. We were there the night he broke it off with her at Josephine Baker's L'Imperial. Miss Baker was quite put out. When she arrived at one o'clock in the morning, fresh from her appearance at Folies-Bergère, and still wearing her ostrich feathers, she expected the usual fanfare. Instead, all anyone was talking about was how Gideon had thrown over *the* Marguerite Muir for an unknown heiress. Josephine had a tantrum and threw the plate of black-eyed peas her chef had prepared for her right back in her face. Gideon made a hash of it, by all accounts. He didn't try to spare her feelings, just told her he was in love with someone else and asked her to return the diamond engagement ring he'd bought her.

'Marguerite stormed off into the night and no one could find her. She was spotted by a passer-by on a bridge over the Seine and Gideon was worried she'd drowned herself in the river. But she turned up a few weeks later, back in Los Angeles, acting as if nothing had happened. Turned out the only thing she threw into the river was her diamond engagement ring. She gave an interview about it to *Variety*, calling Gideon the Playboy Archaeologist. Not any more it would seem.'

'It appears Gideon Rivers had a talent for breaking hearts. Marguerite wasn't the only one. I'm afraid it gets worse. He was also having a love affair with a young man of our acquaintance, a jazz musician by the name of Bobby Bassey.'

'Never heard of him,' said Roland.

'The day after Gideon's funeral, Bobby was found dead. Drowned in the plunge pool at Charleston. It's just too dreadful to think about.'

Nessa put her head in her hands. Valentine put a hand on her back, and the warmth of her palm was reassuring. Nessa looked up again and took a sip of the *café au lait* the waiter had just brought her.

'There's your man, then,' said Roland. 'A clear case of a crime of passion, in which the murderer, filled with regret, goes on to take his own life.'

Nessa shook her head slowly. 'There were signs of foul play, marks on the ground suggesting a struggle before Bobby entered the water, probably already unconscious. Jasmine was staying with us – she'd only just arrived – and when she fled at the same time as the murder it looked suspicious, especially as she and Bobby were both in love with the same man.'

Roland took a packet of cigarettes from his pocket, lit one and took a drag, then blew out the smoke as he took in what Nessa had just told him.

'It sounds a total mess. I see why you don't trust the police to find the killers,' he said.

Valentine's eyes shone with concern. 'You must take care.

Whoever has committed these terrible crimes is extremely dangerous. You don't want to end up as their next victim.'

'I'm not worried on my own account. No one takes any notice of an old drab like me. But I feel I simply must get to the bottom of it, for the sake of those two young men and their families, and I know Ginny feels the same.'

Looking at her watch, she saw she'd better leave if she was to have time to take in the gallery and the Louvre.

'Thank you, darlings. You two have been a real tonic, but I must go. Do come and visit us in Charleston. I have a feeling you'll like it there.'

With kisses all round, she left the young couple drinking their coffees and watching the world go by and continued to Marcel's gallery.

As she walked in, he had his head under the counter looking for something, but when the door jangled he looked up. Seeing her there, he ran over to the door, waggling his finger at her.

'Nessa, you naughty woman, you left without saying goodbye last night. Did you run off with some young lover?' he said.

'You know Duncan's the only man for me. Even if I'm not the only man for him. The truth is I was suddenly desperate to go to bed, *alone*. I'm sorry, Marcel. Did anything happen after I left?' she replied.

'Your young friend Jasmine is not quite as grief-stricken as you thought, it appears. She was partying all night long and I'm willing to bet *she* did not go to bed alone. I thought you said she was devoted to Gideon.'

Nessa let out a loud sigh. Had she been taken in by Jasmine? Could she be guilty? After all, she was the only person they knew of who had the opportunity in both deaths. And yet, could someone so slight really have done away with two men, much bigger and stronger than herself? Perhaps she was underestimating the strength of the young woman.

'Come, I'll show you around the gallery and we can talk about how I'll hang your pictures,' said Marcel. The dear man was trying to distract her.

'I'm determined this exhibition will be the *crème de la crème*. Paris needs to know your work. To my mind, you are a talent up there with such greats as Cézanne and Monet. Have you been to his garden at Giverny? I think you'd like it there.'

For the next half-hour, she let Marcel lead her round his gallery, talking about which of her paintings they should show and explaining to her his philosophy of how to hang great art. His chatter was soothing and, for a while, she almost forgot why she was in Paris.

'Let me take you for lunch,' he proposed when the tour was finally at an end.

Nessa shook her head. 'I only have a few hours before I must catch the train back to London, and I haven't been to the Louvre for years. I promised myself this morning I would go there today.'

'Then let me accompany you.'

She put two hands on his arms. 'Marcel, you are a dear man, but I need to be alone for a while to have time to think. So much has happened in these last few weeks. It's difficult to get my head round it all.'

With a wistful look, he nodded in agreement.

'Very well, until the next time, *cherie*. Hopefully then we will meet in happier circumstances. The exhibition that will make your name. And you'll bring that delightful daughter of yours. She looks so very like her father. Duncan and Angelica, a pair of beautiful angels.'

Nessa put a finger to her lips and smiled. 'You know very well Angelica has my husband's name even though it's many years since we've lived as man and wife, and she believes Clive to be her father.'

'Your wish is my command. I am silence itself. *Adieu*, Vanessa.'

By the time she reached the Louvre, she was ravenous. Directly after paying her entrance fee, she went to the museum restaurant, where she ordered a plate of *steak-frites* with a green salad and a glass of Beaujolais to wash it down.

A waiter brought the glass of wine, and she'd just taken her first sip while waiting for the food to arrive when she saw a familiar face walk past the door leading from the restaurant to the museum. It was Jasmine, and she was pretty sure she hadn't seen her. What was she up to? Her stomach said stay and eat, but her brain reminded her she was here in the capacity of amateur sleuth and couldn't let this opportunity pass. She got to her feet just as the waiter returned with her meal.

'Keep it warm – I'll be right back,' she said. The waiter in his starched white jacket looked most put out.

'But, madame, the chef has prepared it medium rare. The steak cannot wait.'

Shrugging, she pushed past him and ran out of the door, leaving him muttering about *les anglaises* under his breath. At the end of the corridor leading into the museum, she could just see Jasmine's back disappearing through a door.

Following at a safe distance, she watched as the young woman walked through the ground-floor galleries until reaching a staircase leading to the museum's private offices.

Glancing over her shoulder and ascertaining there was no one around except for a sleepy-looking security guard at the far end of the gallery, Nessa followed Jasmine up the stairs and through a set of glass double doors just in time to see her entering one of the offices. Glad of the espadrilles that enabled her to pad silently, she made her way along the corridor until she was right outside the door, where she could just make out what was being said inside.

'Mademoiselle Zain al-Din, what a pleasure to see you again. Please tell your father we're most grateful for the financial support he's given to this exhibition,' said a man's voice.

'I'll pass it on. Both he and I believe it's of the utmost importance the role of our people in the Crusades is accurately reflected. It wasn't just a case of civilising Christian knights arriving to enlighten the natives. There was already an ancient and advanced civilisation when they arrived,' came Jasmine's impassioned reply.

'A band of thugs from Europe, you mean?' said the man in an amused tone. He was presumably a member of the museum's curatorial team.

'Far be it from me to say such a thing, but the tablet we speak of shows a culture in which poetry and philosophy were very much at the fore,' answered Jasmine.

'And you say this tablet was found on a hill in the English countryside. May I ask how it got to be there?'

'I believe it has something to do with the third Earl de Warenne, who fought in the Second Crusade. He didn't make it back alive, but his colleagues returned his possessions to his wife and daughter, Isabella, who went on to marry the king's illegitimate half-brother and become a considerable power in her own right. They must have been buried at Lewes Castle and not discovered until now, nine hundred years later.'

'Most unfortunate. A priceless artefact is found, and a man is killed. Do you think there's any connection between the two events?'

'Merely a tragic coincidence,' said Jasmine. 'They've already arrested someone for the murder. The husband of a young girl who worked for Gideon's mother. There had been a youthful indiscretion between them, and she fell pregnant. The man in custody must have somehow found out the child wasn't his and killed poor Gid in fury.'

There was silence for a moment or two, followed by the sound of gentle sobbing.

'There, there, don't upset yourself,' said a man's voice. In response came the loud blowing of a nose.

At that moment, Nessa heard footsteps coming up the stairs. Looking around, she saw a small stock room opposite, and hurried inside, closing the door behind her and crouching down between shelves stacked with piles of dusty books. Whoever it was knocked on the door of the office where Jasmine was talking to the unseen curator. Nessa didn't dare come out from her hiding place and stayed there crouched in a most uncomfortable position, until she heard the door opposite open again and the voices of three people emerge. Only once the sounds of their voices had faded away completely did she dare to emerge, opening the door just a crack to begin with and peeping out to make sure the coast was clear.

She hurried back to the museum gallery and from there to the restaurant, where her half drunk glass of wine was still on the table. A couple of minutes later, the waiter who'd served her before reappeared, frowning. He slammed a plate of *steak-frites* down in front of her.

'We'll have to charge you for a second steak, madame. The chef said it was *incroyable* to keep the first one warm for you.'

Nodding in resigned agreement, Nessa picked up her knife and fork. But as she cut into the steak and saw fresh blood seep out on to the plate, the image of Gideon Rivers being hacked to death sprang into her mind and she suddenly found she had no appetite.

26.

Virginia

Rodmell, East Sussex

Leonard's plants had arrived from the nursery on the back of a horse-drawn cart.

'Heard you've had a murder in the village,' said the delivery man as he helped to unload wooden trays containing hardy perennials and biennials. Ginny imagined them flowering with abundance the following year.

'A young man from the village was found dead in Lewes. It's a tragedy for the family, but the whole of Rodmell has felt it,' replied Leonard.

She made a face indicating he should be quiet, as at that very moment Fred Hobbes was advancing up the lane towards them. Thankfully, they'd just finished unloading.

'I'm afraid I have no time to stand and gossip, got to deliver all of these by lunchtime, or I'll be in trouble with the boss. Old Sally here doesn't move as fast as she used to,' said the man, climbing back on to the driver's seat and tugging the reins to let the mare know it was time to go.

184

He pulled off as Fred reached the front gate, oblivious to the connection between the murder he'd just mentioned and the man who was currently the chief suspect in the case, who would still be in jail if it weren't for her and Leonard persuading the inspector to let him out on bail.

'Fred, there was really no need for you to come. We could have managed the plants by ourselves. You must be exhausted after your ordeal,' said Leonard.

'I'd rather keep myself busy if it's all the same to you, sir. Can't bear sitting at home with the missus, twiddling my thumbs.'

Together, Leonard and Fred began carrying the trays of plants round to the back of the house. Feeling herself to be redundant, Ginny thought she might as well leave them to it and get on with some writing. She retreated to the safety of her hut and spent a happy hour during which the words flowed from her pen.

At eleven, Nellie brought tea out into the garden and the three of them stopped work and sat in the low sunshine on the grass, enjoying the last of the year's warmth. The two men had already planted half the new stock in the flower borders and were admiring their handiwork. Leonard remembered something he'd left in the house and went off to fetch it, leaving Ginny and Fred alone.

'What are those ones there?' asked Ginny, pointing to a group of plants with heart-shaped green leaves.

'Those are hollyhocks, Mrs Woolf. By next summer, they'll produce tall spires of yellow and pink flowers, most attractive to the bumblebees.'

Hollyhocks. Why did that ring a bell? Then she remembered.

'By the way, my sister said to say thank you for the hollyhocks you took over to Charleston the other day. You should have let me know you were going.'

Colour rose to Fred's cheek, and he mumbled, 'Sorry about that. It was a last-minute sort of thing, or I would have mentioned it.'

She paused a moment before adding, 'Are you sure the hollyhocks were the only reason for you going to Charleston that day, Fred?'

The gardener stared hard at his feet. He seemed to be making his mind up about whether to tell her something or not. Eventually, he spoke.

'I wanted to get a look at Mr Grant's young friend. I'd heard rumours, you see, that there was something between him and Mr Rivers and I wanted to look for myself, suss out whether he might be linked to the murder and that might get Danny off the hook. But I didn't know he was going to go and get himself killed that very evening.'

Ginny's heart sank. Much as she wanted to believe Fred, it didn't look good that he'd been in the same place at the same time as not just one, but two murders.

He must have guessed what she was thinking because the next thing he said was, 'I know it looks suspicious, but I promise you I had nothing to do with either death. Ask anyone, I'm not a violent man. I saw something when I was at Charleston that I haven't been able to mention to anyone. You see, if I did, it would put me on the scene, which would lead the authorities to assume exactly what you've just been thinking. But there was someone else there who shouldn't have been that day: young Mr Dryden.'

'You saw him at Charleston?' asked Ginny.

'From a distance, but it was him all right, walking across the fields from the direction of Lewes. I recognised his floppy hair and he's got a singular way of walking.'

Fred was right. Harry Dryden's long legs meant he walked with a fast lollop, making him look ungainly, like a young deer. She'd noticed it that time she'd followed him over the Downs. If what the gardener said was true, that put a whole new perspective on things. Harry had told her and Nessa he hadn't visited Charleston before he came there looking for Jasmine. If he'd been there on the day of Bobby's murder, that was highly suspicious and would surely elevate him to number-one suspect in the case. Was it possible he'd murdered his best friend, and Bobby had seen them, or found out, so had to be silenced?

'Did you tell this to Chief Inspector Gripe?' she asked.

Fred looked thoroughly miserable and shook his head. 'I've only told you because I don't want you thinking I'm a killer. But how would it look if, after all the hours of questioning I've already been through, I hadn't mentioned something which could be so relevant to the case? It would put me on the scene of both murders, and the police would think I was just making it up about Mr Dryden to get myself off the hook.'

He had a point. It didn't look good that he hadn't said anything about it earlier. But there was something about the way in which he told her so now that made her believe he really had seen Harry that day.

'Are you going to say anything, ma'am? You and Mr Woolf have been so good to me that I'm willing to put myself at your mercy and do whatever you think is best.'

She heaved a deep sigh and looked out over the fields

to the river valley and the Iron Age fort of Mount Caburn beyond. They would have to tell the inspector sooner or later, or he could accuse them of withholding information too. But she was willing to hold off a bit longer to see if she and Nessa could make any sense of this new revelation and fit it into what they already knew.

Leonard had reappeared. Leaving him and Fred to get back to work, she went back inside and had just gone upstairs to change out of her gardening clothes when she heard a knocking on the door. Nellie went to answer it, and she could hear muffled voices, but couldn't make out who it was or what was being said.

A minute later, she heard Nellie's footsteps clomping up the wooden staircase followed by a tap on her bedroom door.

'There's someone here to see you, ma'am. A Mrs Doodley.'

'I don't know anyone called Mrs Doodley,' called back Ginny through the closed door. Then with a sharp bite of annoyance she realised who it was.

'Do you mean Mrs Dudeney?' she asked.

'That's right, Mrs Dudeney,' replied Nellie. 'Shall I tell her you'll come down?'

Alice Dudeney was the last person Ginny wanted to see right now, but it couldn't be avoided, and the woman might have some information.

'Show her into the sitting room and tell her I'll be down in five minutes,' she said.

188

27.

Alice

Here she was at last, in the inner sanctum. Virginia Woolf's sitting room. The shape was not so very different from her own drawing room. They both inhabited houses that were centuries old and had bits added on to them here and there over the years. But while the Dudeneys had opted for a traditional boiled beef-brown on the walls, the Woolfs proved their modernist credentials with a choice of arsenic green, the colour of bandstands in the rain. The furniture was nothing special. Solid pieces handed down through the family, presumably, or bought at auction in Lewes. The books, however, were cutting edge and eclectic. The latest volumes of poetry by young Thomas Stearns Eliot and his friend Ezra Pound, printed by the Woolfs' own Hogarth Press with covers designed by Vanessa Bell, sat alongside *The Lives of the Great Victorians* by Virginia's late father, Sir Leslie Stephens.

Alice hated the fact that she was so intrigued by the younger writer; Virginia was sixteen years her junior. Mrs Dudeney was a bestselling novelist in her own right with far more books under her belt than Mrs Woolf. But these days Alice no longer made the newspaper lists of the best writers, whereas Virginia was always right up there at the top.

The door opened and despite herself she felt a flutter in her chest as Mrs Woolf walked in. There was something about her upright posture, the way she held her head high above her tall, slender frame, so one could see right up her long, narrow nostrils that made Alice feel as if she were back at school in the presence of the head girl. She was followed by a flustered-looking maid, weren't they all, who put down a tray of tea and milk – no biscuits – on a side table, then left the room.

'Mrs Dudeney, what an unexpected visit. How can I be of assistance?' she asked. There was no warmth in her words. Really, the woman was a cold fish, but she'd made the effort to come all this way; she must persist.

'I wanted to ask your advice. I've heard you're taking a keen interest in Mr Rivers's murder.'

'His mother lives in the same village and is an acquaintance and I was with the young man shortly before his death. It's only natural I should want to keep myself apprised of the case,' said Virginia.

Did Alice detect a slight defensiveness in her tone? She cut straight to the point.

'There's something I haven't told the police inspector investigating the case. Namely, because he hasn't thought to ask, which I must say seems rather an oversight when I live right at the location where the crime was committed.'

Virginia's grey eyes took on a new intensity.

'Detecting a murderer in a case of this sort requires a subtlety of mind I'm afraid Chief Inspector Gripe lacks,' she said, following these words with a small disdainful snort. 'What is it that you haven't told him?' she added, a new curiosity in her gaze.

'It's about the other young man who sadly lost his life, your sister's house guest.'

'Bobby Bassey?' asked Virginia sharply. 'What about him?'

'A few days before all these terrible events took place, I saw Mr Rivers from my window. It was late in the day, dusk was falling, and it looked as though he was the last one on the dig. He was just locking the gate leading from Brack Mound to the street when the other fellow came along and called out to him. I was sitting writing at my desk in the window, and one doesn't often see a person of his sort in Lewes.'

'By *his sort* I suppose you mean a Black man,' said Virginia, raising one thin eyebrow.

'Yes indeed. I mean he stuck out, but it wasn't so much the colour of his skin as what he was doing. He appeared to be trying to embrace Mr Rivers, but Mr Rivers was having none of it. Pushed him away and they raised their voices. There was no one else around at that time, or they would have attracted attention, and I don't think they noticed me sitting in the window, watching them. They exchanged heated words and then something Mr Rivers said seemed to pacify him and they ended up embracing one another. In a way that men don't usually embrace, if you get my drift.'

'I see, and you think it has something to do with the murders?'

'Two young men, possibly committing a mortal sin. Could it be that someone decided to deliver divine punishment?' asked Alice.

'We are none of us perfect, Mrs Dudeney,' said Virginia, giving her a knowing look. Alice blushed; it was common knowledge she'd left her husband for her lover when she was a younger woman. But that was a different sort of affair altogether.

Then she thought about the equally scandalous rumours that Mrs Woolf had taken a lover of her own sex, the aristocratic Vita Sackville-West. Neither of them could claim the moral high ground, she supposed.

'What do you think I should do about this information?' she asked, returning to the safer ground of the investigation.

'Will you allow me to mention it to my sister before you tell the inspector? Bobby was her and Duncan's guest and now that he's dead too there may be little point in tarnishing his reputation and that of Mr Rivers. There's his poor mother to think about as well. But it is interesting to hear they met when Bobby insisted to my sister that they hadn't seen one another during his stay.'

'Indeed,' said Alice. 'I'll leave it with you and let us pray there is soon a satisfactory conclusion to this matter.'

28.

Vanessa

Shortly after returning from Paris, Nessa found herself behind the wheel of her huge charabanc hurtling down the road to Newhaven. The hedgerows were rusty with hawthorn berries, and in the sharp October sunshine it felt wrong to be saying goodbye to one who had died too young.

Duncan sat on the seat beside her carrying the urn containing Bobby's ashes. The previous day he and Nessa had gone together to the new Downs Crematorium near Woodingdean to pick them up and he'd kept the urn on the mantelpiece in his bedroom the night before.

Not long ago, Bobby had been in his bed. At the time, Nessa had felt the usual fear that this time Duncan would fall in love for good and leave her. It was a worry she was experiencing more and more these days as her good looks faded into matronly middle age. Duncan had always preferred men to women when it came to that side of things, but she couldn't help thinking it was her beauty that had attached him to her and now she was losing that she might lose him.

In the back sat Maynard and Lydia. Julian had gone back to Cambridge and Quentin had gone to stay with a friend. There had been quite enough death recently, and she was more than happy for her sons to go off and enjoy the benefits of being alive.

Her sister and her husband had been meant to join them, but Ginny had sent a message to say she had a headache and naturally Leonard had stayed with her. So, it was just the four of them in the vehicle when it drew to a halt beside the harbour in Newhaven. Nessa had arranged for a local fishing boat to take them out to sea. After enquiring at the harbourmaster's office, they soon found it and their little party climbed aboard. The fisherman was a weather-beaten fellow missing a front tooth, who reminded her of a piece of driftwood, carved by the sea. He didn't speak much but made an 'argh' sound in response to whatever was said to him, which she supposed was a form of local seafaring dialect.

From the shore, the water looked calm, but once the boat had gone a little way out the waves grew decidedly choppy. Duncan said a few words, half of which were lost on the wind, then tried to make his way to the side of the boat, holding the urn aloft before him.

Saltwater splashed on to the deck, making him slip and he only just managed to stop himself from falling. He waited for a break in the waves before trying again. This time he had better luck. He reached the side of the boat, unscrewed the top of the urn and tossed its contents into the air. Most reached the surface of the sea, but some flew back, landing on his face, giving him the appearance of one of the bodies found at Pompeii. Without saying a word, Nessa passed him her shawl – the faded white one inherited from her mother – with which to wipe his face.

By the time they arrived back at shore, everyone was cold and wet and ready for tea. No one spoke as Nessa drove home. Lydia filled the silence by crooning an old Russian folk ballad. The rest of them didn't understand the words she was singing, but there was no mistaking the mournful nature of the tune.

When they got back to Charleston, they piled into the dining room, where their spirits were lifted by a jolly fire and the hearty spread that Grace had prepared for them. There was boiled ham, poached salmon, warm potato salad and crusty bread fresh from the oven, which they washed down with tumblers of red wine and whisky.

They devoured the food and took turns to make increasingly drunken toasts to Bobby's memory. Maynard was starting up a new toast, slightly slurring his words, when they heard the purr of an engine coming up the drive. Nessa, feeling a little light-headed, went over to the window to see who it was. A familiar vehicle came into view. It was Leonard, behind the wheel of his new motor, but when she craned her neck to see where her sister was, she realised he was alone.

At once, she sobered up and ran to the front door, her heart beating double time. Had something happened to Ginny? As she crunched over the gravel towards the now stationary automobile, Leonard must have seen the stricken expression on her face.

'Don't worry, Nessa. Ginny is fine,' he said as he got out of the car and removed the key from the ignition.

Nessa put a hand to her chest in relief. 'In that case you

must come inside and toast Bobby's life with the rest of us. I know one's not meant to drink while driving, but I'm sure one glass won't hurt.'

Leonard followed her inside and accepted a glass of red wine and a plate of ham and salad. As he took a seat at the table, in front of the grey-painted fireplace she and Duncan had decorated with geometric black markings, she couldn't shake off the feeling there was a reason for his visit, and not a good one.

'I'm afraid I come bearing bad news,' he said, forking a buttery new potato into his mouth.

'I knew it,' said Nessa. 'What's happened?'

'It's Harry Dryden. He's been found up at the castle, unconscious. Ginny's with Mrs Rivers now. She's in a terrible state. Almost worse than when she heard her own son had died. Apparently, she fainted when Chief Inspector Gripe came to tell her the news.'

'You say he's unconscious, though, not dead?' asked Nessa.

'He's in hospital in a bad way. It looks as though someone knocked him out then bludgeoned him with a heavy instrument. It was lucky Mr Briggs was doing his evening rounds of the castle and scared them off before they could finish the job. He found him and called an ambulance immediately. He's fighting for his life, but they say he's in with a chance.'

The jolly atmosphere dissipated just as quickly as it had arrived. No one had any more appetite for food or drink. The Maynard Keyneses made their excuses and left, and Grace started clearing the plates while Duncan went outside for a smoke.

'Will you come back with me? Ginny could do with your support. The whole business is taking its toll on her,' said Leonard.

He and his sister-in-law exchanged glances. They both knew how fragile Ginny's state of mind was, how easily she could be plunged into a depression that lasted for weeks, making her physically ill.

'Of course. I'll come at once,' said Nessa, and went to fetch her coat.

It took them half an hour to drive back to Rodmell in the dark, a few flecks of rain soon turning into a downfall. Leonard searched around for the button to activate the window wipers and couldn't find it. He nearly veered into a ditch as Nessa located it for him and it was quite a relief when they finally pulled up in front of Monk's House.

They both rushed inside, but there was no sign of Ginny.

'I'll see if she's in her writing hut,' said Nessa.

Thankfully, the door of the hut was open, and she found Ginny inside, sitting on a wooden chair, her knees pulled up against her body in the pose she used to adopt when she was a girl. The air was cold, and she had only a thin crocheted blanket pulled around her shoulders. Nessa crossed to where she was sitting.

'Come on, Ginny. It sounds like you've had a bit of a day. Let's get you back to the house and tucked up in bed.'

Obediently, her sister let her lead her back along the garden path to the house, where they went upstairs to her bedroom. Nessa helped her to take off her clothes, then watched as she got into bed. Leaning over, she pulled the heavy eiderdown over her and plumped up the pillows behind her head.

Leonard popped his head round the door.

'I've made you both hot cocoas. Thought you could do with warming up,' he said, handing Nessa two steaming mugs.

When he'd gone, Nessa perched on the end of the bed.

'Tell me all about it. How was Mrs Rivers?'

'Oh, Nessa, it was awful to see the poor woman. It brought back all the grief of her son's death and I thought she was going to have a nervous breakdown. Apparently, it was supposed to be Harry's last night with her before he had to go back to his job in the City. He was upstairs packing when a note came for him and he dashed downstairs and told her he was going to walk into Lewes to meet someone who might be able to shine a light on Gideon's death. She begged him not to go, saying they should tell the police and let them deal with it. But he insisted and said it was perfectly safe. That was the last she saw of him and the next thing she knew was Chief Inspector Gripe turning up on the doorstep of Hollybush House to tell her Harry was unconscious in hospital. Stanley Briggs found him, and it looked as though he'd been hit over the head with a blunt instrument. If old Briggs hadn't turned up when he did, he could have met the same fate as Gideon. Daphne fainted on the spot and had to be put to bed. As soon as I heard, I went to see her. She's as pale as the moon, but she's insisting she wants to go and visit him at the cottage hospital in Lewes in case he wakes up. I told her she needs to rest.'

'As do you. The whole thing is a mess. I suggest you get some sleep, and we think about it in the morning. Harry is in the best place with nurses to look after him. I suppose this rules him out as a suspect.'

Ginny nodded. 'I suppose it does, and just as I was starting to think you might be right about him being involved.'

She told Nessa what Fred had said about seeing Harry at Charleston on the day of Bobby's murder. Then something occurred to her, and she grasped her sister's arm with fingers that felt a little too bony.

'It was Briggs who found him, but you don't suppose he had something to do with it, do you? What if it wasn't simply a case of him doing his nightly rounds and scaring the culprit away? What if that was just a story that he told to Gripe? Maybe he was the one trying to bludgeon Harry to death and he was interrupted, then made up the rest as a cover story.'

Nessa thought about it, then shook her head.

'I can't see it. That would run the risk of attracting all the attention to himself. I don't much like the man, he's a pompous fool if you ask me, but I don't see him as the type to knock someone out and leave them for dead.'

Ginny wasn't listening to her, and her eyes were shining in a way that Nessa had seen before when one of her ideas had got hold of her.

'But don't you see?' she asked, gripping on to her sister's arm again. 'It all fits. If Briggs contacted Harry saying he had information about Gideon's death, he would have hot-footed it up there without suspecting anything.'

As she tried to picture the scene, something clicked in Nessa's mind. When she'd overheard Jasmine speaking to the curator at the Louvre, she'd said something about her 'associate'. What if Harry was that associate and he'd gone to see Briggs, not to find out about who killed Gideon, but in search of the tablet that seemed to be behind everything in this case? It seemed as though Ginny might just be on to something.

29.

Virginia

At breakfast, Ginny sneezed three times and feared she was coming down with a chill. As a precaution, she forced down a teaspoonful of cod-liver oil and it seemed to do the trick as by lunchtime she felt well enough to call on Mrs Rivers at Hollybush House to ask if there was any update on Harry.

A housemaid in a neat black dress and starched white apron showed her into the large oak-panelled drawing room, where she took a seat upon a canary-yellow chaise longue. She'd barely had time to glance around the well-proportioned room, which smelled of beeswax and lavender, taking in the expensive china on walnut bookshelves and showy landscapes hanging on duck-egg-blue flocked wallpaper, when Mrs Rivers bustled in, wearing a handsome black mourning gown and a small black hat decorated with a single rook's feather.

'Mrs Woolf, I cannot thank you enough for your kindness yesterday,' she said.

'Is there any news from the hospital?' asked Ginny.

The feather waggled from side to side as Mrs Rivers shook her head.

'I'm afraid they've had to keep him heavily sedated because of his injuries. If Mr Briggs hadn't arrived when he did, he might not have survived. Thank goodness, the doctors say he will make a full recovery.' She placed her palms together in a prayer-like position.

'I'm very glad to hear he will be all right,' said Ginny.

Mrs Rivers shook her head slowly. 'His body will, perhaps, but how could he ever forget such a vicious attack?' she said.

Ginny nodded and made a sympathetic noise. 'Did he say anything else about who he was going to meet and why?' she asked.

'Not apart from what I've already told you about someone who could shine a light on Gideon's death,' said Mrs Rivers. 'No, wait, he did say something else just before he left the house. I couldn't understand what he was saying, and it was as if he were talking to himself. He said, "I will have it, you devil." I thought he was talking about information that could lead him to the killer, but now I think about it, I suppose he could have had a physical object in mind, something that he wanted to take from whoever it was he was going to meet.'

'Could he have been talking about a clay tablet, like the one they found at the dig on Brack Mound?' asked Ginny.

Mrs Rivers thought about it for a moment or two. 'Yes, I suppose it could have been that. He's almost as passionate about archaeology as Gideon was, you know. Finding that tablet meant a great deal to my son. It's no wonder his best friend might want to get hold of it after his death.'

She sat down on the chaise longue next to Ginny, so close

she could feel her substantial thighs pressing against her own thinner ones through the material of their respective skirts. Leaning in towards her, she spoke in a confidential tone of voice, so close that little flecks of spit from her mouth landed on Ginny's face and she could smell her scent of old roses, and was that brandy?

'I haven't said anything yet to Harry or anyone else – in fact, you're the first – but when everything has calmed down, I'm thinking of changing my will, making a substantial sum of money over to Harry to enable him to pursue the career he's always dreamed of in archaeology. He's wasting away at that insurance company, poor boy, trying to please his impossible father. I'm a widow who has lost my only child. I've no one else to leave it to aside from my brother's family and we're not close.'

'Where is the tablet now?' asked Ginny.

'As far as I know, it's still in the possession of Mr Briggs. He refused to hand it over to Gideon before his death, even though it was my son who discovered it, so I see no reason why he would offer it up now unless it was in his own interest. No doubt he has plans to use it to seal his reputation in the field. But the credit for its discovery should go to my son.'

Ginny sensed an opportunity.

'I quite agree. My sister and I were there when he found the artefact and would be willing to vouch for his legacy. I don't suppose Gideon left any notes about his work on the dig that would support the case for his recognition?'

Mrs Rivers shook her head.

'I'm afraid his research was kept at the museum, which means Mr Briggs oversees that too.'

She suddenly got to her feet. 'No, wait a minute, there

is something. His notebook. He always kept that with him, and he had it in his pocket on the day he . . .' She trailed off here, still unable to say the words. 'Stay here and I'll go and fetch it. It's in my dressing-table drawer.'

She disappeared and Ginny heard her go up the stairs and then the creaking of floorboards. Mrs Rivers's bedroom must be right above the drawing room. A couple of minutes later, she reappeared, clutching a small black leather notebook, which she held out to Ginny.

'I haven't been able to look at it. I don't suppose you would mind reading it for me?'

Closing her fingers around the notebook, Ginny opened it at a random page. The writing was scrawled and difficult to read.

'I'd be happy to. Do you mind if I take it with me? I'll need my reading glasses.'

'No, of course not, take it for as long as you like. I'm just glad to know my son's work isn't going to be wasted.'

Ginny waited until she was safely ensconced back in an armchair in the sitting room at Monk's House before looking at the contents. Much of it was indecipherable, or in academic jargon that made little sense to her. But throughout the pages were little sketches and it soon became apparent that Gideon had not just been a first-rate archaeologist, but also a talented artist.

There were scenes from Syria, depicting fragments of stone lying on the sand, etched lines showing a hazy sun in the sky above. Later, were tiny tableaux from the dig in Lewes, revealing the trench at the top of the mound at different depths. Towards the end of the booklet, she found what she was looking for, a sketch of the tablet itself, its edges were worn away in parts, but there was no denying the beauty of the Arabic characters carved into it.

Beneath the drawing were some notes, which looked as though they'd been made in haste.

Found by William de Warenne III? In Antioch? Or the desert nearby? How did they get to Lewes, poss. brought back by his companions. Significance of this found with Kufic coins – evidence of links between England and Holy Land. Why this tablet? What is its meaning?

Then there was an attempt to translate from the Kufic script into English:

The Eagle soars above the desert, back to his Eyrie high on a rock, flying past the Eye of God, All praise be to His Name.

Were these words significant? They reminded her of the reading about eagles' wings at Bobby's funeral. Could there be a connection? She didn't see how – it was Duncan who'd chosen the reading, saying it was Bobby's favourite. How could he possibly have known about this inscription?

Flicking back to the start of the book, she saw a dedication written on the frontispiece.

To G, all my love, B.

With a start, she realised the notebook must have been a gift to Gideon from Bobby. She thought back to Mrs Dudeney's visit and her account of seeing the two men embracing. And yet, before he'd died, Bobby had told Nessa he hadn't seen Gideon since he'd been in the country. Why had he lied and what was it about their relationship that had seen both men cut down so young?

'Ginny, Leonard said I'd find you here.'

She looked up from her desk to see Nessa peering through the window.

'Stop lurking inside here like a bat and come outside with me to get some fresh air. You look awfully pale,' said her sister in the bossy tone that always got Ginny's back up.

'You don't look too healthy yourself,' Ginny retorted petulantly.

Nonetheless, she got up from her chair and followed Nessa outside. It was warm for October, and bees from the hives nearby rode the gentle air currents through the orchard. Their disagreement forgotten as quickly as it had erupted, the sisters linked arms as they walked along the turf path past apple trees losing their leaves, with just a few wrinkled fruits still hanging from their spindly branches. Spiders' webs glistened in the long grass. They reached the brick path Leonard had laid himself and made their way along it to a bench overlooking the tiny pond fringed by yellowing reeds. Here she showed Nessa her find.

Her sister took her spectacles from the top pocket of a blue cotton artist's jacket.

'Is that a new coat?' Ginny asked, as she hadn't seen it before.

'What, this? No, it's Duncan's old one. He bought himself a new smarter one, but I hated to see this one going to waste and so I've adopted it,' explained Nessa.

'Can't you afford a new one of your own?' asked Ginny.

'That's not the point,' Nessa said, looking affronted. 'Let's talk about this notebook.'

'What do you think about the inscription? Doesn't it remind you of the reading at Bobby's funeral? How did you choose it?'

'Duncan said it was Bobby's favourite verse. Now I come to think of it, I believe he said it was Gideon's favourite too.'

'Then it could be a clue. We need to look at the real thing. Doesn't Briggs have it in his possession?' asked Ginny.

'I believe he does,' said Nessa.

'Then I propose we pay him a visit,' replied Ginny.

Leonard had driven back to Richmond for another meeting about the printing press and so the sisters had to walk into Lewes. Nessa was still wearing the blue artist's jacket, over a rustic white linen shirt, together with a broad-brimmed black straw hat. Ginny put on one of Leonard's old gardening jackets over a pistachio green shirt. Walking through the Sussex countryside, they stood out like a pair of exotic birds who had strayed off course on their migration to a far-flung land.

Mr Briggs lived in a large Edwardian house on the outskirts of town. Miss Bramble answered the door. She wore the dreadful brown felt hat even when she was at home.

'I'm afraid Mr Briggs isn't here. Can I take a message for him?' she asked.

'Just tell him Mrs Woolf and Mrs Bell called. Do you have any idea when he will be coming back?'

'I believe he's taken the train to London, and he usually stays over when he goes up to town, so I'm not expecting him back until tomorrow. At least I hope not as I'm going to visit my elderly aunt tonight,' she added, this last bit said more to herself than to the callers.

They walked away down the leafy suburban street.

'What shall we do? Come back tomorrow?' asked Nessa.

But Miss Bramble's words had planted the seed of an idea in Ginny's mind.

'Don't you see, Nessa, we might never get a better opportunity than this?'

'To do what?'

'Break into Mr Briggs's house tonight while it's empty and look for the tablet and any other incriminating material he might have lying around.'

'You really think he's guilty, don't you? To such an extent you're willing to commit a crime to find him out. What if he has nothing to do with this whole affair? I'm very much afraid you're going to get us both landed in prison for breaking and entering.'

'Nonsense,' said Ginny. 'You heard what Miss Bramble said. She's going to visit her aunt tonight, which means the house will be empty. I had a quick scout around as we were standing talking to her. All we need do is smash a panel of the stained glass in the front door, then we can put our hand inside and open the lock. The beauty of it is that it will look like a burglary and who would ever suspect two respectable middle-aged women of such a thing?'

'It will look like a burglary because that's what it would be,' said Nessa. 'Absolutely not.'

'You're willing to pass up the chance to unmask a murderer just because of social niceties?' asked Ginny. Nessa sighed, and she knew that if she continued to argue with her for just a little longer, Ginny would eventually wear her down.

There wasn't a criminal bone in her body, but unlike her sister, who was always clouded by emotion, she was able to look directly through such concerns to see the bigger picture. And, in this case, that was the crucial element that Chief Inspector Gripe and his men seemed determined to overlook. If they could just get into Briggs's study and look at the tablet, she felt sure it would reveal something new about the affair.

She leaned in against her sister.

'Go on, Nessa. Can't you stop being so cautious just this once? What happened to my radical big sister who cared nothing for convention? Don't tell me you've turned into a respectable old maid?'

Even as she said it, she could hear the familiar mania in her words. It was the same energy that powered her when she was working on a new book she believed in, and when it seeped away would leave her bedbound and even more exhausted than before. Nessa was right to tell her it was insanity to talk about breaking into a house under cover of darkness. She would go home, return to her writing hut and pour all that energy into a new piece of writing. Leave the investigation to the police. Why did she ever imagine she could uncover something they'd missed. It was time to give up this mad pursuit.

'All right, then,' said Nessa.

'What do you mean, *all right, then*?'

'Just what I said. Let's do it. We'll go back tonight. It's a new moon, so we're unlikely to be seen. But I have one condition.'

'What's that?' asked Ginny.

'We break in by the back door. It would be such a shame to smash that lovely stained-glass window.'

30.

Vanessa

There was barely a sliver of moon, and the garden of Stanley Briggs's house was in almost complete darkness when they returned at eight o'clock. Not wanting anyone to spot them, they'd bought sausage rolls from the butcher's shop earlier that evening, then walked up on to the Downs and devoured them as the sun was setting.

Sitting in the long grass, being eaten alive by insects, they looked back at Lewes, a toy town in the valley below. The castle was perched like a child's drawing on its tall motte, and next to it, a little way off, Brack Mound looked like little more than a thicket from this angle. They munched on the flaky pastry and meat and talked about business at Ginny and Leonard's printing press, and Nessa's children, as if they were together on a jolly outing and not planning a break-in. They waited until the sun had dipped beneath the hills before making their way back down the path through the fields to the western edge of town.

No one was in sight in the tree-lined street where Briggs lived. Opening the gate, they hurried up the path into the garden, which was hidden from the street by high hedges. Just in case Miss Bramble had changed her mind and stayed at home, they rang the bell, but after five minutes when there was still no answer, they decided it was safe to make their way round to the back. Before breaking any glass, they tried the handles of all the windows and doors. They were in luck. Miss Bramble had forgotten to lock the conservatory door. Once inside, they found another key under a mat, and they were in. Nessa was so pleased they hadn't had to force entry that when she heard a noise in the garden behind them, she ignored it. It was probably just a cat or a fox. They'd prepared a story in case a nosy neighbour called round to find out what they were doing. Ginny still had Gideon's notebook in her pocket, and they were calling on Mr Briggs to ask his opinion. As his secretary was out for the evening, he'd told them to come round the back.

They had to try a couple of doors before they found themselves in the study, a narrow room at the side of the house with a large desk underneath the window. To one side were shelves adorned with multiple artefacts from Mr Briggs's long career. Lumps of limestone gathered by early geologists, fragments of pottery left over from the ruined Lewes Priory after it had been destroyed by Henry VIII's engineers, a bronze torque from an Iron Age dig on the South Downs.

It was hopeless. How would they ever find the tablet amidst all this chaos?

'Where would a man like Briggs keep such an artefact?' asked Ginny.

'If it were me, I'd display it on the mantelpiece,' said Nessa.

'Of course you would, between a daubing by Angelica

211

and a week-old cup of tea, but I'm talking about someone with a methodical mind,' snapped her sister.

'There's no need to get personal,' sniffed Nessa.

Then she spotted it. The tablet Gideon Rivers had discovered on the day they'd first met him, when his mother had persuaded him to show them the dig on Brack Mound. It was smaller than Nessa remembered. Forgetting that it might be fragile, she picked it up and felt it with her artist's hands, sensitive to every subtle contour. For a moment, she forgot it had travelled all the way to Lewes from a distant desert and felt it simply as a lump of baked clay, of the same kind that she and Quentin loved to mould into living sculptures, seeing what stories came to mind when they looked at the stone, what pictures they saw when they ran their fingers over it.

'Don't just stand there caressing it. We're breaking and entering, not attending a sculpture night class. Is there anything else that might tell us something about its origin, or why it's so important?' asked Ginny.

Nessa felt stupid. She'd been so carried away by the sensual, tactile nature of the object that she'd forgotten why they were there. She put it down and hastily looked around. There was something nearby, a letter, with a red stamp saying 'Permission Denied'. She was just about to pick it up when she felt a sharp pin prick and everything went black. The last thing she saw was her sister slumping to the floor.

31.

Alice

A wistful autumn light illuminated the trees, showing off their turning colours in a last hoorah. Alice decided to take Nelson for a longer than usual walk over the Downs. Up on the tops, she felt free from the social niceties one was obliged to observe within the confines of the town. There was a breeze, not strong enough to be enervating, but sufficiently lively to lift one's spirits. As she strode over the fields, the dog running a short way ahead, she breathed in deeply and felt almost young again.

Once, she'd walked the Downs with David, when they hadn't been able to keep apart from one another. For all too brief a moment, she and her lover had been as free as the skylarks soaring on the air currents above. Leaving respectability behind, they'd fallen into one another's arms, abandoning their respective spouses. But it had proved too much to live like that for long. The pressure of not caring what other people thought of them grew too much. It turns out human beings are creatures of habit, who like other creatures must retreat to their dens once the mating season is over. She'd crept back to Ernest, and now they were tied to one another until death did them part. He a grumpy old soul and she a contrary harridan. She was not unaware of her own failings, not that it made them any easier to bear.

A rabbit ran across her path and paused for a second, twitching its small black nose, scenting Nelson on the breeze. Spying potential prey, the stupid dog darted towards it and Alice held her breath, fearing the worst. But Nelson was too slow, and the cottontail escaped into the undergrowth, through a fence and out of sight.

It was growing dark, and she called Nelson to her side, not wanting to lose him if he spotted any more bunnies and decided to give chase. Woman and hound soon found themselves back in civilisation, entering the town from the west, and making their way towards the castle. At this hour there weren't many others around. Those few who did pass nodded a greeting. Lewes was small enough that most of its residents recognised one another, by face if not by name. One had to be on one's guard, or risk being trapped in conversation with a local do-gooder.

Before too long, they were back at the castle precincts. As he always did when they approached home, Nelson strained on his leash, eager to get back to his basket and the promise of food.

Alice usually left the front door open, but Ernest had been out when she left and it was the maid's afternoon off, so it was locked. Fumbling around in her pocket for a key, she got the distinct impression she was being watched, and hoped it wasn't the neighbour who'd been pressing her to cut her bushes back. She looked round at the long, low flint hop barn next to the bowling green that had once been the castle's tilting ground. Behind that rose Castle Gates House, and its walled gardens, and on the other side Castle Lodge, an example of high gothic architecture that paid homage to the ruins of the Norman castle that rose above it. The entire area had once been the site of the castle, a town within a town that was home not only to its lord and lady, but to their legions of servants, as well as squires and knights who came in from the surrounding countryside. On the far side of the raised platform from her own house was a handsome cottage, and a tall old house that stood alone, reminding her of the sort of building you might find in Shropshire or Herefordshire rather than Sussex. Finally, on Castle Banks, an eclectic collection of cottages tumbled down the hill towards the spire of St John's sub Castro.

Having surveyed the whole area, she could see no one. Apart from the other residents tucked away inside their houses, she had the place to herself.

It occurred to her to check on the Old Poor House, next door to her own house. It had once been home to the destitute of the parish, and she'd bought it off the previous owner to avoid undesirable neighbours. Money was always tight, though, and she had soon realised that renting it out would be more profitable and had found a young couple from London eager to take it off her hands. She still felt a proprietorial concern for the old house, though, particularly as it backed on to her own garden.

Much to Nelson's disgust, she tugged him away from her own front door and carried on a few paces down the street. The lights were on in the Poor House, but the new tenants had finally got around to hanging curtains, so she couldn't see inside. She paused and from inside she could hear vague strains of music as if someone were listening to the wireless or a gramophone. From the exterior, all looked well cared for and maintained.

Satisfied, she turned round to make her way back to her own home when she saw them. A dark figure, moving through the dusk away from her. She couldn't see their face, but whoever they were was diminutive in stature, wearing a long black dress and hood. Female, then, but who could she be, alone at this hour?

Nelson whimpered and strained as they once again walked past the front door to the end of the street where a couple of gentlemen were sitting drinking ale on the steps of the Lewes Arms.

'Good evening, Mrs Dudeney,' said one of them.

'Good evening, Bert. I don't suppose you saw a woman pass by just now?' she replied.

'Matter of fact I did, a slip of a thing dressed all in black, but she had a hood pulled up close around her face and I couldn't see who it was. Doesn't seem right her being out all by herself at this time of night. No disrespect meant to you, ma'am.'

'None taken. At my age I know how to take care of myself. I wonder who she was,' said Alice.

She wished the men good evening and returned to her house. Nelson finally got his wish to go inside, where he flopped gratefully into his basket. Before closing the door, Alice took one last look around, as if she might be able to glimpse the mysterious woman out there in the dark night. But there was nothing to be seen and so at last she shut the door, locking it behind her for good measure.

32.

Virginia

When she came round, Ginny found she was no longer in Briggs's study, but in a much larger room. Morning light seeped in through the windows, with heavy drapes that were only half pulled back. Where was she, what time of day was it and who had brought her here? These questions occurred to her, but she wasn't in any great hurry to find out the answers.

Sleep still enveloped her like a warm blanket, and she felt pleasantly dreamy as she took in her surroundings. The walls of the room were covered in sketches of what looked like archaeological sites. Immediately in front of her was a baize green wall and an elaborately curlicued white fireplace. Above this hung an impressive collection of arrowheads in all different shapes and sizes. Shelves to either side of the mantelpiece were adorned with shards of pots and rough bowls with peeling glazing. There was no mistaking this was the home of an archaeologist, suggesting she was still in Briggs's house. And she appeared to be lying on a settee.

Nessa! She remembered she'd persuaded her sister to

come with her, led her into danger. Where was she? Raising her head to look around, she saw with relief that Nessa was sprawled on an armchair nearby, apparently dead to the world, but still breathing if the rise and fall of her bosom was anything to go by.

The sound of a door opening awoke her more fully and she attempted to pull herself up to a seated position, realising the reason she was so lovely and warm was someone had covered her with a blanket.

When she saw Briggs walk through the door, closely followed by Chief Inspector Gripe, her dream state dissipated in a flash and she sat upright, pulling the blanket around her.

Everything came back to her at once. What they'd been doing before everything went black. They must have been caught breaking and entering a house and, quite rightly, Briggs had summoned the law. The newspapers would have a field day. 'Famous novelist Virginia Woolf revealed as a common thief.' Her ego well and truly pricked. What was worse, she'd persuaded Nessa to come along too. Now they would both end up in prison. She wouldn't be surprised if they tried to pin the murders on them too.

The men didn't seem to realise she was awake. Taking one look at Nessa still slumbering in her chair, they carried on talking to one another as if there was no one else there.

'You say you came home from your evening out and found them here like this?' asked the chief inspector.

'Not here, no. I found them slumped on the floor of my study next door. I waited until Miss Bramble returned from her aunt's house, and together we managed to pull them in here where we thought they would be more comfortable. But we couldn't wake them, try as we might.'

'Harrumph.' Ginny tried to speak, but all that came out of her mouth was a peculiar sound. She felt as though she'd been drugged.

'I suspect they've been administered a drug to render them unconscious,' said the chief inspector.

'Arrugh,' came her next attempt at speaking. It did at least have the result of making the two men turn to look at her and see that she was awake, after all.

'Mrs Woolf,' they both said in unison, hurrying over to her side.

'Are you all right, ma'am?' asked Gripe.

'So . . . so . . . so . . .' she tried. Eventually she managed to spit out the word she was trying to form. 'Sorry.'

'Sorry for what?' asked Briggs, then as it dawned on him, he said, 'Oh yes, that. Well, the least said about what you and your sister were doing in my study the better. I imagine you have some decent explanation, but let's not worry about that now. What I want to know is who rendered you unconscious. That's why I alerted the chief inspector here because I feared the worst, that you and Mrs Bell might never wake up.'

Hearing her name, Nessa's eyes blinked open at long last. Ginny would have liked to get up from the settee and go over to her, but she found her legs weren't working. It felt as though she had nothing but cotton wool below her waist.

'I think these ladies need a strong cup of tea before they do anything else,' said Mr Briggs. He rang the servant bell next to the light switch and a moment later Miss Bramble appeared through the half-open door. Her spectacles had steamed up and she took them off and rubbed them, then balanced them back on her thin nose and peered at the two prone women in her employer's drawing room. Ginny felt like an exotic animal on display.

'Miss Bramble, it appears our house guests have finally come to. Would you be so good as to bring them each a cup of tea, and perhaps a slab of pound cake?'

His secretary muttered something under her breath and left the room, reappearing a few minutes later with a tray laden with a china teapot decorated with mauve roses, a matching milk jug and cups and saucers for four and a plate piled high with thick slices of cake. She put this down on an occasional table before pouring and handing out four portions. This done, she retreated to the doorway, where she hovered, as if reluctant to miss out on whatever was said next.

Ginny's mouth still felt fuzzy, the same sensation one had after climbing off the dentist's chair. She had a sharp headache around her temples and felt nauseous. Judging by Nessa's silence, she felt the same. But she managed to sip a little of the tea and tasted the sweetness of the cake on her tongue. Having wolfed down his own plate and drained his cup in record time, Chief Inspector Gripe did most of the talking.

'I've got a couple of my men interviewing the neighbours as we speak. They've already had a word with the old dear next door, who remembers seeing you two come in for the second time. The first time she saw you talking to Miss Bramble at the front door, so when you came back she assumed it was prearranged and thought nothing of it. But she kept on insisting there was someone else with you.

Whether it was a man or a woman, she couldn't say. All she could tell us was this person was slightly shorter than you, Mrs Woolf, and they were wearing a black cape. Nor could she say whether they were young or old, although she did describe them as sprightly, whatever that means. Whoever they were, I think we have our attacker. The question is, how did they know you were going to be here at that time?'

Ginny tried desperately to speak and eventually she managed to form the words.

'We didn't even know ourselves until the last minute. It was an ill-conceived plan, entirely of my own making, Chief Inspector. You mustn't blame my sister for any of this.'

Nessa made a sound as though she would have liked to protest at this point, but, having come round later than Ginny, she still wasn't at the stage of being able to form words. Throwing her hands up in the air, she fell back against the seat of her chair, surrendering to her temporary muteness.

'In that case, the suspect must have been following you, and when you entered the house, they crept in after you and pounced on you while you were least expecting it.' Having delivered these words in a tone of some not inconsiderable melodrama, Chief Inspector Gripe scratched his sideburns.

'What beats me is how one person managed to render two people unconscious. Surely there must have been more of them, who went unseen by the elderly neighbour.'

'I'm no expert, but have you considered the use of intravenous barbiturates?' asked Briggs. 'I believe in sufficient dosage they could have that effect.'

'I'll instruct Sergeant Hamsey to investigate. Now, I assume you ladies have a perfectly good explanation for why you entered Mr Briggs's house in his absence?' said Gripe, putting his hands in his trousers pockets and hoicking up the waist.

Ginny fought another wave of nausea.

'We've been utter fools. *Mea culpa*. We got it into our heads that the murders of Gideon Rivers and Bobby Bassey had something to do with the antique tablet uncovered at the dig on Brack Mound in our presence. Believing it to be in your possession, Mr Briggs, we took it upon ourselves to find it and see whether it presented any clues as to the murderer. I now see quite clearly that we've been reading too many detective novels,' she said.

Mr Briggs looked unamused by her confession. 'I suppose in your lurid imaginings I was the murderer?' he enquired.

Ginny bit her bottom lip and said nothing.

Chief Inspector Gripe pulled himself up to his full five foot ten and puffed out his chest, holding his hands behind his back like a weapon.

'In my experience, Mrs Woolf, it never does for members of the public to take it upon themselves to investigate a crime. They – and in this case I mean you – are entirely lacking in the necessary training and skills to make a good job of the matter.'

Hanging her head, Ginny nodded in agreement.

'I know. I see that now,' she said.

'For your information,' said Mr Briggs, 'I'm keeping the tablet safe in my study, until a decision has been made about what to do with it next. Before Mr Rivers met his untimely end, I offered it to the Director of the British Museum. Gideon had also been in touch with him, however, and he didn't want to see it until we had agreed between ourselves

222

whose discovery it was. I haven't been back in contact with him since, as there has been so much to sort out with the dig being on hold. It's about time I did, as there's no dispute now that Mr Rivers is no longer with us.'

There was something about his tone that jarred with Ginny. Surely Gideon's death didn't alter the fact of who had found the tablet? But she wasn't about to argue with a man whose house she had just broken into. There was something he wasn't telling them – she felt sure. Just as she was wondering what it could be, the door burst open, and Miss Bramble entered in a state of great excitement.

'Mr Briggs, sir, it's the tablet,' she said, panting.

'What about it?' he replied.

'It's disappeared.'

'What do you mean *disappeared*? It was there when we found Mrs Bell and Mrs Woolf and no one else has been in the house since, have they?'

He left the room and a few moments later they heard an anguished cry. The chief inspector ran out into the corridor. Ginny's legs still felt woolly, but she followed him into the study, where they found Briggs with his head in his hands.

'Is something the matter, sir?' asked Chief Inspector Gripe.

Briggs turned and bestowed a withering look upon the inspector.

'I should say so. A priceless artefact has been stolen from right under our noses.'

Ginny wondered how they were going to get home, but she needn't have worried.

'I'd be grateful if you could both come down to the station

to make a statement, when you're recovered from your ordeal,' said Chief Inspector Gripe as he took his leave of them. 'In the meantime, there's someone waiting outside who is very eager to see you.'

A concerned face appeared round the drawing-room door. It was Leonard.

'Ginny, I've been beside myself with worry. I thought something terrible had happened to you.'

'Something worse than being knocked out while breaking into a house in search of a priceless antiquity?' asked Ginny drily. 'But I'm very glad to see you, Leonard.'

Utterly humiliated by the entire affair, she was desperate to get back to her own home where she could bury herself in a book and forget about everything that had occurred in the last twenty-four hours.

Nessa was having difficulty getting to her feet. Leonard took her arm and half pulling, half supporting her, they followed Ginny as she wished Mr Briggs and Miss Bramble a hasty goodbye and retreated down the garden path as quickly as was seemly.

The automobile parked out on the street greeted her like an old friend. Leonard helped Nessa on to the back seat, while Ginny took her place beside him in the passenger seat. Her husband fussed around them both, tucking them up in blankets, which he produced from the boot of the vehicle.

As they drove out of town in the direction of Charleston, to take Nessa home before returning to Monk's House, they passed beneath Brack Mound. Ginny couldn't help looking upwards, past the thickly wooded slopes to the bare summit, where to her surprise she saw a solitary figure. From this distance she couldn't determine their age or sex, but there was one detail that made her shiver despite the blanket. The figure was dressed in a black cape, just like the one Briggs's elderly neighbour had described.

As they drove out of Lewes, into ancient rolling country-side between towering Downs, Leonard's story about the tablet inflicting a curse on those who discovered it came to mind. But as the motor emerged into the river valley, illuminated by the harsh autumn sun, she told herself firmly that was mere superstition.

33.

Vanessa

'What were you thinking of?' cried Duncan, running to meet Nessa as Leonard pulled up to the old barn in front of the farmhouse. He helped her out of the car and supported her weight as they walked together towards the house.

It was almost worth the events of the previous twenty-four hours for the proof that he still cared for her.

'I thought I'd lost you,' he said, holding her at arm's length and looking at her as if she might not be real, then pulling her to him. It was a long time since they'd been so physically close. She could feel his heart beating through his thin chest.

Leonard had telephoned ahead to explain the situation, so there was no need for Nessa to do anything other than let Duncan lead her inside. It was good to be back in the familiar surroundings of the home they'd made together.

He led her to her bedroom, looking out on to the garden, where he put her to bed and pulled the cover over her with great gentleness. Through the French window, she had a view down the garden path, edged with flame-coloured chrysanthemums, culminating in a stony-eyed bust carved by Quentin.

Leaving her side only to ask Grace to bring her a cup of beef broth, Duncan returned and pulled up a stool by the bed, where he perched like some magical creature dancing attendance upon her, a faun or dryad.

'I think it's time you stopped playing the amateur detective, Nessa, if it's going to get you into scrapes like this. From what Leonard told me, it sounds as though Chief Inspector Gripe let you off this time without interrogating you too closely about what you were doing poking around a strange house in the dark. Next time, he might not be quite so patient.'

'Gripe is a fool. If he had anything about him, he would have apprehended the murderer by now. Don't you care about finding the person responsible for Bobby's death and bringing them to justice?'

Duncan bit his lip and she saw his eyes were moist with tears.

'Of course I care, desperately, but that's not going to bring Bobby back, is it?'

'Our experience last night has shown that person is still at large. They could be a threat to you, to me, to Angelica.'

As if she heard her name being called, at that moment her small daughter burst into the room.

'Mummy, there you are. Quentin said you might have been murdered,' she said, flinging herself on to the bed and pressing her small warm body into her mother's.

'Don't listen to anything your brother says. He's just trying to wind you up, and he usually succeeds. I'm perfectly fine, just a little tired,' said Nessa, putting her arms round her daughter and hugging her. She rested her chin on the top of her head and smelled her sweet, dark hair, which still retained some of its baby softness.

'You should have taken me with you. I would have found the murderer. I know all sorts of clues, but no one ever asks me,' said the child.

Nessa laughed.

'Really, what sort of clues?' asked Duncan, poking Angelica affectionately.

She sat up on the bed, dangling her feet over the edge and placing her hands together primly on her lap.

'Like about your friend Bobby. I spoke to him, you know, on the day he died. It must have been just before it happened.'

She paused and her already big dark eyes grew even wider.

'Wait, do you think I might have been the last person to see him alive?'

The smile had left Duncan's face.

'What did he say?' he asked sharply.

'That he was going to meet someone, out in the court-yard, someone who had walked all the way from Lewes to see him, but that I wasn't to mention it to anyone because he didn't want to be interrupted.'

'Is this true, Angelica? You're not just making it up? Why didn't you mention it before? It could be a vital clue in the case and we need to tell the inspector if it really did happen,' said Nessa.

The child nodded vigorously.

'I swear it's true. Cross my heart and hope to die,' she said.

'Don't say that,' snapped Duncan, crossing himself even though he wasn't a Catholic.

228

'Do you have any idea who he was meeting? Did he say whether it was a man or a woman?' asked Nessa.

Angelica shook her head.

'No,' she said, 'but whoever it was, I do remember one thing. He said they were coming in disguise.'

That was just the sort of detail that appealed to a child. Nessa turned to Duncan.

'A disguise? That means whoever it was clearly didn't want to be recognised, suggesting the murder was premeditated,' she said. Overcome by the effort of trying to puzzle it out, she let her head fall back against the pillow.

'Run along and play now. Mummy needs to rest,' said Duncan, lifting Angelica off the bed.

When she'd run out of the room and clattered down the hallway, they looked at one another.

'Who do you think it could have been? Who could have walked all the way here from Lewes without anyone recognising them?' asked Duncan.

'I don't know. Ginny's gardener Fred said something about seeing Harry here, when he came over to drop off some hollyhocks. But now he's been attacked that seems rather unlikely. It's a relief that it wasn't Jasmine at least,' said Nessa. 'What's important is that we find whoever is behind these dreadful crimes.'

She turned her head back to look out into the garden, where birds were swooping down to drink from the little rectangular pond on the lawn. It was so beautiful here, so peaceful, that it was difficult to believe that just a few days earlier it had been the scene of a brutal murder.

It really was all too much to bear. Duncan tucked her up and left her to rest, and as she drifted off to sleep images swirled around her mind. Breaking into Briggs's house in search of the tablet; the body found on Brack Mound; Bobby's distorted features when he was dragged out of the plunge pool. Somehow, they were all connected. But how?

34.

Virginia

It was a great relief to be back in her favourite armchair in the green sitting room, with her feet tucked under her, a fire blazing in the grate and a book on her lap. A pile of other books sat by her elbow; in case she grew tired of the one she was reading.

Nellie, who was being unusually conciliatory, brought her hot buttered toast and a cup of beef broth, which was exactly what she needed to build her strength back up. The effects of whatever drug she'd been administered at Briggs's house still hadn't worn off entirely.

She tried to concentrate on the words in front of her, but when she'd read the same sentence five times over, she gave up and let it rest on her lap. Leaning backwards in the chair, she closed her eyes.

What had happened to the tablet? That was the question that had been on her mind since leaving Briggs's house. His distress at its disappearance had seemed genuine. She had little doubt that whoever had knocked out her and Nessa had also taken the precious artefact.

She was pondering this when there came a loud knock at the front door. Bother. Someone was very determined to gain entry, because they repeated the knock not once, but twice. Nellie answered the door and she heard her speaking to someone, but couldn't make out who it was through the thick walls. A moment later, she popped her head round the sitting-room door.

'Mrs Rivers is here to see you, ma'am.'

There was no getting rid of a grieving mother.

'Show her in, and then bring tea.'

She'd barely finished speaking when Daphne Rivers entered the sitting room without waiting to be shown in. Still dressed in mourning, she seemed much reduced from her former self, having lost a considerable amount of weight. But there was a new determination in her eyes.

'Are you all right, Mrs Woolf? You look dreadful,' were her opening words.

'Thank you for your concern. I've just been through a minor ordeal, but nothing that beef broth and bed rest can't cure,' she replied.

Mrs Rivers looked at her uncertainly, then carried on talking.

'I had to come at once to let you know the news, after you so kindly offered to help with the investigation into my son's murder. Not that there's been much progress on that front. I hear you bailed out Fred Hobbes. I dislike the man intensely, but I have to say I agree with you. I don't think he's the person responsible for Gideon's death.'

'Is that what you came to tell me, Mrs Rivers?' asked Ginny a little wearily. It wasn't news to her that the investigation was progressing slowly, or that she and Leonard had bailed out their gardener.

But her visitor shook her head vigorously as she lowered herself into the chair opposite Ginny's own.

'No, my dear. I have something of far greater import to impart. It's regarding Harry.'

'How is he doing? Is he still unconscious?'

Once again, Mrs Rivers shook her head, so the netting on the small black hat pinned to her grey hair nearly came loose.

'Far from it. Oh, Mrs Woolf, Harry has disappeared. I'm at my wits' end. I couldn't bear to lose him too after what happened to Gideon. Do you think there's someone out there who is preying on young men?'

Ginny thought it highly unlikely. An alternative solution immediately presented itself to her. One in which Harry Dryden was far from the feeble victim. It seemed highly suspicious that he'd gone missing at the same time as the tablet. Could it have been him who followed her and Nessa, then injected them with a sedative and took the relic? If so, what were his plans for it? Did he intend to sell it on the black market for antiquities? Was Briggs in on the act?

She couldn't say any of this to Mrs Rivers, however. The woman adored her late son's friend and wouldn't hear a bad word said about him.

'Is it possible that he came to, and, being disorientated, discharged himself? He might be on his way back to London at this very moment. One does hear in such cases of people blocking out whole chunks of time. He may not remember the attack, or even what went before.'

Mrs Rivers gasped.

'You mean, in poor Harry's head dear Gideon might still be alive?'

'Let's not get ahead of ourselves, Mrs Rivers. This is pure conjecture, after all. But what I mean to say is that it's impossible for us to know Mr Dryden's state of mind. He's an adult male, however, and perfectly capable of looking after himself. Look, here's Nellie with the tea. That should calm your nerves. You've been through a great deal in the last few days.'

Mrs Rivers nodded and accepted a cup of tea.

'How sensible you are, Mrs Woolf. I've probably got myself in a panic about nothing.'

They drank tea and talked about the village and fifteen minutes later her visitor departed, her mind put as much at rest as it could be.

Once Mrs Rivers had gone, Leonard came in from the garden, where he'd been maintaining a safe distance.

'What did she want?' he asked her.

Putting down the book, which she'd only just picked up again, she told him.

'Disappeared? From the cottage hospital? Sounds unlikely. He probably woke up and wanted to get the hell away from Lewes after everything that's happened here in the last few days.'

'That's what I told her, and she seemed to accept it. But I think there's more to it than that. It's too much of a coincidence that Harry Dryden and the tablet have both gone missing at the same time.'

Ginny sat beside Nessa on the canvas deckchairs that they'd moved to the croquet lawn. Pinka was curled up at her feet, the sun reflecting off her sleek brown mane, a droplet of pure white fur on her canine forehead.

'I don't know what to make of it all, Nessa. The deeper we get into it, the more confusing it becomes. I'm starting to wonder whether we should just leave well alone,' she said.

'I'd be inclined to agree with you if it weren't for the fact that two young men have so cruelly lost their lives, and there could have been a third. Although to my mind Harry Dryden's disappearance is highly suspicious. How do we know he didn't fake the attack on himself to divert attention?' asked Nessa.

'I can't believe Harry Dryden is the killer,' said Ginny.

'You have a blind spot when it comes to that young man,' said Nessa. 'For what it's worth, Duncan agrees with you. He also thinks we're getting ourselves into something that could prove dangerous and should leave it to the professionals.'

'Old Gripe and his men? So far, they've proved spectacularly useless.'

'If we're going to continue hunting for the murderer, where do we look next?'

They both sat and contemplated this in silence. A single magpie alighted in front of them, and Nessa saluted it.

'Still as superstitious as ever,' said Ginny, but her tone was affectionate rather than disapproving. 'Leonard and I must go up to London tomorrow. I've dallied in the country too long and there's urgent business at the Press that we can't neglect a moment longer.'

Nessa clapped her hands together. 'Why, that's perfect. I'll be in town too, preparing for a new exhibition. Why don't we meet in the afternoon and do some sleuthing? I'm sure there's more to be squeezed out of Diana Underhill at the Sylvan Rooms, which might shed light on Gideon and Bobby's relationship.'

'What about the British Museum?' asked Ginny, whose mind was still very much on the tablet and its possible significance. 'We could go there and talk to the curator who Briggs has been dealing with, see if he can tell us anything more about its importance and whether there's anyone who wants it so much, they might be willing to kill for it.'

Pinka suddenly got to her feet and ran down the garden, yapping. Ginny rose to her feet, wondering what could have disturbed her, hoping it wasn't another visitor. She was looking forward to some time alone in the garden with her sister. Fortunately, it was just Grizzle snuffling his way down the path to greet them.

'That's decided, then. We will resume our investigation in London. Until then, let's enjoy the rest of our day here amid the perfection of Hesperis,' said Ginny. Hesperis was the name she and Leonard had given to the old apple tree on account of its golden fruit, like the tree of legend. Feeling the sun on her face, she enjoyed a moment of perfect peace. But then a cloud passed in front of the sun, and she remembered the trail of death that still hung over them. There would be no true peace until they'd unmasked the killer.

35.

Vanessa

Bloomsbury, London

Gordon Square, where Nessa lived, and Tavistock Square, where Ginny had her London home, were planned as adjacent garden squares, opening out on to a map of the city like the two wings of the moths they'd collected as children. They used to pin the creatures to the bark of the trees in the garden of Talland House, their childhood Cornish holiday home.

Nessa waited for Ginny on the corner of the street. As her sister approached, her tall, thin figure accentuated by her long skirt and short jacket, Nessa worried that all this murder business was wearing her out. Her hooded eyes were sunk even deeper than usual into her pale face.

'Are you sure you want to do this? I can go alone if it's too much for you?' she asked.

'Nonsense, I'm not the one who's nearly fifty,' said Ginny, linking her arm into Nessa's.

'There really is no need to keep harping on about one's

237

age. You're far more of an old woman than I am,' retorted Nessa. But it was true that the following year she would reach her half-century, and yet she didn't feel old at all, apart from the occasional ache and stiffness.

Ginny pulled her along Bedford Way towards Russell Square and beyond that to the neoclassical façade of the British Museum. When they got to the main entrance, the porter recognised her.

'Here for the Reading Room, Mrs Woolf?' he asked.

'Not today. We have an appointment with Samuel Ferrers, Curator of Middle Eastern Antiquities,' Ginny replied.

'Take the staircase on the right up to the first-floor corridor. His name will be on the door of his office. From memory, it's the fourth one along,' said the porter.

They followed his instructions and soon arrived at the office, where Nessa knocked on the door. A moment or two later, it opened and a small man, unshaven with grey hair sticking out of his head at peculiar angles, opened the door. He was wearing a jacket and tie at least, but his shirt was half hanging out.

'Do we have an appointment?' he asked, scratching the back of his head with one hand as if struggling to remember.

'We do indeed, Mr Ferrers,' said Ginny, stepping forward and making her way into the room on the other side of the door before he could protest.

'Ah, Mrs Woolf, I didn't recognise you, and this must be your sister, Mrs Bell. I'm a great admirer of your art. Do come in and take a seat.'

He ushered them in and drew a couple of chairs into the centre of the room, where he placed them opposite a desk stacked high with books and papers in piles that looked perilously close to toppling. Walking round the desk, he took a seat opposite them, and their view of him was only partly obscured by the paperwork.

'How can I help you?' he asked, leaning forward and placing his palms together, nearly knocking over one of the book stacks.

'We'll get straight to the point, Mr Ferrers,' said Ginny. 'We're after information about a clay tablet, discovered in an excavation taking place on one of the mottes of Lewes Castle. I believe the chief archaeologist there, Stanley Briggs, has been in touch with you already regarding the artefact.'

'Ah yes, one of the few Norman castles to have a double motte, most interesting. Not to mention this connection with a crusading knight, which is extraordinary. From what I've heard about the tablet in question, it's the sort of thing one would expect to find in the middle of the desert, not on a rainy English hilltop,' said Mr Ferrers, his voice speeding up with animation.

'So, you haven't seen the tablet in person?' Nessa asked.

He shook his head vigorously. 'Not yet, no. Mr Briggs was keen to bring it to me for safekeeping, but I believe there's some controversy as to who discovered it, and I'm afraid we must be most particular at the museum about what we will accept. Unfortunately, the black market in stolen antiquities is rife at present and we can't afford even the slightest whiff of scandal. We have a reputation to maintain, however tempting it might be to lay our hands on such an object. I told Mr Briggs we couldn't even countenance looking at it until the debate over who found it was completely cleared up. Now, I believe the situation is even graver, with the artefact sitting at the centre of a police investigation into a murder. No, we must keep away until the whole affair is resolved.'

'I'm afraid that's looking unlikelier than ever,' said Ginny, interrupting Mr Ferrers, who gave the impression he could ramble on for hours. 'You see, the tablet has disappeared.'

That shut him up. He ran both hands through his unruly mop of hair.

'But this is terrible news. Mr Briggs assured me it was being kept in a safe place, until such a time when we had secured the necessary permissions and could look at bringing it into our permanent collection.'

'It was taken from the study of Mr Briggs's house in Lewes. We were there at the time but met with an unfortunate incident. My husband suspects the object is cursed,' said Ginny.

Samuel Ferrers narrowed his eyes and regarded the two women with suspicion. Nessa saw that he'd initially dismissed them as genteel artists who couldn't possibly understand the niceties of archaeology, but was now starting to wonder whether that really was the case.

'Here at the British Museum we deal in facts, not superstition. What exactly is your role in the whole affair?' he asked, speaking more slowly this time.

'We don't have an official role,' said Nessa in the appeasing tone that came so easily to her and not to her sister. 'But Lewes is a small place. We both live nearby and have close connections with the two men who were murdered, so, you see, we do have an interest in the case.'

Samuel Ferrers sat back in his leather-backed chair.

'Two murders, you say. I'd only heard about that of Gideon Rivers, such a promising young archaeologist,' he

240

said, shaking his head. 'I'm not sure how much help I can be though, as I've never laid eyes on the object.'

'You mentioned a black market in antiquities. Do you think it possible that it's been stolen to order?' asked Ginny. The pupils of her hooded eyes were as sharp as pencil leads, her nostrils narrowed, as she applied the full force of her intellect to the question at hand.

Samuel Ferrers nodded. 'Yes, that's entirely possible. But who would do such a thing?' he asked.

Nessa cleared her throat. 'When I was in Paris, I saw an advertisement for a new exhibition coming up at the Louvre entitled *Les Trésors des Croisades*. You don't suppose it could have anything to do with the disappearance of the tablet?'

'You're not suggesting the Louvre, the greatest museum in the whole of France, would have anything to do with stolen antiquities?' asked Samuel in a tone of outrage.

'Not exactly,' replied Nessa hesitantly. She told them about overhearing Jasmine in conversation with one of the senior members of staff of the Paris museum, although she left out the bit about following her undercover from the restaurant and hiding in a broom cupboard.

Samuel listened intently as she spoke, resting his chin on a hand propped up by his elbow. When she'd finished her tale, he swept his hands through his hair again.

'There's only one way we can find out. I'm close to my counterpart at the Louvre, Roman Leclerc. I will telephone him now and see what I can find out. I'm sure he's involved with this exhibition you've talked about.'

There was a black telephone sitting on the desk. He picked up the handset and spoke into it.

'Paris, please, Operator. *Le Musée de Louvre*.'

A couple of moments later, he was connected.

'Can I speak to Roman Leclerc, *s'il vous plaît*? This is Samuel Ferrers from the British Museum.'

There was a pause and a crackle, and then a booming voice speaking English with a strong French accent could be heard at the other end of the line, loud enough for the two women to hear every word that was being said.

'Samuel, what a pleasure to hear from you. How can I be of assistance?'

'Roman, is that you? I need your help with a sensitive matter. It's to do with your upcoming exhibition on the Crusades. It's come to my attention that it might somehow be linked to the disappearance of an ancient artefact on my side of the Channel.'

'And what is it, this artefact?'

'A clay tablet, dating back to at least the twelfth century. It was found here in England, in Sussex on the south coast. But it is presumed to have been brought back by a knight who visited the Holy Land.'

There was a long pause at the other end of the line, as if Roman Leclerc was weighing up what he should say. Did he think Samuel completely mad? Or was he hiding something after all?

'I've heard of this object,' came the disembodied voice at last. Nessa and Ginny let out a sigh in relief that they weren't on a completely wild goose chase.

'How? Who told you about it?' asked Samuel, a little sharply. He'd clearly suspected the sisters of making the whole thing up, and yet here was a respected fellow member of his profession backing up their story.

'A promising young archaeology student, Jasmine Zain

al-Din,' said Monsieur Leclerc, and a shiver ran down Nessa's spine. She hadn't expected him to confirm the name so easily. 'But she told me it wasn't yet in her possession. She was waiting for her contact in London to get back to her. It's rather unconventional, I know. We wouldn't usually accept such a recent find before its provenance had been fully established. But this is a cutting-edge exhibition. We are aiming to show what an exciting and forward-looking time the Crusades were and how Christianity and Islam once co-existed in the Near East. If we could get our hands on it, this would show our research is completely up to date. Is there a problem at your end?'

'I must be honest with you, Roman: I haven't set eyes on the tablet yet. At present, it's pure hearsay to me that it exists at all. However, I have a couple of ladies with me now, who tell me that it's gone missing. What's more, the disappearance might be linked to a pair of murders that were recently committed in the town where it was found.'

There was a sharp intake of breath down the line. '*Mon Dieu.* I wasn't aware. This puts things in a very different light. I will have to talk to my superiors, but if what you tell me is true, we can't possibly include the tablet in our exhibition, even if it is found. Do you have any idea who could have taken it?'

'None whatsoever. That's why I called you. I wondered if you might be able to shed any light on it?'

'Samuel!' Leclerc sounded shocked. 'I hope you aren't suggesting the Louvre would have anything to do with stolen goods?'

'Of course not, my dear Roman. But if someone thought

243

it was worth their while, they might steal it to extract a fee from you.'

'On that count, I can reassure you. When we borrow artefacts for display, it is done as part of a reciprocal arrangement of trust between us and other institutions such as your own – you know that. It would be unheard of for us to pay cash for an item without being certain of its provenance.' Leclerc sounded agitated.

'I would have expected no less, and intended no offence,' said Samuel, trying to soothe him. 'Nonetheless, if the tablet should happen to fall into your hands, by whatever means, I would be grateful if you could let me know.'

'You can rest assured I will do so,' said Leclerc, and with some polite formalities, the exchange was at an end.

He put down the telephone and turned to the two women, who had moved to the front of their seats to listen to the conversation.

'There's certainly something strange afoot here. If I hear anything more, I'll let you know, and I'd be grateful if you could do the same. We need to get to the bottom of what's happened to the tablet for the sake of posterity, not to mention two murdered men.'

How could such a small object wield such power? Perhaps Leonard was right, and the tablet was cursed. If so, would they too pay the price for pursuing it?

36.

Virginia

By the time they left the museum, it had started to rain, so they decided to take the omnibus to Tottenham Court Road. There was one passing as they reached the stop, and they only just managed to scramble on board, pay the conductor for their tickets and clamber up the winding stairs to the front of the top deck where Ginny elbowed Nessa out of the way and collapsed, giggling, into the window seat.

'You beast,' cried Nessa, to the bemusement of their fellow passengers.

The view of London pavements from the top of a bus was one of her favourite things. Down below, smartly dressed ladies hurried along, their umbrellas blowing inside out in the gusty wind. On a street corner, a wizened old man turned the handle of a barrel organ, and they could hear the strains floating on the air through the open window as they passed by. Young clerks who'd escaped from their desks leaned against buildings, smoking, despite the showers.

Even though the rain slowed the traffic down, it didn't take them long to reach the busy shopping street. They were nearly thrown down the stairs as the bus screeched to a halt at their stop and they got off, pulling their hats a little closer over their heads against the rain. Nessa took Ginny's hand and dragged her away from the crowds towards one of the side streets.

'Come on – the Sylvan Rooms are this way,' said her sister.

It was amazing how quickly the busy thoroughfare gave way to quiet alleyways. They passed a man sitting hunched on the pavement, his dirt-stained hand outstretched, his eyes dead. Ginny stopped and felt in her purse for a coin.

'Bless you, ma'am,' he muttered as she pressed it into his palm.

Nessa gave her a sharp look. 'Come along, you'll only encourage him,' she said, taking her arm and tugging her away.

Before long they arrived at a set of cast-iron railings leading down to a nondescript black door. Up above them, suspicious moaning noises emanated from an open window. It wasn't a part of town either of them was used to frequenting. Ginny drew her coat a little closer around her, as if it might give her protection from unseen threats.

Nessa rapped loudly on the door. For a moment or two there was no reply and Ginny was tempted to suggest they abandon the visit. Then the door opened, just a crack at first, then more fully, and from the shadows stepped Diana Underhill, wearing a green silk dress that clung to her curves, and a small, navy pillbox hat perched at an angle on her red curls, with just the right amount of netting.

'Mrs Bell, I didn't expect to see you back here so soon, and Mrs Woolf, I'm honoured indeed. What brings you to my humble establishment?'

'I hope you don't mind, but we have a few more questions about the murders. As someone who knew both Gideon and Bobby, we thought you might be able to help,' said Nessa.

'You'd better come in, then,' said Diana, ushering them inside. With a quick glance up the stairwell to the street, she closed the door behind them.

She led them along a darkened corridor to the bar. In the corner, a pianist was playing scales. It was only four o'clock in the afternoon and a few hours until the club opened. The lack of light and air made Ginny feel distinctly claustrophobic, but she took the high stool Diana indicated.

'Can I get you a glass of champagne, ladies?' Diana asked, lifting the hatch and walking round to the other side of the bar.

Ginny looked at Nessa, who shrugged.

'Why not?' she said.

Taking a bottle from an ice bucket, Diana popped the cork with an expert flick of thumb and forefinger and poured out three generous glasses. Then she leaned on the bar and lit a cigarette.

'They've not found the murderer yet?' she asked, blowing out a smoke ring.

Nessa shook her head. 'The police are proving useless, which is why we're on the case.'

'Go ahead, but I told you everything I know last time,' said Diana with a bored expression.

'It's about Jasmine Zain al-Din, Gideon Rivers's fiancée,' Nessa began.

'As I said, I barely knew the woman. She only came here once or twice,' replied Diana without missing a beat.

'We have reason to believe she may be involved in the

247

smuggling of stolen antiquities and wondered if you knew anything about that,' Nessa continued.

'Wait a minute. Are you accusing me of being involved with an illegal trade? I'll have you know both I and my establishment are completely law abiding,' said Miss Underhill.

'We don't doubt it for a second, but you're a woman of the world with your ear to the ground, and we merely want to know if you've heard anything, any piece of information that might shed some light on this whole sorry affair.'

Diana Underhill took another drag on her cigarette, somewhat appeased. 'I'm not naïve and it would be foolish to suggest that such things don't go on. But I think you're barking up the wrong tree with Jasmine. From what I've heard, she's from a highly respectable Parisian family. Why would she need to get involved in anything untoward? Do you suspect her because of the colour of her skin?'

Nessa had the decency to blush. 'Absolutely not. I can assure you neither of us is prejudiced against anybody based on their complexion. It's just we suspect we're not seeing the whole picture where Jasmine is concerned.'

Ginny had been dying to use the bathroom ever since they'd left the British Museum, and the champagne hadn't helped. She feared what the state of the washrooms might be here, but could hold it in no longer.

'Would you mind if I used your facilities?' she asked.

'Second on the left,' replied Miss Underhill.

Ginny got to her feet and left her sister and the club owner glaring at one another in an uneasy silence. She found the bathroom and to her relief it looked recently scrubbed with a strong odour of carbolic soap. Entering one of the cubicles, she locked the door behind her, and it was only as she was relieving herself that she noticed a collection of photographs on the wall, which looked as though they'd been taken in the club. Examining them idly as she sat there, one of the pictures caught her attention. Getting up from the seat and making use of the scratchy toilet paper, she rearranged her clothing and moved closer to get a better look. She realised her first instinct had been correct and the photograph did indeed show what she thought it did.

Back in the bar, Nessa and Diana were sipping champagne and listening to the piano player, who had launched into a ragtime tune.

'If Jasmine Zain al-Din only visited your club on a couple of occasions, Miss Underhill, can you explain why there is a photograph of her in the ladies' bathroom?' said Ginny, interrupting.

Diana held her gaze, but she'd picked the wrong target. In an outstaring contest, Ginny would win every time.

'I think there's something you're not telling us,' Ginny added.

Shrugging, Diana took another drag on her cigarette.

'So what? I said she'd been here once or twice. The photograph must have been taken on one of those occasions.'

'Except she looks completely at home. And she has her arm draped around someone you told us she barely knew – Bobby Bassey.'

At the mention of this name, Nessa started and looked at her sister, her eyes wide. Ginny nodded to confirm what she was saying was true.

Pursing her lips so lines cracked through her thick foundation, Diana leaned forward to stub out her cigarette in a large smoke-green ashtray, then stood up straight. She walked over to the optics hanging above the bar, and refilled her champagne glass with neat gin, took a swig, then turned back round to face them. Her voice took on more of a Cockney lilt.

'All right. I admit it. Jasmine was a regular here. The Sylvan Rooms was her home from home when she was in London. She and Bobby were the best of friends. That's what made it so hard when she and Gideon got engaged. It felt to Bobby like the ultimate betrayal.'

'And she didn't mind that Gideon and Bobby had been lovers?' asked Nessa.

'Of course not. I'd have thought you of all people would appreciate that,' said Diana with a toss of her head.

Ginny remembered what Nessa had told her about meeting Jasmine at Le Boeuf sur le Toit. How she'd mistaken her at first for a young man. There'd been a time when she was naïve as to such things, but after her affair with Vita she now knew differently.

'Why didn't you tell us this before?' she asked, still convinced Diana was hiding something.

'In my profession you get used to deflecting questions. It's a force of habit,' said Diana.

Nessa, who'd been quiet until now, spoke up. 'This puts Bobby's death in a very different light. When I invited Jasmine to Charleston, I thought they were strangers who had a reason to dislike one another. Now I know they were close . . . Don't you think they must have spoken while she was with us? Perhaps I misjudged her when I assumed she could have nothing to do with the murders.'

'Jasmine isn't capable of hurting anyone, least of all

250

Bobby,' blurted out Diana with uncharacteristic passion. 'She's the sweetest, most thoughtful . . . If you must know, I was helping her. One of the reasons she accompanied Gideon to the dig was because she was hopeful it might turn up something unique that her fellow archaeologists working in both Syria and France had never seen before. That's what makes her so good. Even though she's only recently graduated, she's one of the best of her generation. Gideon used to say he didn't love her for her beauty, but for her mind. He admitted she would make a far finer archaeologist than him, and he wasn't a man known for his modesty. Sometimes I wondered if he was jealous of Jasmine and worried she would eventually outshine him in his field. She had an inkling they would turn up something interesting in Lewes, and they did. This extraordinary tablet shows there were strong ties between England and the Holy Land nine centuries ago. Jasmine wanted the discovery to be at the heart of this exhibition being held at the Louvre next year, the largest ever of its kind. She explained it all to me, treated me like someone with a brain, which is more than most people do. That's why I was willing to do whatever it took to help her get the tablet to Paris.'

'Where is it now?' demanded Ginny, who was finding Diana's eulogy a tad irritating.

'What do you mean?' asked Diana, looking genuinely confused.

'It was taken from Stanley Briggs's house. While we were there. Someone wanted it so badly they were willing to knock us out to take it,' said Nessa.

Diana looked horrified. 'But Jasmine is relying on the tablet to make her reputation. She's promised it to the Loover,' she

251

said, pronouncing the name of the museum to rhyme with the vacuum cleaner. 'All she's ever wanted is a permanent position there, and she's hoping this will be her passport.'

She stopped speaking and looked from one sister to the other, clearly wondering if she'd said too much.

'Who was your contact? When Jasmine was in Paris, who were you dealing with in Lewes?' said Ginny, trying to think as a proper detective might.

'I honestly don't know. There was a postal box number I was to go to where it would be, and from there I was going to pass it on to my usual contacts to take it across the Channel without arousing suspicion,' said Diana.

'Usual contacts?' asked Ginny, arching her eyebrows.

'Come on, Mrs Woolf – you're the writer. Use your imagination as to what business an establishment like mine might have that one wouldn't want the law involved in.'

In some ways, Ginny was very much a woman of the world, but she now saw that in others she was a complete ingenue. She could only guess at what Diana was talking about, and even then, she wasn't sure she'd be right. If she was going to play detective, she would have to cast off some of the prejudices of her age and class.

The pianist had switched to playing a mournful tune. Despite herself, Ginny started to sway her shoulders.

'Do you fancy a dance, Mrs Woolf?' asked Diana, noticing her moving in time to the music and laughing.

Ginny shook her head, but Nessa, always the more sensual of the two of them, got to her feet and held out her hands to pull her on to the dance floor.

'Come on, Ginny, let your hair down for once,' said her sister.

252

Seeing them get to their feet, the pianist picked up the pace. He was an accomplished musician and, despite herself, Ginny let Nessa lead her round the room twirling and jiving. She was surprised to find she wasn't quite such a terrible dancer as she'd feared.

Then she remembered why they were there and stopped, patting down the front of her dress. They were here to investigate a double murder and instead they were prancing around like showgirls. This wasn't a game, she reminded herself. Death is a serious business.

37.

Vanessa

Charleston farmhouse, Firle, East Sussex

When she arrived back at Charleston, Nessa found Duncan waiting with his bags packed in the hall. He was pacing up and down, running his hands through his black hair, and looked pale and drawn.

'There you are, Nessa. I was wondering whether you'd be in time to give me a lift to the ferry at Newhaven,' he said.

Having just caught the train back from London, then driven through the rain from Lewes, narrowly avoiding swerving off the road on several occasions as she still wasn't used to the mechanics of steering in a downpour, the last thing she felt like was making the round trip to the port town, which was a good half an hour's drive away. She hadn't eaten since breakfast and was faint with hunger. But she could never deny Duncan what he wanted.

'We need to leave straight away if we're to make the six o'clock crossing. I'm meeting my mother in Paris in the morning,' he said.

'Paris?' repeated Nessa.

'I'm taking her down to Cassis. I need a break after everything that's happened, and George will be there.'

Nessa felt as though she couldn't breathe, but she tried to ignore the sensation. She'd resolved long ago never to interfere in Duncan's love affairs. It was her only hope for keeping him in her life. She knew she should have more self-respect, but she couldn't help loving him, and part of that meant recognising his weakness when it came to matters of the heart.

Usually, she rubbed along fine with his boyfriends. When the affair petered out as it inevitably did, several of them had stayed close to her and still corresponded with her, seeing her as a sort of open-minded mother figure. But George was different. There was a pompous quality to the young American she just couldn't bear. How could Duncan leave her with everything that was going on to spend time in the south of France with him? Then she reminded herself that his mother would be there too, and she at least was deserving of her son's company for a week or two.

She forced a smile, turned round and headed back out through the door, without removing her hat or coat.

'Come along, then. What are you waiting for?' she called to him.

Duncan dashed away then reappeared, holding up a small package wrapped in brown paper. 'Sorry, there's something I almost forgot,' he said.

'What is it?' she asked.

Duncan looked flustered. 'Oh, just a little sketch I had framed. It's a present for George,' he said, blushing.

An hour and a half later, having dropped Duncan at

the ferry terminal, where he'd just made his crossing, she returned to an empty hallway. She was so tired she felt ready to collapse.

'I've made you supper,' she heard Grace call out from the kitchen, and felt better at once. Home at last, a bowl of soup and hunk of bread waiting for her on the well-loved table, she finally allowed herself to relax. The wood of the table was marked with stains and scratches, each one containing a memory. Bunches of onion and garlic brought back from Cassis earlier that summer hung either side of the stove.

As she sat there, letting the warmth of home seep into her veins, a question began to niggle at her mind. Why had Duncan been in such a hurry to leave? Was it just because he was exhausted and would benefit from the warmer air of the south in the company of a handsome young man? Or was he running away, and if so from what?

'Mummy!' Angelica ran into the kitchen and threw her arms round her mother, burying her head in her shoulder like a small ram. The next hour was spent taking her back upstairs, settling her into bed and reading her a story, the familiar routine a salve to them both.

It wasn't until much later when Nessa went to bed herself, in the quiet room she and Duncan had painstakingly decorated, that she wondered if this was how it would always be from now on. The sex had stopped some years ago, not long after Angelica's birth – she'd already accepted that. But she'd hoped their love and companionship would be enough to see them through their middle years and into old age. Now what she feared most was facing the future alone. She had to accept that at the age of nearly fifty, she was mother to all, lover to none. At least she still had Ginny and the adventure of trying to track down a murderer.

As she lay there, relishing the cool cotton of the pillow on her cheek, listening to an owl hooting somewhere in the tall trees that surrounded the farmhouse, her mind was still worrying away. The same questions circled round her brain. Why did Duncan look so grief-stricken it was making him ill? Why was he so eager to get out of the country following the death of his friend? Could there be more to it than simply a desire to sun himself on Mediterranean shores?

She thought of him walking up the gangway when she'd left him at Newhaven, striking a solitary figure with a battered suitcase in one hand and the brown paper package in the other. Suddenly, it came to her what it had reminded her of. The dimensions of the parcel, which he'd said was intended for George, were the same size and shape as the missing tablet.

257

38.

Virginia

After coming into Lewes to pick up some supplies, Ginny decided to walk home via the priory ruins. Once the richest religious establishment in England, a daughter house of the great Abbey of Cluny in Burgundy, the priory was now reduced to a romantic pile of stones.

She liked to imagine what life must have been like for the monks living and working there: sleeping together in dormitories, eating together in the dining hall in silence apart from a solitary brother reading aloud from the Bible. Each of the monks had their own individual task, one tending the herb garden, another caring for the sick in the infirmary, yet another overseeing the fishponds. Life went on like this for centuries, until fat old Henry VIII decided he wanted a new wife and lost his temper with Rome. So intense was his fury with the Catholic Church that he hired an Italian engineer, Portinari, to bring down the walls of Lewes Priory so decisively they could never be reconstructed. And yet it was impossible to erase all traces of a building that had once been a seat of such power.

Four centuries on, its mark was still indelibly left on the landscape.

Eighty years earlier, navvies cutting the Brighton to Lewes railway line had dug right through the priory's former chapter house, uncovering two lead caskets containing the bones of William de Warenne and his wife Gundrada. William was right-hand man to the Conqueror, and they were the founders of both castle and priory. It might be ancient history, but the echoes of the past still resounded around the wide river valley stretching between Kingston Ridge to the west and Firle Beacon to the east.

It was late afternoon, and the sun was beginning to lower in the sky, casting a soft golden glow on the ruins as she walked through them, taking her time, dreaming of the past. Stopping, she sat upon a pile of stones, despite the sign expressly forbidding one to do so, and laid a hand on the mossy surface, feeling the warmth it had absorbed from the sun. Looking around, she couldn't see another soul, and yet she had the distinct impression she wasn't alone. Could it be the ghosts of the monks who had once inhabited this place?

As she got to her feet, from the corner of her eye she saw a dark figure moving nearby. Her heart pounded as she contemplated the possibility that she'd conjured an actual ghost out of thin air. When she turned her head, however, there was nothing there. What nonsense. It was just her imagination playing tricks on her. Giving herself a firm telling-off, she placed one foot in front of another, the sight of her grey worsted stockings and brown brogues bringing her back to reality. But she couldn't shake off the sensation of being followed. This time, she turned round rapidly, hoping to catch out whoever it was, ghostly or otherwise. Now she was convinced there was someone, or something, watching her. For the next few minutes, she stopped every few paces, turning round as quickly as she could in the hope of catching them, but still she saw nothing. Then she spotted an opportunity. At the turning out of the priory ruins there was a blind corner. As soon as she'd rounded this, she stopped, making sure she was concealed from anyone behind her, and leaned over as if to tie her shoelaces. She remained bent in this position for what seemed like an age, although it was probably no more than a couple of minutes.

She was about to give up and carry on her way when a figure dressed all in black rounded the bend. It was a woman, a veil over her face, but before she could get close enough to see whether she was young or old, the dark lady turned and fled back the way she'd come.

Ginny considered pursuit, but short of physically apprehending the woman and unmasking her, she was unsure of what she would do if she caught up with her. She could hear her heart pounding in her ear drums. At least she wasn't going mad. There had been someone pursuing her, it hadn't been just a ghostly figment of her imagination.

Ridiculous as it sounded, she couldn't shake off the feeling that the woman was somehow connected to the murders. Could the curse of the clay tablet be about to strike again?

Who was she and why was she following her? Moreover, why didn't she want to be identified? She pondered these questions as she plodded through the fields back to Rodmell, taking care to avoid the mud. Every so often, she looked over her shoulder, even though it was unlikely the mysterious person would continue to trace her steps. Still, she felt relieved when she reached the main road where it was not too far to go until the next place of habitation.

When she finally reached Rodmell, the sun had sunk behind the hills and the village lay in shadow. She was always glad to see Monk's House, and on this autumn evening the white weatherboard exterior of their little cottage stood like a beacon in the valley. As she approached, she felt like a boatman reaching the safety of a lighthouse.

Leonard was sitting at the writing desk in the living room composing dull but necessary letters to do with the business of the Hogarth Press. Their little publishing imprint was gaining quite a name for itself, but with success came extra duties. When he heard his wife come in, he looked up, glad of the distraction.

'Cup of tea?' he asked, offering to make it himself as it was Nellie's afternoon off.

Taking off her coat and hanging it on a peg in the hall, then entering the drawing room, she flung herself down into the comfiest armchair, kicked off her brogues, and shook her head.

'I think I need something a little stronger,' she said.

Leonard rose from his seat and crossed the room to the old oak cupboard, bought from a lawn sale of the belongings of the previous occupants of the cottage, where they kept a bottle of good Courvoisier together with a couple of glasses. It had been a gift from a grateful poet, whose slim volume they had published with surprising success. He poured them both a glass, then brought hers over and handed it to her. Then he sat down in the chair opposite, leaned forward and put a hand on her knee. It was a delicate hand for a man, with long, slender fingers, but his nails were dirty from working in the garden. His brow was furrowed with concern.

'Ginny, are you sure this whole murder business isn't proving too much for you? I know you and Nessa feel some sort of responsibility towards the young men who have lost their lives, but it's not up to you to find out who killed them. That's a job for the police. You can't bring them back.'

She told him what had just happened as she walked home through the priory ruins, but even as she spoke the words she could tell he wasn't convinced. He clearly thought at worst she was hallucinating, or at best had got the wrong end of the stick.

'I tell you, there was a woman in black following me,' she insisted.

'But you couldn't see her face because it was covered by a veil?' he replied.

She sighed, knowing he had reason to doubt her. Her dear, sweet Leonard, who'd nursed her patiently through many bouts of depression and illness. How could she make him believe this time was different?

'I know it sounds unbelievable, but honestly, although I'm a little shaken right now, I feel more alive investigating this business than I have done in a long time. It's not just police officers who can have an opinion on how a murder might have happened and why. Have you never heard of private eyes?'

Leonard sat back in his chair and laughed heartily. Then he raised his glass in the air.

'I must toast you, Ginny. I didn't realise that was how you and Nessa see yourselves. It's as if we were on the mean streets of Harlem, rather than living in a sleepy country

262

town. I see it now: a smoke-filled office, a sign on the door saying: "Messrs Woolf and Bell Investigate".'

'Misses, if you please,' said Ginny, trying to join in the joke, but feeling rather peeved at her husband's reaction. She lit a cigarette and made a fuss of Pinka who'd come in from the garden to greet her with the distinct smell of wet dog.

'Do you honestly think Gripe is up to the job?' she added.

Her husband thought about this for a moment, putting down his brandy glass and rubbing the palms of his hands together.

'Presumably the man has experience with such matters. And he has a team of trained men underneath him,' he said.

Ginny snorted. 'He's a country policeman looking for an obvious solution, such as sexual jealousy, but this is a case with links to the world of archaeology, and the demimondes of London and Paris. It's far outside his usual remit. I'm not saying Nessa and I would make good policemen, simply that with our knowledge of the people involved and the circles in which they move, combined with a certain artistic temperament that I think we can fairly claim, we might uncover relevant facts that don't immediately present themselves to Gripe and his men,' she said.

Leonard nodded, but still didn't look entirely convinced.

'I'm just asking you to be careful, Ginny. You know how easily you can run yourself into the ground and then it can take weeks or even months for you to recover.' He paused, then added, 'If this woman in black really was following you, do you think she meant you harm?'

Ginny shook her head. 'I've been thinking about that all the way home. From the way she reacted when I stopped to catch her out, I'm almost certain she didn't mean me any physical harm. She was shorter than I am, so there would be no guarantee she would win in any sort of combat. But I suspect she wanted to scare me, and if that was the case then why? What does she have to gain by making me think a ghost is pursuing me?'

'Isn't it obvious?' asked Leonard. 'She wants to warn you off the case. Somebody doesn't want you poking around in these murders, and I have to say I agree with them.'

Ginny took a sip of the brandy, relishing the burning sensation as it slid down the back of her throat. Was Leonard right? Should she take the appearance of the woman in black as a sign that she shouldn't interfere in matters that weren't directly related to her? Then she thought of Nessa and how worried she was about Duncan. She owed it to her sister to help her find out the truth about Bobby's death, if nothing else. It had happened at Charleston, her home from home, and directly impacted members of her own family, the people she loved most in the world after her husband. Since the death of their mother, Nessa had been more than a sister to her – she was her safe place, her rock in a stormy sea. If her sister was threatened, she simply had to do something about it.

There was another thought too, hidden further away in the recesses of her mind, a less honourable one. Leonard was right, she was rather relishing the role of detective. It was an intellectual puzzle that strangely soothed her whirring mind, and she wasn't ready to give up the chase just yet.

39.

Alice

She rose early, while Ernest was still asleep, and, before breakfast, took Nelson's lead and summoned the eager dog to join her on a dawn stride across the Downs. The sun was peeping over Mount Caburn, sending out golden beams that called her up on to the slopes of Malling Down, part of the same rocky outcrop. She felt decidedly pleased that at the age of nearly sixty she still had no problem in walking at a fast pace up the sides of the steep combe leading to the summit.

The walk improved her mood, which had been rather black. The death of the young archaeologist remained unsolved. The first suspect in the case had been released without charge, and the second bailed. As the immediate neighbour of the crime scene, she felt a certain responsibility and wouldn't rest easy until the killer was brought to justice. All these thoughts, which had been spinning round in her mind for days, dissipated with the simple action of placing one foot in front of another to climb the grassy slope, making her heart beat all the stronger as she did so. The view from the top over the village of Glynde to Windover Hill and Firle Beacon was its own reward.

As she came back down the steep road that continued to the clifftop golf course, known as Chapel Hill, she swung her arms in exhilaration, Nelson trotting alongside her wagging his tail. She navigated her way home through a series of narrow twittens, which she had grown to know as well as the veins on the back of her hands. It was only when she took the cut-through leading between two public houses, the Lamb and the Lewes Arms, past the Star Brewery, that she saw she was not alone. The figure in black whom she'd seen a few days previously was standing on Castle Banks, watching her house.

Heart pounding, with fear now rather than exertion, she turned round and walked back towards the High Street, much to Nelson's confusion. Here she found a bench, where she took a seat while she decided what to do next. Nelson sat dutifully on the pavement beside her, his tail still as he tried to work out why his mistress had nearly returned home and then changed her mind.

Finally, she let out a long decisive breath.

'Alice Dudeney, you are a fool. Nothing bad is going to happen to you outside your own home in broad daylight,' she said aloud, getting to her feet. Fortunately, there was no one around apart from a couple of delivery boys who were probably out of earshot, and even if they weren't, they were too focused on their work to worry about an elderly woman talking to herself.

When she arrived back home, the figure had gone, and she began to doubt herself. Was she seeing things? She pinched the fore of her arm until it hurt to reassure herself that she wasn't going mad. No, she was quite sure there had been someone there, hadn't her reaction proved that? But what should she do about it? If she told Ernest, he wouldn't believe her.

As she released a relieved Nelson from his leash, a thought came to her. She would write to Mrs Woolf. They may not always see eye to eye, but Alice knew she was taking an interest in the case, together with her sister. She felt sure the figure in black had something to do with the murder on the mound. If anyone was going to take her seriously, it would be Virginia Woolf. She had the distinct impression that Mrs Woolf and that sister of hers were following the murder investigation extremely closely. For all their differences, she respected Virginia's opinion, which was more than she could say for most people whom she found to be insufferable fools.

She sat down at her writing desk, Nelson curled up in his basket at her feet, took a sheet of her best paper and her fountain pen, and began to write.

Dear Mrs Woolf,

Twice now I have been followed or observed by a mysterious figure in black. I feel sure the figure is a real human being, not a ghost or my own imagining, and what's more that they are connected to the murders in which you are particularly interested. Why else would they have appeared at this time?

If I tell Chief Inspector Gripe about what I have seen, or indeed my own husband, they will dismiss it as the fancies of an overactive female mind. Whilst you and I may have our differences, I believe you will have greater sympathy with my

predicament and I would be interested to know your thoughts
on the matter, if only to reassure myself that I'm not going mad.

Yours faithfully,
Alice Dudeney

She signed the letter, and sealed it in an envelope, then placed it on the hall table for the maid to post later that morning. That done, she found she had an appetite for breakfast, so made her way to the dining room, and called for scrambled eggs and toast, washed down with a pot of strong coffee. Now all there was to do was to wait for Mrs Woolf to respond. Would she think Alice crazy, or might she be able to shed some light on the mysterious woman in black?

40.

Vanessa

She arrived in Lewes in a bad temper. It had taken three attempts to start the motor and on the road from Charleston she had been so busy worrying about Duncan she'd nearly collided with a tractor driving in the other direction. The farmhand driving the beast had made an extremely rude gesture as she sped off, cheeks burning, swearing under her breath in language her late mother would have been appalled by.

Parking badly on Castle Banks, she got out of the car and breathed in the crisp autumn air in relief. It made a nice change from petrol fumes. She still didn't know why Ginny had wanted to meet her at Brack Mound with such urgency. When the messenger boy had arrived on his bicycle – in the absence of a telephone both the Woolfs and the Bells still relied on hand-delivered letters – she had been at the far end of the walled garden, weeding the narrow flower beds around the piazza where she was attempting to recreate the Mediterranean planting she so loved at their home in the south of France. The pink cistus and blue Russian sage were thriving, but all her efforts to grow lavender here had so far failed.

The urchin had handed her a scribbled note, which she'd unfolded and read.

Nessa,
Mrs Dudeney has written to me regarding a matter of some concern that might relate to the murders. I told her I would meet her at her house at four o'clock this afternoon. Can you come?

In haste,
Ginny

It didn't suit particularly, and at first she was minded to send the boy back with a letter declining the abrupt invitation. But the more she thought about it, the more she was intrigued. Perhaps what Mrs Dudeney had to say would shed light on the murders. They couldn't pass up on that opportunity.

Two minutes later, she'd made up her mind.

'Any message, ma'am?' the boy asked.

'Yes, please return to Mrs Woolf and tell her I will meet her at Castle Banks at four o'clock. Can you remember that?'

The boy, who couldn't have been much older than ten or eleven, nodded, but he didn't immediately get back on his bicycle. Nessa felt around in her apron, and found five pennies, which seemed to satisfy him, as he leaped on to the rickety contraption and pedalled off at top speed.

Four hours later, Nessa found herself standing on the doorstep of the house on Castle Banks, about to ring the doorbell. As she hesitated, the door was flung open and Mrs Dudeney emerged, dressed in a sprigged cotton frock that made her look as though she were trying to appear both younger and slimmer than she was.

'Mrs Bell, so good of you to come at such short notice. Your sister is already here.'

She ushered her inside the house, where Ginny was sitting in the drawing room, her sharp brown eyes darting around in a fashion that her sister knew meant she was taking in every detail and committing it to memory to be judged at her leisure.

'Can I offer you a cup of tea?' asked their hostess.

Nessa was about to accept, but Ginny shook her head. 'What is all this about?' she demanded.

Mrs Dudeney didn't immediately reply, but drew in a deep breath, as if she were summoning up the courage to speak.

'I fear that I may be going mad, and I wanted to ask your advice. This whole murder business has got to me, and I wonder if I'm starting to see things.'

'What manner of things?' said Ginny, a little too sharply for Nessa's liking.

Mrs Dudeney cleared her throat. 'A woman dressed all in black. It sounds crazy, but she has appeared to me three times now, and I fear she is some sort of bad omen.'

Nessa half expected Ginny to exclaim 'what nonsense', but her sister was quiet, merely nodding at Mrs Dudeney to continue.

'On two occasions, I was walking Nelson when I got the distinct impression I was being followed. Each time I caught a glimpse of her, and once this was confirmed by townspeople out that night. I feel certain that she is not supernatural, that if I were to reach out and touch her, she would be flesh and blood, though she vanishes as if she might have been a ghost.'

'What about the third occasion?' asked Ginny. 'You said you saw her three times.'

'It was in the middle of the night. I was woken by the sound of something banging, like the gate closing and I got up and went over to the window. At the time I thought it was just a trick of the light, but now I am sure it was her I saw standing opposite like an angel of death. Who do you think she could be?'

Nessa had been taking all this in with incredulity. This was why they had been summoned here so urgently. To hear about Alice Dudeney's spectral imaginings. Appraising their hostess with an artist's eye, she took in her owlish features, the grey hair looped in an unflattering bun, the sagging chin. It was difficult to believe this was the same woman who'd left her husband for a scandalous love affair. The woman had clearly gone completely mad.

Lowering her gaze to Alice's hands, she noticed they were trembling, ever so slightly. Suddenly, she was overcome with a wave of sympathy. There was a raw emotion in her that could not be ignored. It was clear she'd been badly frightened. Nessa glanced at Ginny, wondering whether she'd seen the shaking too, but her sister was looking straight ahead.

'It pains me somewhat to admit it, Mrs Dudeney, but I believe entirely in your woman in black, for the simple reason that I have seen her too,' said Ginny.

Nessa let out an involuntary gasp. Her surprise was

followed by the familiar concern for Ginny's state of mind. To the outside world, she wore a hard shell, but Nessa knew the soft creature that lay within. She put a finger on her arm and this time Ginny met her eyes and nodded.

'I'm sorry I didn't tell you before, Nessa. This dark lady has now appeared to two of us. We were both with Gideon Rivers shortly before his death, so I think it is safe to assume this woman in black also has a connection to the murder,' Ginny continued. 'If we were to approach Chief Inspector Gripe and lay the facts of what we have seen before him, I agree with Mrs Dudeney that his limited imagination would dismiss it as the mere fancies of hysterical women. Therefore, our only recourse is to tackle the situation ourselves.'

'And how exactly do you propose to do that?' asked Nessa.

'Assuming our dark damsel is flesh and bone and not a demon, we must trick her into revealing herself. So far what we know is that she has followed both Mrs Dudeney and me when we have been out walking. Furthermore, she's only appeared to us when we've been alone. In some way, she must be tracking our movements. I suggest that if I walk from the priory ruins where I first saw her, up here to the mound, she will be unable to resist the temptation to come after me, albeit at a distance. That's when we'll catch her in a pincer movement. Mrs Dudeney, you must wait inside your house, out of sight without any lights on to see if you can catch a glimpse of her. If you do, exit through the side gate to approach her. Nessa, you need to appear from another angle – I suggest coming up from the castle. She can't possibly be looking in both directions at once. One of you will come up in front of her and if she tries to get away the other will be there to block her path. In the meantime, I will turn round from the door and try to get a good look at her.'

Nessa let out a hearty laugh. 'Ginny, I think you've been watching too many music-hall routines. What you suggest sounds utterly farcical,' she said. But the look on her sister's face was anything but amused. Her nostrils narrowed as they did when she was inclined to take offence. Nessa saw she was going to have to agree to the ridiculous scheme.

'All right. When are we going to carry out this plan?' she asked.

'This afternoon. In about an hour's time, to be precise. First, we must split up and each take our position. Mrs Dudeney, you stay here and watch out from your window without being seen. I'll walk down to the ruins and back again in the hope of hooking her. Nessa, you must make yourself busy for a while. We will reconvene here at a quarter past five.

It sounded completely crazy, but Ginny's brown eyes were focused in a way her sister knew meant she'd closed off all argument. There was no choice but to busy herself in town until the allotted hour and see the plan through. She only hoped no one would get hurt.

Mrs Dudeney showed them to the door. Ginny marched off in the direction of the priory and Nessa, finding herself alone, set off at a slower pace along the cobbled street leading under the two Norman archways, one earlier and one later, towards the High Street. As she passed the entrance to Barbican House, she saw it was open, and a light was on inside. Although not raining, the day was overcast and there was a welcoming appearance to the interior that drew her

274

in. According to her watch there were still fifty-five minutes to pass before she could make her return. There was no one in the entrance hall.

'Hello?' she called out, but there was no reply. The door was open and the lights on, so there must be someone around, perhaps in the library on the top floor. She began to climb the stairs, the old wooden treads creaking loudly as she did so. When she got to the third floor, the lights were also on there, so she made her way past the dozens of shelves of books on history and archaeology to the office looking out over the High Street.

Miss Bramble was sitting at the desk poring over a book. The funny old thing seemed so oblivious to the world around her she didn't notice Nessa until she was standing right over her. Looking up, she stared at her through her thick-rimmed spectacles, not appearing to recognise her at first. Then she pushed back her seat with a scraping sound and got to her feet, nearly knocking the book she'd been reading off the desk.

'Mrs Bell, you must forgive me. I thought I was quite alone. I get so carried away when I'm reading. How can I help you?'

'Do you have any books on the art of the Middle Ages?' Nessa spluttered, quickly coming up with an excuse for what she was doing there.

'Let me see ... Where do we keep the art books?' said Miss Bramble, crossing over to the bookcases on the other side of the room. 'No, this section is about the geology of Sussex. Let me try next door.'

She led Nessa into the next cramped attic room, but they had no joy there either. The poor woman didn't seem to be much good at her job, but eventually they located a single shelf of books on medieval art. Pretending that was exactly what she'd been looking for, Nessa selected a volume at random and took it over to a desk by the window, where she took a seat.

'Do you mind if I leave you to it?' asked Miss Bramble, who was evidently dying to get back to her book. Nessa smiled and shook her head, glad of the time to consider what had just happened with her sister and Mrs Dudeney, and prepare herself mentally for the encounter to come.

When Miss Bramble had disappeared back into the next room, she laid the art book on the desk and looked down at the street below. The draper's shop opposite was closing for the day and she watched as the owner, Mr Clayton, whom she knew vaguely, stepped out looking as smart as ever in a grey tweed suit and brown leather hat with a feather tucked into the brim. Unaware that anyone was watching him, he turned the key in the lock of his shop, then took a packet of cigarettes from his front pocket and a matchbox from another. Leaning back against the shop window, he lit one, took a drag and closed his eyes.

Nessa felt as though she could easily have a little snooze sitting here in the late afternoon sun in the quiet of the old library. But she couldn't afford to. She had to stay alert until the time came to return to Brack Mound and see whether Ginny had succeeded in tempting the lady in black into their trap. Instead, she focused intently on some detail of French fourteenth-century portraiture, wondering if she could copy the way in which the long-dead old master had captured the light falling on the cheek of a young woman. Wishing she had her sketchbook on her to copy the image to refer to later, she was about to ask Miss Bramble whether she had any paper and a pencil she could borrow, when her eye was caught by a figure gliding along the now nearly empty street below. It was a woman, small in stature, who stood out because she was dressed entirely in black. From this high angle, it was impossible to see her face. Her heart started thumping. Could this be the person they were looking for? Hastily replacing the art book on the shelf from which it had come, she dashed past Miss Bramble, who looked up from her reading in surprise.

'Sorry, I've just remembered something important,' she said, springing down the stairs, taking them two at a time until she reached the front door. But when she got out into the street the woman in black was nowhere to be seen.

41.

Virginia

She felt a bit of a fool parading around the ruins all by herself. Before, she'd had a purpose, a direction – she'd been walking swiftly home like an arrow flying towards its target. Now, she was more like a drunken bluebottle zigzagging between the crumbling stone walls of the old priory. There was no sign of their mysterious lady. She resolved to make one final tour then climb back up the hill to meet the others. It had been a foolish notion of hers to catch the spectre in this manner. Perhaps she and Alice Dudeney were suffering from a shared illusion that only affected female writers, regardless of literary talent.

When there was still no sign of the woman, she sighed and turned round, making for the path leading through playing fields back up past the Victorian station building and the bridge over the rail tracks, then up a steep twitten with ancient brick-and-flint walls hiding a warren of gardens behind.

When she emerged opposite the cobbled street leading up to the castle, she saw Nessa coming out of Barbican House.

She was about to call out to her sister when she realised there was someone trailing behind her. Nessa was being followed by the very woman they were searching for.

She hung back in the shadows so as not to be seen. When both figures were far enough ahead not to notice her but still in sight, she crossed the road. Maintaining a safe distance, she continued like this until they were at the mound, where Nessa approached Mrs Dudeney's door and rang the bell. While she waited for an answer she glanced around her, but evidently did not see either her pursuer or her sister further behind. The door opened and Nessa went in. Ginny hung back to see what the woman would do next.

To her surprise, the moment the door was closed, the woman in black surged towards the gate leading to the top of the mound and by some unknown means opened it and disappeared through it.

Heart pounding, Ginny waited a moment or two before hurrying towards the house. Alice answered the door.

'No joy, then?' she asked, her face downcast. Nessa was standing just behind her.

Shaking her head wildly as there was no time to explain, Ginny stepped into the cool, dark hallway.

'Can we access the mound through the house?' she asked.

When Alice nodded, she grabbed her sister by the forearm, tugging her along.

'Show us the way. There's no time to explain.'

Opening her eyes wide, but asking no questions, Alice obliged and led them through the house to the back door, then out into the garden and from there up the path leading to the top of the hillock.

Running now, her sister and Mrs Dudeney in tow, she

was quite out of breath as they approached the summit. She really must cut back on the number of cigarettes she was smoking. One after each meal would suffice, with exceptions made for parties.

As soon as they reached the top, they saw her. The woman in black was lying on the turf.

Alice let out a horrible little gasp. Turning to see her stricken face, Ginny realised it must be bringing back the memory of finding Gideon's dead body in this same spot.

But she doubted the woman would have had time to die. Marching towards her, she stood over the prone body and prodded it with her walking stick.

'Ouch,' came an indignant voice, confirming the woman was very much alive and not at all a ghost.

Ginny saw now that the outfit worn by the crumpled figure on the ground was of a cheap black material cut to look more expensive than it was. The dress was curiously long, a throwback to an earlier epoch, recovered no doubt from a grandmother's trunk. The hat that accompanied it was equally anachronistic, fitted with a small netting veil that obscured the woman's face. As the mystery person pulled herself up, Ginny saw she was of a petite but curvaceous build.

'Reveal yourself,' she commanded.

The woman's small, plump body started to convulse in sobs as she sat on the ground.

'Leave her alone, Ginny,' said Nessa with one of her looks, pushing her sister out of the way and throwing herself down on to the ground beside the sobbing female.

'May I?' she asked, putting her arm round the woman.

The woman nodded and with one long, paint-stained finger, Nessa pushed back the veil.

Now it was Ginny's turn to gasp. The woman in black was none other than Betsy, her gardener's daughter.

For a few moments, they all sat or stood in silence, staring at one another, none of them knowing what to make of the situation.

It was Nessa who broke the silence.

'Can you explain yourself, my dear?' she asked in a motherly tone.

Tears still streaming down her cheeks, Betsy shook her head.

'I loved him,' was all she would say.

Ginny was about to say something, but Nessa put a finger to her lips.

'This is about Gideon?' she asked kindly.

Betsy nodded. 'We were in love. Even after the baby arrived and I married Danny. We met here several times. He even pressed a key for me so I could come up here to wait for him when no one was about. But I swear I had nothing to do with his death. I wouldn't have hurt a hair on his sweet head. I still can't believe he's gone. I keep thinking there's some way I can bring him back. This must be what it feels like to be a widow. I've been doing the only thing I can do, which is to put on my grandmother's mourning dress, which my mother kept in the attic, and come here to remember him at dusk. Sometimes, when I close my eyes, I think I can hear him whispering to me, feel him touch my arm like he used to do.'

Ginny looked at her sister and Mrs Dudeney, their expressions a mixture of pity and horror. Poor girl. What she was saying was complete madness, but also utterly believable. She had loved Gideon with all her heart, and in his own way it sounded as though he had been fond of her too. So much for pledging himself to Jasmine. Being engaged to be married hadn't been enough to pin him down.

Not for one moment did she believe Betsy had murdered Gideon. Her love seemed so innocent, so true. But what she'd just told them opened all sorts of other possibilities. If Gideon had a key cut for his lover – for one of his many lovers – that meant he probably had one himself. Access to the mound had not been as restricted as they or Gripe had previously imagined. Could Betsy's father have followed her and killed Gideon in a fury because the entitled young fellow was still leading his daughter astray? Or could Danny, jealous that his wife was in love with another man, have taken the key from her pocket and come here to meet his rival, then dashed his brains out?

For an instant, she found herself wishing she'd let things be, that she'd never insisted on pursuing this mystery of the woman in black, which seemed only to have released a series of darker imaginings. But she forced herself to shake off that feeling. This is what true detective work meant: confronting the blackness of the human soul, with all its strangeness and vulnerability. A writer's imagination could be a curse, but it also provided insights that the humdrum brain of a Chief Inspector Gripe could never understand.

42.

Vanessa

It was warm for October, almost too much so for the Pither stove, which she'd lit to heat her while she worked. Here in their studio was the place she felt closest to Duncan while he was away. They'd lived at Charleston for a decade, and nearly lost their tenancy, before she worked her magic and negotiated a longer lease. That had made them confident enough to build the studio as an extension to the old farmhouse, where the chicken run had once been. Even with north-facing windows, the room was filled with light, which they'd tempered by painting the walls an earthy brown. As with so much in the house, they'd decorated the fireplace she was working beside together. Duncan had painted the caryatids supporting the mantelpiece and the still lives above it; she had coloured the tiled surround in azure blue and yellow.

Duncan's easel stood empty, a reminder of his absence, in front of the antique fairground stand they'd picked up in Italy before the war. Was he painting now, she wondered? It wasn't like him to go for more than a day or two without picking up his brush. But the presence of his mother might be putting him off. Or the company of George could be proving too distracting.

She found herself unable to concentrate on the vase of asters and black-eyed Susans she was trying to paint. Instead, the soft light drew her out from her studio to the garden. There was something so wistful about this time of year. Crimson haws glistened in the autumn sun and the leaves on the trees were turning from green to gold and rust. But there was beauty in the decay, the silhouette of blackened seedheads, the joy of the final few roses defying the season. She decided to move her easel outside, to the top of the path, and attempt to paint what she saw, although no amount of artistry could capture the quiet splendour of the dying year.

Her reverie was broken by Angelica arriving with the post. Her daughter was slight for her age, with big dark eyes like those of her father. Sometimes she wondered if she should tell Angelica Duncan was really her father, even though it was easier for everyone to maintain she was the child of Nessa's estranged husband, Clive, the father of her two sons.

'There's a letter from France. It must be from Duncan. Open it and see if he's sent me some pictures,' said the child.

Whenever Duncan was away from Angelica, he would sketch little details from everyday life – a bird, the view from a window, a funny person he'd seen in the street – and send them to her, a way of keeping a connection between them. Their lives were so intertwined. Surely he wouldn't give all that up.

Nessa returned to the studio for the sharp knife she kept with her paints, then brought it back outside where she sat down upon the plain wooden chair she'd placed before her easel and used it to open the envelope. Three little pieces of paper fell out, which Angelica snatched up and clutched to her chest. She took them a little distance away to a low staddle stone, which she perched upon in an improbably elastic position to examine them in privacy. This gave Nessa the space to read Duncan's letter. He was usually a man of few words, so the fact that he'd managed to cover a whole page made her heart sink. Was this it, the communication that would inform her he was breaking away from her for good?

Dear Nessa,

Being away from you and from Charleston has given me the space I needed to gather my thoughts about everything that has happened recently. If I was difficult or distant before I left, please forgive me.

Bobby's death has shaken me even more than I realised. He was a young man for whom I felt responsible. It was I who invited him to stay in the country, and if he hadn't come he might still be alive today. In my darkest moments I believed it was some sort of divine retribution for my sins. But being here in France, away from it all, has made me realise it was no more than an unfortunate coincidence.

It's still as warm as midsummer in Sussex here in Cassis. The cicadas sing loudly in the undergrowth, and Mother and George and I are cooling down with the crisp white wine from the chateau.

George is quite extraordinary. I sensed that you didn't like him when you met him, but I hope over time you will come to appreciate him for the talented artist he is. He is becoming very dear to me and it would mean a lot for two of the people I love the most to become bosom friends.

Let's use this time apart to reflect on what it is we want from the future. Neither of us is young any more. Of course, there will always be Angelica, but perhaps you and I need to find a new way of being together.

Yours as always,
Duncan

She felt the words on the page as a body blow to her belly. Did that cold winter's day when she brought Angelica into the world, just as the world was celebrating peace, mean nothing to him? Had George replaced her in his affections as easily as that? She was used to playing second fiddle to his lovers, but this felt different somehow.

'What's the matter, Mummy?' asked her daughter who, having absorbed the pictures herself, was now coming over to show them to her mother.

'Look at this funny frog,' she added, thrusting one of the pieces of paper under her mother's eyes.

Nessa looked at the peculiar expression Duncan had given the amphibian in his sketch and couldn't help but smile at it. No, he would never abandon Angelica – she knew that. But as for her . . .

She drew the little girl close to her and rested her chin on the dark silken hair of her fragile head. She knew one thing after reading Duncan's letter. She was not going to give him up to George without a fight.

43.

Virginia

She dashed around the cottage moving items from one place to another, seeing how they looked in their new position, then changing her mind and putting them back again. Pinka followed her around with a look of confusion on her face as if to say, what's happening? What is this mad human being doing? What the spaniel didn't know was that Vita was coming and before her visits Ginny was always in a flutter, worrying how their humble abode would look to her aristocratic eyes.

As soon as her motor pulled up outside and Vita stepped out, cigarette dangling from her mouth, wearing the thick bloomers she preferred for driving, her hostess remembered how oblivious Vita was to her surroundings. For a moment, she wondered why Vita had left the car door open, then she realised she was waiting for Pippin to jump out and join her.

Pinka at her ankles barked with joy at the sight of her mother and the two dogs ran towards one another. After an initial tentative sniff, they were soon tumbling around together. Grizzle, who had come to see what all the fuss was about, wandered off again in a huff.

Ignoring them, Vita marched into the house, handed her gloves and coat to a disgruntled Nellie and threw herself down on to the most battered of the armchairs. After giving her daughter a thorough lick, Pippin came and settled at her owner's feet.

Leonard had made himself scarce, having long ago accepted the effect Vita had on his wife and the special relationship they enjoyed, which did not include him. The early intensity of their affair had passed, but Vita still had the ability to make Ginny feel like a schoolgirl. Fascinating rather than beautiful, with dark curls plastered to her high forehead, large Spanish eyes and a haughty nose, her gestures were quick and hypnotic as she waved her arms around, making the simple account of her journey from Kent to Sussex sound like the most interesting story ever told.

Even though it was only ten o'clock in the morning, Ginny felt she ought to offer Vita a drink, and showed her the selection of spirits they had on offer in the drawing-room cupboard.

'I'll take a Kummel,' she said, pointing to the bottle of liqueur flavoured with caraway, cumin and fennel seeds, which Leonard had brought back from a trip to Germany the previous year. Ginny poured them both a glass and they carried it out into the garden, where they sat on one of the old millstones in the sunshine, the dogs at their feet.

Vita reached out the hand that was not holding her drink and took Ginny's in her own, looking her directly in the eye.

'There's something you're not telling me,' she said.

'How do you mean?' said Ginny, pulling her hand away,

desiring Vita's touch, but at the same time feeling it to be too intense.

'There's something different about you since we last met, and I'm determined to get it out of you.'

Ginny hesitated, unsure how much to tell her about the murders.

'Nessa and I have been playing at being detectives.'

'Detectives? Sounds intriguing.'

'It's not really a game. Two young men of our acquaintance have been murdered.'

'Murdered?' Vita placed her glass down on the ground beside her a little too firmly.

'Yes, I'm afraid so. One of them was staying at Charleston with Nessa and Duncan. We have no confidence the police will get to the bottom of it, so we've been making investigations of our own.'

'And what have you discovered? Have you found out who the murderer is yet? Or murderers? I suppose there could be more than one.'

'If only it were that simple,' Ginny sighed. Picking one of the Mexican fleabane daisies out of a crack between the bricks and twirling it between finger and thumb, she told Vita about the arrests and consequent releases, about Jasmine and her flight to Paris, of the clay tablet and the possible connection with the black market. Finally, she told her how they'd caught and unveiled Betsy, and how heartbroken the poor girl still was over the death of her lover.

Vita listened in silence, occasionally taking large sips of the Kummel. By the time Ginny had finished her story, her glass was empty, and Ginny had to go back inside to fetch the bottle.

'It sounds to me as though you're too close to see what's really going on. You and Nessa are both intimately connected to the people and places involved. How can you possibly gain any proper perspective on it? You need to step back and find a way to look at things differently,' said Vita as Ginny refilled her glass.

'But how do we do that? It all feels like a horrible jumble in my brain, and I know Nessa feels the same.'

'I can't say for sure, except I know for myself being out in the garden always helps me to see things differently. Being with plants helps me to step back and gain perspective on the complicated world of people,' said Vita.

Pinka got up from where she had been lying and started barking. Ginny looked around to see what had disturbed her. There was someone in the churchyard, leaning over the wall and chatting to Leonard, who had got up from where he was bending over the flower bed weeding. From a distance, it took her a moment or two to work out that it was Harry Dryden.

'What on earth is he doing back in Rodmell?' she wondered.

'Who?' asked Vita.

Ginny realised she'd spoken her thoughts aloud.

'That young man who Leonard is talking to was Gideon Rivers's best friend, and is close to his fiancée, the beautiful Jasmine,' she explained in a whisper. 'Suspiciously close,' she added.

'Is he a suspect?' asked Vita.

'He was, until he was bashed over the head and left for dead at the castle. He was in hospital unconscious for a couple of days until he discharged himself and disappeared.'

290

'Left for dead, *but not killed*?' said Vita with meaningful inflection. 'Perhaps it was merely a tactic to divert attention from himself.'

'It could be, but he was in a pretty bad way,' said Ginny, sounding uncertain.

Vita jumped to her feet and took her elbow.

'Come on. Let's go and speak to the fellow and I'll let you know my opinion.'

Sighing, Ginny realised she had no choice in the matter, and followed Vita as she strode over to where the two men were talking. When they got there, she stood there expectantly until Leonard introduced them.

Harry looked paler and more tired than the last time Ginny had seen him. There was still a visible scar on his forehead from where he'd been struck, and there were worry lines engraved on his young brow.

'Mr Dryden, this is my wife's friend Vita Sackville-West. Vita, meet Harry Dryden. Harry, we all wondered what happened to you when you disappeared from your hospital bed.'

The young man looked at his feet. 'I'm afraid when I came to I was desperate to get away from Lewes, so I got out of bed, dressed and hopped on the first train back to London. When I came to my senses, I wrote to Mrs Rivers asking for her forgiveness and she asked me to come back. I felt I owed her that at least. She wanted me to stay with her at Hollybush House, but I'm staying at the White Hart. I didn't want to be too much of a burden on Mrs R. Plus, it reminds me horribly of Gid.'

Ginny studied his face. Did she detect guilt?

'She's asked me to come back to help her sort through

Gid's things. She's pressing me to take some of his stuff, and I don't want to offend her, but I don't really want it. Too painful a reminder, if you know what I mean?'

Leonard made a soothing noise.

'I'm so sorry to hear of your loss. Losing a friend is never easy, even harder when you're young,' said Vita. 'Tell me, Harry – may I call you Harry?'

He nodded.

'Who do you think did it?'

Harry looked taken aback and didn't answer for a moment or two.

'I'm sorry,' he said at last, shaking his head as if to rid himself of a thought. 'The truth is, I can't imagine anyone killing Gid.'

'He was popular, well-loved, is that it?' asked Vita, with the persistent manner of one who was not directly impacted by events.

'Ye-es,' said Harry, sounding less certain.

'Did he have enemies?' jumped in Vita, sensing a certain diffidence.

'More that he was too well-loved, if you know what I mean?'

Vita said nothing, but looked at him with those dark Spanish eyes, making it clear she expected him to expand on what he'd just said.

And what Vita expected, Vita got, thought Ginny, who had often been on the receiving end of that same gaze.

'Gid was good at making people fall in love with him. He made a habit of it. Sometimes I think it was all just a big game for him. He enjoyed watching people become besotted with him and then stringing them along. It was

292

quite cruel. He couldn't see that he was toying with people's feelings, real emotions, the stuff of life. And death as it turned out. That was why I was so relieved when he met Jasmine. At last, he seemed to have found someone who was his equal, who could stand up to him. I don't mean she's a heartbreaker; she's not at all like that – she's a very serious person. But she was in a different class to his other lovers. He recognised that, which is why he asked her to marry him so quickly.'

'He didn't completely give up playing the field, though,' said Ginny, speaking before she thought, the memory of Betsy and her midnight meetings with Gideon still fresh in her mind.

'What do you mean?' asked Harry, turning to her, his voice sharp, almost angry.

'I don't want to pry into other people's business, but I have reason to believe he was still carrying on romantic assignations outside of his engagement to Jasmine,' she said, trying to think of the best way to put it without giving too much away.

Harry put a hand to his forehead and swept back his hair.

'I really thought Gid had changed this time, that he was serious about being faithful to Jasmine. Do you think that had something to do with the reason he was killed?'

'Not directly, but it does rather complicate matters,' said Ginny.

'Have you told the police?' asked Harry.

Ginny snorted. 'Chief Inspector Gripe doesn't strike me as a man who understands the inner workings of the human heart,' she said.

'Nevertheless, if you have suspicions, you have a duty to

report them, otherwise you could be accused of withholding evidence,' said Vita.

Pinka let out a loud woof, indignant at being ignored. Her mother Pippin joined her.

'I think these two hounds could do with a long walk across the Downs. How about it, Ginny? It's what I came for, after all,' said Vita.

Feeling a spark of excitement at the thought of an hour or two alone, just them and the dogs, Ginny nodded.

'I'll go and fetch Pinka's lead,' she said.

'Good day, Mr Dryden. How nice to meet you and I hope you are a comfort to poor Mrs Rivers,' said Vita, extending a languid hand.

As they left Harry behind and walked back down the garden towards the house to ready themselves for a hike, Ginny realised he'd managed to avoid answering Vita. Harry Dryden had entirely dodged the question about who he thought had murdered his best friend.

44.

Vanessa

Grace came out into the garden still wearing her apron as if she'd been interrupted in the middle of working in the kitchen. She was holding a folded white piece of paper in her hand.

'This just came for you, Mrs Bell. A young boy on a bicycle arrived, quite out of breath he was, said he was under strict instructions to get it to you by lunchtime. He's waiting to be paid.'

Glancing at her watch, Nessa saw it was already coming up to midday. She unfolded the paper and took her reading glasses from the front pocket of her smock coat. Although she didn't immediately recognise the handwriting, it only took her a line or two to realise it came from Stanley Briggs.

Dear Mrs Bell,

I hope you are recovered from the unfortunate episode at my house. Once again, I must apologise for any misunderstanding.

The reason I'm getting in touch with such haste is that there's been an important development concerning the clay tablet found on Brack Mound. A discovery that may shed some light on the recent terrible events. I know you and your sister have shown an interest in helping to solve these crimes and would like to take the opportunity to convey this information to you in person. I would be grateful if you would meet me at five o'clock this evening on top of Brack Mound. Bring Mrs Woolf with you and I will explain all.

Yours sincerely,
Stanley Briggs Esq.

Laying the piece of paper down on her lap, she looked up to see Grace watching her expectantly. She felt about in her pocket, but found no change there.

'I'll go and see if I have any money in my study,' she said to Grace, who raised her eyebrows.

'The boy's waiting at the front of the house,' she said.

Nessa headed round to the front door, where the messenger boy had propped his bicycle up against the wall and was leaning next to it, whistling a tune.

'Can you deliver a message to my sister in Rodmell? I'll pay you extra,' she asked.

At the prospect of more money, the boy's eyes lit up and he nodded enthusiastically.

'Wait here while I go and write her a note,' she said.

She went inside to the study and sat down at the desk. Taking a sheet from her writing pad, and dipping her fountain pen in the inkwell, she composed a message.

Ginny,

Stanley Briggs has asked us to meet him on Brack Mound at five o'clock this evening. No time to explain further, but he will shed light on the tablet, and possibly the murders too.

See you then,

Nessa

She found her purse in the desk drawer and took it with the note back outside to where the boy was leaning over the water to inspect the carp in the pond, which had come to the surface and were opening their mouths in expectation of food. Opening the purse, she fetched out a few pennies and counted them into his outstretched hand, alongside the note.

'Take this to Mrs Woolf at Monk's House and cycle as fast as you can,' she instructed.

Then she went back inside to the study to put away the writing pad, which she'd left out in her haste. Above the little bookshelf, filled with an eclectic mix of volumes gathered by her and Duncan, together with some left behind by their many visitors, hung a charcoal portrait of her late mother. How she missed her soft touch, her gentle understanding eyes. She could have done with her unassuming wisdom right now. What would she make of her daughters, grown women with lives and families of their own, investigating murders as if they were detectives in a paperback novel? She doubted Julia Stephens would approve, and yet sometimes, events conspire to push one outside one's usual sphere. The world was changing in ways in which her Victorian parents could not even have conceived.

Whatever it was that Briggs had to tell her and Ginny, she

hoped it wouldn't take too long, and that it would bring a new perspective that might allow them to move on, because, placid as she usually prided herself on being, this whole affair was starting to take a toll on her nerves.

There were still a few hours to go before it was time for them to meet Briggs, however, and, unable to settle to anything, she found herself drawn to the pottery yard. She hadn't been there since the night they'd discovered Bobby's body. The police had cordoned it off for days while they combed it for evidence, but they had found nothing and now they were gone.

Making her way along the passageway between outbuildings that led to the yard, Nessa felt her pulse quicken at the memory of the last dreadful time she'd been there. But when she emerged into the little walled garden it was empty, and nothing remained to suggest what had happened there except some scuff marks on the gravel. She kicked at these aimlessly, feeling angry at the intrusion into her idyll, when her toe encountered something shiny. Bending down to pick it up, she saw it was a needle. What a strange thing to find out here. She kept her sewing kit indoors, or if she did take it out to do some mending on a sunny day she might place it on a basket chair in the main walled garden, but never here in Duncan's domain. Putting it in her pocket, she decided there must be some reasonable explanation. Then again, nothing about this case seemed to be making sense.

45.

Virginia

There's nothing quite so exhilarating as marching over the Downs on a crisp autumn day, clouds fleeting through the sharp blue sky overhead, casting their shadows on the bright green turf. Pinka and Pippin ran ahead, sniffing the ground, rejoicing in being alive in their doggy way. She and Vita talked and talked, of mutual acquaintances, of the literary world, and about the lecture she was about to give in Cambridge arguing that women need a space in which to work that gave them both physical and mental freedom.

By the time they had walked the loop up to Kingston Ridge and back round via Swanborough, taking two and a half hours in total, Ginny had almost completely forgotten about the murders. Her mind was feeling as free as the skylarks that hovered above the fields singing their sweet song. They must be preparing to migrate soon.

As they turned into the village, however, they were met by the sight of Mrs Rivers still wearing full mourning, standing outside the post office.

'Good morning, Mrs Woolf. I was just sending a letter

to my solicitor, tidying up my affairs now that I have no living direct heir,' she said in a matter-of-fact tone, tinged with great sadness.

Ginny introduced her to Vita and the two women politely said hello. She wouldn't have dreamed of asking her who she was leaving her not-inconsiderable wealth to, but to her surprise the older woman volunteered the information.

'I'm settling my estate on Harry Dryden and giving him a sizeable advance. At last, he will be able to get away from that monster of a father of his. At least something good will come out of this whole dreadful affair and I feel sure Gideon would have approved.'

So that was why Harry was still hanging around. Men have killed for much less, she thought, but how could he have known how Mrs Rivers would choose to dispose of her wealth in this way?

'I saw Harry this morning in the churchyard,' was all she said.

'Yes, he was visiting Gideon's grave. He's such a devoted friend. I feel sure that when I'm gone I'll be leaving my son's memory in the best of hands. He's brought Jasmine with him too, the dear sweet girl. They've both been so badly affected by everything.'

'I didn't see her with him,' said Ginny.

'No, I believe she went into Lewes, to the castle to meet Mr Briggs. Something to do with her archaeological studies. Such a serious young woman. I can understand now what my son saw in her.'

They bade Mrs Rivers farewell and made their way back to Monk's House.

As they walked through the front door and released the hounds from their leashes, Leonard called from the kitchen.

'Ginny, a note arrived for you from Nessa,' he said. She went through and he handed her a slip of paper bearing her name. She opened it and scanned the brief message.

'Briggs wants to meet me and Nessa in Lewes this evening,' she said.

She shivered involuntarily. She had a strong feeling something wasn't right. But what could she do except meet them at the appointed time?

She didn't have much appetite for the lunch Nellie had prepared. Vita left soon afterwards, catching her up in a strong embrace of tweed and cigar smoke. She got into her motor, Pippin on the seat beside her and tooted the horn. She started the engine, but just before she drove away, she wound down the window and handed a folded bundle to Ginny.

'I almost forgot – I brought you this magazine. Harold brought it back from America, but I don't have much use for Hollywood gossip.'

Ginny looked suspiciously at the magazine, featuring some starlet or other on the cover. It wasn't her usual kind of read, but it might prove a pleasantly mindless distraction, so she accepted it, hugging Vita goodbye.

Exhausted after their walk, she took herself off to bed, mindful that it did her no good to get overtired. She didn't set an alarm, sure she would only sleep for an hour or two, but when she awoke, still in the cloying grip of her dreams, she slowly became aware the sun was sinking in the sky outside her bedroom window, silhouetting the substantial spire of Saint Peter's Church.

Unwilling to rouse herself just yet, she leaned over to where she had placed the magazine Vita gave her on the bedside cabinet. She propped herself up on her pillows, and idly flicked through the articles inside. One caught her eye, and she was shaken awake in an instant. Without hesitation, she swung her feet out of bed and made her way down the stairs, having to steady herself on the banister as her legs had not yet adjusted to the impatient speed of her mind.

'Leonard, you must drive me into Lewes straight away,' she called out, and was relieved to see he was sitting at his desk. He looked up.

'Ginny, what is it? Are you feeling all right?'

'It's Nessa. We must get to her as quickly as possible. I fear she might be in danger.'

46.

Vanessa

She told Grace where she was going and asked her to put Angelica to bed. Kissing her daughter goodbye, she got into the motor car just after four o'clock and set off down the bumpy farm track that led to the Lewes Road. She got stuck behind a tractor, and it took her about forty minutes to reach the town, where she drove up to the High Street and parked illegally right outside the castle.

The door to Barbican House was ajar and the hallway lit up within. She pushed it fully open and found Miss Bramble seated at the desk in the entrance hall, still wearing the unflattering brown felt hat. Did she ever take it off?

'Hello, I'm looking for Mr Briggs. Is he around?' Nessa asked.

Miss Bramble looked up, a little startled, and peered at her through her thick-rimmed spectacles, as if trying to remember who she was.

'Oh, Mrs Bell, yes, Mr Briggs mentioned you were coming. He's up at the dig. Are you all right to find your own way up there? The gate up on to Brack Mound should be open. I think there was something he wanted to show you.'

What could it be? Nessa wondered. Well, there was only one way to find out. Thanking Miss Bramble, she turned round and headed back out of the museum door.

'Watch out for the thorns,' Miss Bramble called after her.

She made her way up the winding cobbled lane that led under the double-arched gateway. There was no sign of Mrs Dudeney as she passed by her bow window, but the wooden gate adjacent to her property was open, as Miss Bramble had predicted. Nessa made her way through it, finding herself at the bottom of the steep grassy path up to the summit. The sound of laughter came from the Lewes Arms public house just on the other side of the fence surrounding the bottom of the mound, and for a moment she wished she were there instead, enjoying a nice cool pint of beer.

But there was nothing for it. She'd come here to find out what Mr Briggs had to say and so she must press on to the top of the hill. It wasn't quite five yet, according to her watch, and so she took her time walking up. How many ancient feet had trodden this same path? Among them those of the crusading knight who had died in the Holy Land, but whose treasures had made their way back, to be concealed here in a deep well on top of a green English hill.

As she reached the top, she saw a figure clad in white, with a straw boater on their head, tied with a yellow band.

'Mr Briggs,' she called out, but as the figure turned towards her she saw that it wasn't the chief archaeologist, whom she'd been expecting, but someone quite different altogether. The face looking back at her from beneath the wide brim of the hat was Jasmine's. From the expression on her face, the surprise was mutual.

'Miss Zain al-Din, I have an appointment to meet Mr Briggs. I thought he was here,' she said.

Jasmine drew her dark glossy brows closer together.

'But I too have an appointment with Monsieur Briggs. He must have brought us both here for a reason.'

There was a note in her voice that didn't ring quite true, and a thought occurred to Nessa that made her pulse quicken. Had Jasmine lured her here under false pretences? Did she mean to do her harm? She must keep her talking until Ginny got here – that was her only hope.

'When did you return from Paris?' she asked, as if making polite conversation.

Jasmine looked annoyed. 'What? Oh, a couple of days ago. I received a letter from Mr Briggs saying it was imperative I return to Lewes to speak with him. He said it had to do with the tablet, that he might be able to arrange for a loan to the exhibition at the Louvre, which is all I've ever wanted. I don't understand, though, why he's invited you here at the same time. Do you have an interest in the tablet too?'

Nessa nodded. 'We, that is my sister and I, wonder if it might shed any light on the murders,' she said. Then she shivered. Perhaps Jasmine knew that already.

It was a little past five, and the sun was sinking. The light was fading fast, and around the edge of the mound, behind where Jasmine was standing, a thicket of overgrown bushes was casting a deep shadow. Nessa thought she saw a movement in the bushes, but when she looked again it was gone. It must just have been some nocturnal animal, frightened away when it detected the presence of humans.

'Where are you staying?' she asked Jasmine, scrabbling around for ways to keep her talking.

'At the White Hart, with Harry,' the other woman replied.

'Is he . . .? Are you . . .?'

Jasmine let out a hollow laugh. 'Why yes. Does that shock you? I know it seems rather soon after Gideon's death, but it just feels right, as if we've always known one another. Life with Gid was thrilling, but after everything that's happened I've realised what I want in a marriage is something more stable. Harry makes me feel safe. We will announce our engagement after a decent period of mourning has passed.'

'In that case, I suppose congratulations are in order,' said Nessa, still playing for time.

'Harry is helping me to secure the tablet,' Jasmine continued. 'He knows how important it is to me that it features in the Louvre exhibition. The chief curator there has promised me I can write the accompanying text, and it will make my name in the world of archaeology. It's about time a woman gave all those men a run for their money, don't you think?'

'Why is the tablet of such great importance, anyway?' asked Nessa, determined to keep the conversation going for as long as possible.

Jasmine sighed. 'Because of what it signifies. A link between East and West going back many hundreds of years, perhaps millennia. Your English gentlemen like to think they invented civilisation, but really it was my ancestors in the fertile basin of the Middle East who built the first cities when the West was still full of forest-dwelling barbarians. The exhibition at the Louvre will show that the true treasure of the Crusades was not bringing the word of Jesus Christ to the heathens, but learning spiritual disciplines in the East, both Christian and Muslim, which they then brought back to the . . .'

Without warning, Jasmine stopped speaking and sank to the ground. Nessa was frozen for a moment in confusion. Had she fainted? It wasn't a particularly warm evening; in fact, she was starting to wish she'd worn a coat as well as a cardigan. It was only as she stepped towards the figure now lying on the turf that she realised they were not alone. There was someone else with them on top of the mound, someone who right now was concealed in the shadows of the bushes.

She turned to run back down the path she'd come up, not pausing to look behind her. Even when she heard footsteps advancing on her, she didn't dare look back to see who was following. There was a part of her that didn't want to know. She just wanted to get away from that place as fast as she could.

But she was too slow. Whoever it was, they were quickly gaining upon her. A hand reached out and grabbed her arm, and she tried to shake it off. But in the half-light, she couldn't see where she was going properly. She stumbled over a tree root and before she knew it she'd lost her balance, and only just managed to put her hands out in front of her to break her fall. As she hit the ground, she remembered Miss Bramble's warning and thought she must have fallen headfirst into a thornbush. The last thing she remembered was a sharp pricking sensation, and then everything went black.

47.

Virginia

'Damnation,' muttered Leonard under his breath as he put his foot on the accelerator and nothing happened. He tried revving the engine again and the motor jolted forward and then came to a stop. This was not the time to have trouble with a hill start.

Ginny closed her eyes and took a deep breath.

'I'll get out here and walk,' she said, opening them again. It seemed like the only solution, and she had to find a way to get to Nessa before it was too late. The decision worked like a spell, as at that precise moment, Leonard tried the engine again and this time it roared into life and he shot up the hill towards the crossroads, then swung the car suddenly and a little violently round to the right. Fortunately, at that time of the evening, they had the road to themselves, although they narrowly avoided knocking an old fellow off his bicycle.

Ginny drummed her bony fingers impatiently on the door handle, willing Leonard to drive faster, aware that every moment might count. As they came into the High Street and approached the castle, she saw Nessa's car parked badly in front of it and her stomach did a somersault. Was she too late?

'Stop here and let me out,' she said to Leonard. The moment he drew to a halt, she flung the door open and leaped from the car. A van behind them hooted impatiently.

Leonard wound down the window.

'You go ahead, and I'll find somewhere to park legally,' he called after her. Unlike Nessa he was a stickler for the rules, even in the midst of a crisis.

She tried the door of Barbican House, but it was locked and there were no lights on inside the building. The iron gate leading to the castle was also locked. There was only one place where they could be. Brack Mound.

As she ran up the hill, ignoring her falling-down stocking, she saw a light on in Mrs Dudeney's house. For a second, she thought to ignore it, then she decided she didn't know what she would find up there and could do with some assistance. She rang the bell and knocked on the door insistently until a maid in a brown dress and a white starched apron answered it.

'Is Mrs Dudeney in?' she asked.

'Who should I say is calling, ma'am?'

Ginny didn't have time for formalities. She stepped into the hall and called out, 'Mrs Dudeney, are you there? It's Virginia Woolf. Come quickly and bring a weapon if you have one.'

The door to the drawing room burst open and Alice Dudeney stood there in a housecoat and slippers, her hair in curlers, a pen in her hand, as if she'd been in mid-flow writing. But she didn't appear to care a jot for her strange appearance.

'Here, you take this walking stick, and I'll bring Ernest's rifle,' she said, handing Ginny a polished wooden walking stick with a heavy metal handle that looked as though it could inflict some serious injury.

'Where are we going?' Alice asked, as if she'd been waiting in all evening just on the off-chance of adventure.

'To the mound. I think my sister is in danger.'

'Come on – this way through the house,' said Alice, leading the way in a rapid charge through the kitchen and out of the back door. Ginny followed her as she ran up the path leading from her garden to the top of the hillock.

As they reached the summit, Ginny's heart sank. They were too late. Although it was almost pitch dark now, she could see not one but two bodies lying on the ground. Both were wearing light-coloured outfits, which shone in the dusk. She recognised Nessa and the other figure looked like Jasmine. There didn't appear to be anyone else around. Whoever had done this must have fled already.

She bent down over her sister, willing her to be alive. To her great relief, when she pressed her fingers to her wrist, she could feel a faint pulse, although she couldn't rouse her.

But Alice saw something Nessa hadn't. She put the rifle she was carrying to her shoulder, cocked the latch and aimed it into the darkness. Then she spoke, in a cool, commanding tone, that even Ginny would have defied anyone to disobey.

'Drop the needle and put your hands over your head,' she ordered. Turning to Ginny, she added, 'It looks as though your suspicions were correct.'

A figure stepped out of the dark undergrowth into a shaft of moonlight. Gone was her usual meek demeanour, and instead she stood there, proud and defiant.

'Miss Bramble, I thought we might find you here,' said Ginny. Turning to Alice, she added: 'You stay here and guard her while I go to the police station to fetch help.'

Ginny didn't like to leave Alice alone, but one of them had to go for assistance, and she didn't have the first clue how to handle a rifle. As quickly as she could in the darkness, she made her way back down the mound, trying to remember the way. The wooden gate leading on to the street was open, and she thought that must be how the others had got up here. Luckily, she didn't have far to go as the police station was just round the corner. She pushed the door open to find Sergeant Hamsey sitting behind a desk.

'Come quickly! We've found out who killed Gideon Rivers, and Mrs Dudeney is holding her at rifle point on top of the mound,' she said, her words tumbling out in a torrent.

Sergeant Hamsey looked at her and narrowed his eyes as though she were mad.

'I'm sorry, ma'am . . . have you been drinking?' he asked.

'You impertinent young fool, I most certainly have not. Get Chief Inspector Gripe on the telephone right now. I'll explain everything to him, then come with me. We need some backup and quickly.'

The young policeman hesitated, but Ginny marched up to his desk and stood over him, until he realised he had no choice in the matter and did as she instructed. Picking up the telephone, he dialled a number, then passed her the handset.

'You'd better explain, ma'am,' he said.

'Hello, Hamsey, is that you?' came a muffled voice on the other end of the line.

'Chief Inspector, it's Mrs Woolf. There isn't time to

311

explain, but suffice to say that Mrs Dudeney and I have apprehended the killer. She's up on the mound now, guarding the suspect with her husband's rifle, but I don't like to leave her alone for too long. Can you tell Sergeant Hamsey to accompany me now, then meet us up at the mound as soon as you can get here? Oh, and call a doctor too while you're at it. There are two other women up there who have been attacked, including my sister, and there's no way of telling how badly hurt they are.'

She passed the handset back to Sergeant Hamsey.

'No, I don't think the lady has been drinking, sir. I can't smell anything on her breath. Should I go with her, sir?'

The reply was clearly in the affirmative, as he replaced the handset, then started to put on the jacket hanging on the back of his chair.

'The chief says I'm to accompany you and he'll meet us there. You lead the way,' he said.

With the sergeant trailing behind her, she moved as fast as she could back in the direction of the mound. As they approached the gate, they saw Leonard coming from the other direction.

'Nessa is hurt, and I've left Mrs Dudeney alone with the killer,' she told him. His eyes almost popped out of his head, but he didn't say anything, just followed her and the sergeant as they made their way to the top of the mound.

But when they got there Ginny's heart sunk. There was no sign of Miss Bramble, but now there were not two but three bodies lying prostrate on the ground. Somehow, she'd managed to get away.

They heard a load groan coming from the direction of one of the bodies. Ginny rushed over to find Mrs Dudeney, with blood dripping from the side of her face. She opened her eyes and reached out a hand to clutch Ginny's arm.

'She's got the rifle,' she said, before closing her eyes and letting her hand fall back down to the ground.

48.

Vanessa

Voices woke her from the deepest sleep she'd enjoyed for some time. Her limbs were heavy, and she could hardly be bothered to open her eyes. It would be the easiest thing in the world to drift back into unconsciousness. But she had a nagging sensation she needed to wake up. There was something she must do, although she couldn't think what it might be. She tried opening her eyes, but when she did all she could see was the black night sky.

Where was she? It felt as though she were outside, but surely that couldn't be. She must be in bed. Whatever was underneath her didn't feel like a mattress, however. It felt distinctly like the cold earth. How strange. Perhaps it was part of her dream.

The voices didn't go away, though – they just grew louder. She forced herself to open her eyes fully and tried to turn her head, although her neck felt like cotton wool. She was sure she could hear Ginny, and when she craned to look, there was her sister, standing above her, looking down. She tried to form words, but nothing came out of her mouth. Ginny spoke for her.

'Nessa, you're alive. Thank God. No, don't try to speak. A doctor will be here soon to examine you. There's plenty of time to tell us what happened. Leonard, take off your jacket and we'll put it under Nessa's head as a pillow.'

A second face loomed out of the darkness, and she saw it was her brother-in-law, who had stripped down to his shirt sleeves despite the chill night air. He rolled up his jacket, crouched down and placed it ever so gently beneath her, lifting her head with his soft hands. Leonard always had made an excellent nurse, she thought, smiling to herself. Whatever had sent her to sleep was still seeping through her veins and it wasn't an unpleasant sensation.

She managed to turn her head now, and the events of the evening slowly came back to her. A little way off, she saw Jasmine, also lying on the ground, but thankfully it looked as if she too was still alive and was being tended to by a young policeman.

'Hello,' came a call from below, and another voice joined the conversation. She recognised it as Gripe's.

'Goodness gracious, Mrs Woolf, what's being going on here? It looks like a battlefield with all these bodies. I thought you said you'd apprehended the suspect,' said the chief inspector. Just behind him was a man in a black coat and trilby with a stethoscope round his neck.

'We had, but while I was fetching help the suspect managed to overpower Mrs Dudeney and get away. Doctor, it's good to see you. You have three patients to attend to, I'm sorry to say. Two of them appear to have been drugged, but are coming round now, and the third has been hit over the head with a rifle. Mrs Dudeney's face is rather a mess, so you'd better see to her first and we'll keep the other two warm.'

Ginny had taken off her own coat and laid it over her sister, while Sergeant Hamsey had placed his jacket over Jasmine and was holding her in his lap with great tenderness. Beauty in distress had that effect on young men.

Chief Inspector Gripe took out his notebook and a pencil.

'You'd better tell me everything that's happened, from the beginning,' he began, but Ginny shooed him away.

'This is no time for taking notes. There's a killer out there and if you're not quick she's going to get away.'

'She?'

'Yes – Miss Bramble. There's no time to explain. Come on, I've got a good idea where she might be. Leonard, can you help the good doctor to look after Nessa for me? All the victims are being attended to, Chief Inspector, so you and I can pursue her. Follow me.'

Now it was Nessa's turn to worry about her sister. She tried to cry out, to stop her from going, but it was no use. Her mouth wouldn't form the words, and she suspected Ginny wouldn't listen to her anyway. Once she'd set her mind on something, she could be very determined. They would just have to hope Gripe wasn't quite as useless as he appeared, and that together with Ginny he would catch the killer.

49.

Virginia

'Where are we going, Mrs Woolf? This is all rather uncon-ventional,' puffed Chief Inspector Gripe as he followed her towards the castle ruins. The heels of her leather shoes click-clacked as she walked as quickly as was safe to do so over the cobblestones.

'Murder is not conventional,' she said impatiently. 'Come on – this way.'

There were easily more than a hundred steps leading up to the Norman keep, but she kept the pace up, ignoring Gripe's increasingly rasping breath.

'Do you carry a weapon, by the way?' she asked. 'It might prove necessary.'

She turned round, pausing for a moment, and seemingly glad of the respite the chief inspector stopped and opened his jacket to reveal the holster of a pistol in his inside pocket.

'I don't carry it as a matter of course, but the missus made me take it when she heard I was being called out in pursuit of a murder suspect,' he replied.

They pressed on and up, until finally they came to a

grassy plateau surrounded by a waist-high wall. Stopping here briefly, they looked out over the twinkling lights of the town, realising just how high up they were. There was no sign they had any company.

'Are you sure about this?' Gripe asked, but Ginny didn't reply. This was not the moment for doubts. This was the time for action. She led him into the ruined castle keep, where she remembered from a previous visit there was a steeply winding staircase leading up to the top. If there was someone up there, they would be able to hear them coming, as there was no way to ascend quietly, but that was a risk they would just have to take. The first two flights led them to rooms of diminishing size with bare wooden floorboards, but still they climbed. Only as she sensed they were at last reaching the top, did she slow down.

'You go first, and be prepared to shoot, if necessary,' she hissed.

The chief inspector took the pistol from the inside of his jacket and released the safety catch.

As they emerged from the top of the narrow spiral stairs on to the open roof of the castle keep, they saw a figure balanced precariously on the stone parapet. It was Miss Bramble, but not as they knew her. Gone was the dreadful brown hat and the mousy hair, and in the moonlight, her head gleamed gold. Gone too were the thick spectacles, and Ginny could see now that, far from being a dowdy assistant, she was a very beautiful woman, with large eyes that in the light of day must have been a dazzling blue.

She'd thrown off the shapeless woollen coat she usually wore to reveal an hourglass figure in a hugging green dress. Her sensible shoes had been kicked off and she was standing barefoot on the ancient flintstones, poised to jump. Over one shoulder was slung Ernest Dudeney's rifle. When she saw them, she raised it to eye level, causing her to teeter precariously.

'Don't come any closer or, I warn you, I'll shoot,' she said in a rich, husky tone quite unlike Miss Bramble's high-pitched voice.

When Gripe lowered his pistol and held up his hands in a gesture of peace, Miss Bramble's mouth opened in a ghastly smile revealing perfect white teeth. She threw back her head, tossing her golden hair behind her, and laughed. In that moment, Ginny saw she was quite crazed.

This didn't faze her. Madness was something with which she was perfectly familiar. Like the woman now standing before them, she knew what it was to present one face to the world, while troubled emotions seethed beneath the surface. Early on in her marriage to Leonard, she'd suffered a total breakdown. Although she now managed to present an external image of success, insanity lurked like a shadow over her shoulder.

'I'll keep her talking – you grab her,' she whispered to Gripe. He nodded, and to her surprise the middle-aged detective disappeared and in his place was a lithe, efficient operator, revealing at last how he'd managed to ascend through the ranks of the police force.

'Don't do anything stupid, Miss Bramble, or should I say Marguerite Muir,' Ginny said to the woman. 'It's a long way down, but, believe me, there's no guarantee you would die instantly. It could be a slow, painful death, and you would never get the chance to present your side of the story. Don't you want to tell the world why you did it? You do crave an

319

audience, after all, don't you? That's why it hurt so much when Gideon told you he didn't love you any more, that he was going to marry Jasmine instead. You couldn't bear the thought that the world would pity you. If you couldn't have him, you were damned if someone else was going to.'

Marguerite Muir's icy blue eyes flashed with anger. She spoke in the seductive transatlantic tones that had made her so famous in the movies.

'You don't know anything about me. Everyone thinks they know who I am, that they can have a part of it, but no one knows the real me.'

'Try me,' said Ginny. 'I know what it is to be in the grip of emotions so unbearable you feel you just can't go on, and to do so while in the public eye.'

Marguerite looked straight at her and could see she was telling the truth. In one respect, they were kindred souls. They both knew what it was to be driven to the brink. But there was an unbridgeable divide between them. However tortured she felt herself, Ginny would never dream of inflicting pain on others.

Lowering the rifle, Marguerite let out a theatrical sob, but real tears were trickling down her porcelain features.

'I loved Gideon, I truly did. That's why I followed him here in disguise. I even managed to fool him for long enough to lure him to meet me at the top of Brack Mound. He still believed I was Briggs's dowdy secretary, a part I played to perfection, if I say so myself. It's amazing how blind men can be when you leave your face unpainted and wear a coat that covers up your figure. Only once we were alone did I reveal who I really was. I begged him to give her up and come back to me. The newspapers would have had a field day – the golden couple back together again. He was surprised at my ingenuity, even suggested I'd gone mad.' She flared her nostrils in indignation at the thought. Ginny could not have agreed more with the poor dead Gideon Rivers.

'But he refused, the fool. He said Jasmine understood him in a way I never would, that he could truly be himself with her, be free. That was his mistake. No one gets to treat me like that. It's I, Marguerite Muir, who spurn lovers, not the other way round. So, you see, he had to die. He took everything from me. My pride, my reputation, my career. How could I carry on acting in films when my heart was so badly broken I couldn't even get out of bed? I injected him with a drug to render him powerless and then I destroyed that beautiful face I'd once loved so much, with his very own trowel. He deserved every blow for the way he destroyed me.'

She spat out these last words, then turned to look over her shoulder at the drop, shuddered briefly and closed her eyes, resigned to her fate, her decision made. Then she opened them again and turned back to face Ginny. The rifle was still slung over her shoulder, but she seemed to have forgotten about it.

'You're right about one thing, though. I'm glad of an audience. I knew you would follow me up here, Mrs Woolf. We clever women understand one another, don't we? And now you can witness my final act. Perhaps you will even write about it and immortalise me.'

She drew in a deep breath, as if she were about to deliver the performance of a lifetime, then took a step backwards.

Ginny let out a cry of horror as Marguerite's beautiful

body started to fall into the nothingness below. But neither woman had noticed that, while they'd been speaking, the chief inspector had advanced gradually closer round the edge of the open rooftop.

'There'll be no immortalising anyone, miss,' came the gruff voice of Chief Inspector Gripe.

'Ouch, get off me,' screamed Marguerite, trying to kick him away, but the chief inspector had gripped her firmly by the ankle and as she attempted to fling herself off the edge with all the force of her lithe body, he braced himself against the parapet and yanked her back down to the roof, removing the rifle as he did so in one deft movement.

'Come and give me a hand, Mrs Woolf,' he said. Ginny hurried over and took Marguerite's other arm. She was pleased to find she had a surprisingly strong grip. Years of writing had strengthened the muscles in her hand. It took all the power they had to restrain the actress. She was writhing around and struggling like a wild animal caught in a trap, gnashing her perfect teeth as if she would have liked to take a chunk out of them if she got the chance.

Glancing over the parapet, Ginny saw several burly young men bounding up the steps towards the keep. Sergeant Hamsey must have called for reinforcements. She and the chief inspector held on to the young woman until the others reached them. When the fresh replacements arrived, Marguerite struggled for a bit, but she soon gave up and slumped to the ground, looking listlessly ahead, and awaiting her fate.

'How did you know she would come up here?' Gripe asked Ginny once the junior policemen had arrived and taken over.

'She's an actress – she was bound to be planning a dramatic exit. We writers may not be good for much, but we have a pretty good understanding of human nature,' Ginny replied.

50.

Vanessa

Half an hour later, they were all seated in Mrs Dudeney's drawing room, a comfortable if old-fashioned place with fine engravings hanging on the sepia walls. Nessa was stretched out on one sofa, Alice on another. The others perched on whatever seats were available.

Nessa was still feeling dozy and not entirely sure how she'd got here. The door opened and Chief Inspector Gripe entered the room, followed by Stanley Briggs. That was it – she'd come to Lewes to meet Briggs, but he hadn't been there. Miss Bramble had told her to meet him up on the mound, but when she'd got there, she'd found Jasmine waiting for him too.

It started slowly coming back to her, how she'd suspected Jasmine was the killer, and had been trying to keep her talking until Ginny arrived. But then Jasmine had collapsed, and there had been something, some*one*, in the shadows. Looking around the room, she saw Jasmine curled up in an armchair, with a blanket over her, looking as sleepy as Nessa felt. So, she couldn't be the killer, after all.

Ginny came over with a glass of brandy. 'Sit up and drink this, Nessa. It will help to revive you.'

She was used to being the one looking after her younger sister, but she did as she was told, glad of someone giving her instructions, as her brain felt too fuzzy to know what to do herself. Bringing the glass to her lips, she took a sip and there was a warm, burning sensation in the back of her throat.

Briggs found himself a seat on a wooden stool by the window, but Gripe remained standing. He cleared his throat and puffed his chest out.

'Now we've got everyone gathered here together, this is a good opportunity to go over the events of this evening. We will need to take statements from you all later, but it would be useful to hear what you all have to say first. Let me re-assure you to start with that Marguerite Muir, whom you all know better as Edith Bramble, is safely in custody. Sergeant Hamsey is watching over her to make sure she doesn't do herself any further harm, having attempted to fling herself from the parapet of the castle earlier tonight. No bail has been offered and she will remain in custody for the foreseeable future, charged with the murder of Gideon Rivers, which she confessed to in front of Mrs Woolf and myself.'

Nessa heard herself gasp.

'Is this true, Ginny? Did Miss Bramble confess to you? Why did she do it? And who is Marguerite Muir?' she asked.

Ginny, who was sitting on the arm of the sofa beside her sister, saw that the eyes of the room were upon her, the same questions upon all lips. Nessa, who knew her sister better than anyone, knew she was thinking about how best to tell her story.

'Imagine you were writing it down in one of your novels,' she said quietly.

Ginny looked at her and nodded, then turned to address the others.

'It was a magazine that revealed the true facts of this sad case to me. A gossip magazine of the kind I rarely look at, but my good friend Vita Sackville-West left it behind for me after she came to visit. There was an article in it all about the Hollywood starlet Marguerite Muir and how she'd had her heart broken by our own Mr Rivers, when he threw her over for a French Syrian heiress. It emphasised how Miss Muir was famous for her ability to transform herself completely into the part of whatever character she was playing, to the extent you wouldn't even know it was the same woman performing different roles. Suddenly, it all fell into place. I think it must have been because I was reading the magazine when I'd just awoken from an afternoon nap. Our minds are more receptive when we've been sleeping, and I realised something I hadn't seen before. The similarity between Muir and Miss Bramble. Of course, on the surface of it, the two women couldn't be further apart. The dowdy secretary and the glamorous film actress. But that was the beautiful simplicity of her plan. If a woman is not considered to have sex appeal these days, no one looks at her twice. Put on a mousy wig, pull an unfashionable felt hat over your features and cover your eyes in a pair of prescription spectacles and you become invisible. It's you who taught me to look beneath the surface, to the true person, a lesson you imbibed at your easel.'

She looked over at Nessa as she said this, and her words sparked a memory. Nessa might not have seen what Ginny saw, but she knew someone who had. Bobby, the day she picked him up from the castle with Duncan. She remembered the look of confusion on his face, and at the time she'd attributed it to being miserable about a doomed love affair. Now she realised he must have recognised Marguerite. Gideon had been engaged to her at the same time he was involved in a love affair with Bobby – their paths must have crossed. If Marguerite realised that she'd been recognised, that meant . . .

'I think she killed Bobby Bassey too,' Nessa said, speaking her thoughts out loud in a strangled voice. When everyone else in the room turned to look at her, she fell silent.

Ginny put a reassuring hand on her arm.

'You can tell us why. We're all friends here,' she said.

'On the day we looked around the dig with Gideon, then came back down to the museum, Bobby went strangely quiet. When I found out he had a history with Gideon, I thought that was the reason, but I realise now he must have recognised Marguerite. She saw it too, and at that moment, his fate was sealed. Angelica said he was going to meet someone in disguise. It must have been her, and she pulled her usual trick, injecting him so he fell unconscious before drowning him in the plunge pool. She would never have had the strength to do it had he been conscious.'

Here she turned to the police chief.

'I haven't had time to tell you, but I found a needle in the pottery yard. I thought it was from my sewing kit and had somehow got mislaid, but it must be a hypodermic needle.'

'And I found a needle up on Brack Mound after Gideon was killed,' exclaimed Mrs Dudeney. She started rummaging around in a desk drawer. 'I've kept it here somewhere.'

327

Chief Inspector Gripe nodded grimly. 'It appears to have been Muir's modus operandi. When we searched her room, we found a silver hypodermic syringe, the kind that uses replaceable needles, together with several vials of barbiturates. I'll instruct my men to ask her about Mr Bassey's death when they question her again in the morning.'

'*The Silent Angel*,' declared Mrs Dudeney so loudly that everyone turned to look at her. 'Ernest and I went to see it together a few years ago. In the end, the nurse kills her beloved by injecting him with a sedative before suffocating him with a pillow. That must be where she got the idea.'

'Of course! I knew there was something about that film that rang a bell,' said Nessa.

'Thank goodness I found you when I did, or you might have met the same fate when you came poking around my study for the tablet,' said Briggs to the sisters.

'Speaking of the tablet, where is it?' asked Jasmine, who'd been silent up until now.

Before Briggs could answer, the door was flung open, and Harry Dryden ran into the room. He looked around wildly and, seeing Jasmine, practically burst into tears and ran over to her, flinging his arms round her without a care for who was witnessing their embrace.

'I heard something had happened to you and I feared the worst. Thank God you're alive,' he said, holding her to him and kissing her in a way that made Nessa blush.

'Perfect timing, Harry,' said Briggs. 'Perhaps you could tell Jasmine about the tablet.'

Reluctantly, Harry pulled away from his lover.

'It was me who took it. Stanley knew all about it, but it had to look as though it had been stolen from his study.

He wanted to keep it safe until the British Museum reached a decision on what to do with it. I'm ashamed to say he and I faked the attack on me. It was a cover to let me take the tablet up to London without arousing suspicion. He's going to let us have it, I mean you, of course, Jasmine, but I hope you'll let me accompany you back to Paris. So long as we say it was found at Lewes Castle and give both him and Gideon a credit in the exhibition notes, he's happy for you to take the glory.'

Jasmine shook her head. 'It's not about glory, Harry, you should know that. It's about being recognised as a woman in a serious academic field,' she said. He nodded like a faithful lapdog and Nessa thought he would do anything she said. How long it had been since she inspired that sort of devotion in a man?

The door opened again. Who could it be now? It was like a game of charades. Feeling immensely weary, she closed her eyes.

'Nessa,' said a voice, which sounded familiar, but it couldn't be, could it? She opened them again to see Duncan, kneeling before her, his big dark eyes looking into her own.

'Oh, Nessa, I've never been so pleased to see you. I'm so sorry I wasn't here for you. I came at once when Grace told me you'd come to meet Mr Briggs at the castle. I just knew something was wrong, and I couldn't bear to lose you.'

'What about your mother and George?'

'Mother will manage just fine without me for a few days, and, as for George, he'll be just fine. He was busy flirting with the Comte de la Roche when I left. I've promised to go back out and escort Mother home again, but I'm not going anywhere until I'm sure you're completely better. As soon as we got to Cassis and I wrote that stupid letter, I realised I'd made a terrible mistake. I turned straight round again and travelled home as quickly as I could. I'm so sorry if I've hurt you, Nessa. You know I could never be without you. I've realised that now.'

He opened his soulful eyes even more than usual in a pleading expression, and she felt rather sorry for him, but she couldn't help smiling. It was gratifying, even if it had taken a close encounter with a murderer to hear him say it.

51.

Virginia

She was supposed to be writing, but her attention wandered to the tiny vase of blooms on her desk, the last of the mauve dahlias together with a spray of purple asters. Ever since the night of Marguerite Muir's arrest, she'd found it difficult to concentrate. Would her attention span improve once the case came to court?

On the desk before her sat a package of copies of *Orlando*, the historical novel inspired by her affair with Vita, recently published by their own Hogarth Press. She must sign one for Vita and send it off, although she feared she was starting to bore her. Next to Vita with her Spanish blood, Ginny felt insipid and English and unadventurous. Yet hadn't she just helped to apprehend a murderer? What could be more exciting than that?

Truth be told, she was worn out. Her sleep was plagued by dreams of Marguerite plummeting to her death from the top of the castle, even though that fate had been narrowly avoided.

A light knocking at the door interrupted her train of

thought. Expecting to find Leonard bearing a cup of tea, she answered it. Standing in front of her was not her husband, however, but Harry Dryden, looking rather sheepish.

'Sorry to interrupt you, Mrs Woolf, but I'm staying the night with Mrs Rivers – there's some paperwork to complete – and I just thought I'd pop by.'

'You're still inheriting, then?'

Harry looked at his feet, embarrassed. Then, as if he thought better of it, he straightened his shoulders and lifted his chin to look her square in the eye.

'Yes, I am. Jolly decent of Mrs R to give me such a boost in life, but I think she gets something out of it too. I won't inherit the house and the bulk of her estate until she dies, of course, but she's giving me an annual stipend until then. It will be enough for me and Jasmine to make a fresh start.'

'You and Jasmine?' asked Ginny, raising her eyebrows in question.

Harry nodded, more confident in himself this time.

'Yes, we were married in Paris last week. She has a placement on a dig, in Egypt this time, and I'm going to accompany her as her secretary. It's unconventional, but it suits us both, and Ma Rivers approves.'

'Well, I wish you a very happy future together,' said Ginny.

'There's something I thought you should know,' said Harry.

'Yes . . .' she said, her heart sinking. She'd known the reason for his visit wouldn't be straightforward.

'Oh, it's nothing to worry about. It's the tablet.'

'What about it?'

'When the curator at the Louvre examined it, he said it was a fake. A good fake, but a fake nonetheless.'

'You mean to say it wasn't even an antiquity?'

Harry shook his head.

'Made within the last few months, was his guess, but by someone with experience in such things. Most likely someone who makes reproductions for a living.'

Ginny's mind raced ahead.

'Someone who works in a film props department, for example?'

Harry beamed.

'I see why you have a reputation for having a quick mind. You're quite correct. When we presented the information to Chief Inspector Gripe, he put it to Marguerite Muir in jail, who confessed at once. She commissioned the piece from a Hollywood props maker she knows to look as convincing as possible, and to distract attention from what she was doing. She wanted Gideon to find it so he would stay in Lewes, giving her more time to try to win him back. When he made it clear that would never happen, she killed him. At that point, the tablet became a focus for the investigation, helping to deflect attention from the real reason for his murder.'

'The forethought required suggests the murder was premeditated all along. She never expected Gideon to ditch Jasmine and go back to her,' said Ginny.

'Let's just say she was hedging her bets,' Harry replied. 'There was something else she confessed to as well. Funnily enough, she admitted to posing as me, wearing a wig to make her hair look like a man's – it seems she had several wigs, because there was another for Miss Bramble – and even copying my limp.'

Ginny thought back to Fred Hobbes telling her he'd seen Harry at Charleston on the day of Bobby's murder. Now it made sense. It had been Marguerite whom the gardener had spied, lolloping over the fields on her way to silence a potential threat. And to kill for a second time.

52.

Alice

Alone in the gravy-brown drawing room, she could hardly believe just a few days earlier it had been filled with all those caught up in the murders of Gideon Rivers and Bobby Bassey. She'd spent two whole days in bed afterwards, sleeping off the effects of the barbiturates Marguerite Muir had administered via a needle before running off with Ernest's rifle.

Ernest had been uncharacteristically affectionate, bringing her tea and toast in bed, although she was sure he must have got the maid to prepare it for him. He hugged her and told her she was his own dear wife, and next time there was a killer running around the mound to come and fetch him first and he would scare them off with a gunshot. Bless him, he utterly failed to understand the intricacies of the case. That took a more subtle, novelist's mind.

She sat down at her writing desk and looked out of the mullioned window, glad to see nothing but the reflection of the sun lowering over Castle Banks. No mysterious woman in black, no bloodthirsty starlet on the rampage, just the rooks circling above the tall trees, preparing to make their beds for the night.

Reflecting on events, one of the most pleasing aspects of the whole dreadful affair was the newfound respect that had arisen between her and Mrs Woolf. She didn't expect they would ever become bosom buddies, but as she and Leonard had departed the night of Marguerite Muir's arrest, she'd turned to Alice and said, in an admiring tone, 'I never knew you were such a dab hand with a rifle.' It might not be literary recognition, but it was something, and, besides which, she knew that the public preferred her books filled with plot and passion to Virginia's difficult modern prose.

For her own part, she still considered Mrs Woolf the most terrible snob, but their recent intimacy had revealed another side to her. She was also brave, and kind, and these were both qualities that counted for a lot as far as Alice was concerned.

There was one thought troubling her, though, and with her usual forthrightness she decided she must address it head on. She was worried she would never feel the same again about her beloved mound. There was nothing for it, but to go out there now and face it. Even though it was already dusk, she put on her jacket and made her way to the back door.

Nelson, who'd been asleep in his basket, raised his head and regarded his owner with a doleful and questioning gaze, as if to say, 'Really? At this hour?' But, when Alice continued, the hound dutifully dragged himself from his bed to accompany her into the garden and up the path to the summit of the mound. She was glad of the company.

A bat swooped over her head, and she could hear cheerful

voices drifting up from the Lewes Arms on the other side of the hill. The sound gave her heart as she took the final few steps to the top. Then she was there, and she saw at once there had been nothing to fear. She was alone, apart from Nelson and the nocturnal creatures in the undergrowth that the dog was busy sniffing out. Putting her hands on her hips, she looked around her at the ancient forms of the Downs circling the town.

Nelson was worrying away at the tarpaulin, stretched out over the now-abandoned dig. She went over to see what was troubling him and lifted a corner of the covering to check beneath, but there was nothing there except an empty gash in the earth. How humans like to leave their mark on the landscape. Then she thought of the knight of old, who'd left this place to travel thousands of miles to the heat of the desert, where he'd lost his life, and of his companions bringing the treasures he had found there back to his widow and child, and how they'd ended up, just like the body of Gideon Rivers, buried in the cold Sussex earth.

Acknowledgements

First thanks must go to my editor at Headline Jessie Goetzinger-Hall, who believed in my story from the start and who has always been so spot on and supportive with all her editorial comments. I have been so lucky to find someone else who wanted to immerse themselves in the world of the Bloomsburys. If Jessie hadn't liked my Twitter pitch in 2023, this book wouldn't be here today.

Thank you to all the team at Headline for everything you have done for *A Deadly Discovery* from fabulous socials to all the behind-the-scenes stuff authors take for granted. Gratitude is due to my meticulous copy-editor Samantha Stanton-Stewart, who sent me scurrying off to check whether they had telephones at Charleston and Monk's House in 1928 (I'm almost certain they didn't arrive at either house until well into the 1930s), and to my proofreader Jill Cole.

I adore the amazing cover designed by Amy Cox, who is such a talented artist, picking out clever details like the bloody trowel in the foreground. Her autumnal colour scheme and tree-lined landscape is so alluring I want to take a walk on the cover. Thanks also to Sarah Weal for taking my cover photo and making the process so easy.

Special thanks are due to my Brighton writing chums, Anna Burtt, and her West Hill Writers, who have been endlessly supportive throughout. The first people to hear me read the opening chapter aloud were the Real Writers Circle, set up by the wonderful Cindy Etherington and Victoria Robson. Sophie Hannah has also been a hugely positive force through her Dream Author programme and timely email advice.

None of this would be possible without my family. My parents Chris and Judith, my first reader, who was also the person who first taught me to read. Jon, with whom I moved to Lewes fourteen years ago and found the perfect setting for my story. And to our children Iris, Molly, and Alfred who put up with me ignoring them while I write at the kitchen table – there's no such thing as a room of one's own in our house. Not to forget Baxter the cockapoo, who would have loved to go for a walk with Alice's Dalmatian Nelson or Ginny's dogs Pinka and Grizzle.

Woolf & Bell return to solve a brand new case . . .

A LETHAL COCKTAIL

Book 2 in The Woolf & Bell Mysteries

Coming Spring 2025

ACCENT